The Secondhand Bookworm

EMILY JANE BEVANS

THE SECONDHAND BOOKWORM

DEDICATION

This novel is dedicated to all my work colleagues and
customers who journeyed with me through the world of
bookselling between the years 2003-2012.
You know who you are.

THE SECONDHAND BOOKWORM

CONTENTS

THE SECONDHAND BOOKWORM

ACKNOWLEDGMENTS

I am grateful for the ten years I spent working in Kim's secondhand and antiquarian bookshops on the South Coast of England, which afforded me greater experience in the world of selling used books.

THE SECONDHAND BOOKWORM

1 CONCERNING RAVENS

In the front room of an antiquarian and secondhand bookshop in a little town in the south coast county of Cole, was a young woman named Nora. She was seated at a cluttered counter surrounded by books that lined the walls while, like a labyrinth, further rooms and stairs spiralled up and up above her, bursting at the seams with books upon books upon books.

Sneakily, Nora was reading a novel on her Kindle, holding the device under the counter so no one could see it. She wasn't supposed to use the sacrilegious item while working in the bookshop, but the evening before she had downloaded an exciting new novel and was keen to read it. And, after all, Monday's in autumn were usually quiet, dreary and dull in The Secondhand Bookworm – just how Nora liked it.

The interior of the shop was silent and the town beyond began to wake up. An elderly man was peering solemnly at a giant ham in the butcher's shop window, two tiny old ladies were examining a tiffany lamp in the front window of an antique shop across the cobbled square, the local Catholic priest strolled cheerfully past having just purchased a black biretta from a vintage shop along the road, and a man stepped out of the delicatessen, almost tripped over another man's Labradoodle and then stood speaking with the owner of the dog about the new A-board that had appeared down Market Street with much shaking of their heads.

Nora glanced up when she heard Bailey, the Labradoodle, barking, and watched a figure loom up to the front door of the bookshop. The door was flung open and a man crossed the threshold.

"I'm looking for a book!" The man exclaimed, tugging off a green bobble hat.

Nora hastily threw her Kindle onto a pile of reserved books under the counter.

"Then you've come to the right place." She replied cheerfully.

The man squashed his hat into a pocket of his jacket and tugged a folded piece of paper out of a pocket of his corduroy trousers, standing before the counter.

"I certainly hope so. Now. Let me see. I wrote the title down so I wouldn't forget it. Here it is. It's a novel and it's by Patrick O'Brian. Have you heard of him?"

"Yes, I have." Nora assured him.

The man peered at her with a doubtful expression and continued.

"Well, he's a grand writer and he penned a series of novels."

"The Aubrey-Maturin series?" Nora guessed.

"It's called the Aubrey-Maturin series." The man said, ignoring her.

Nora suppressed a growl.

"I'm looking for the fourth novel titled 'The Mauritius Command'. Can you check your computer and see if you have it in stock?"

"I'm sorry." Nora shook her head. "We don't have our titles listed on our computer."

"You don't have your titles listed on your computer?!" The man screwed his slip of paper into a ball. "Well that's no good. You should do you know. How do you ever find a book in here then? Sssssss!" He surveyed the room, annoyed.

Nora edged back.

"Erm…well, all of our books are sorted into sections, so if it's an art book then you can look in the art section or if it's a sports book we have a sports section." She explained.

"So where are the novels kept?"

"In the attic room."

"*Attic* room? Do you have an elevator? How far up is it?"

"The attic room is at the top of three and a half flights of stairs." Nora indicated to a walkway that led to a small room containing the start of the staircase. "The books in the attic room are all organised A-Z of author so Patrick O'Brian is quite easy to find."

"If I don't die of asphyxiation before I get there." He shoved the ball of paper back into his corduroy trouser pocket. "Can't you go and look for me?"

"I'm on my own at the moment so I'm not allowed to leave the till unattended."

"Why? Are you afraid I'll rob it?"

Nora looked awkward.

"Erm…"

The man sighed dramatically.

"Fine. I'll climb the metaphorical mountain. You should list your titles on the computer, you know."

"Well, the last stock check we undertook in The Secondhand Bookworm yielded a result of about twenty-seven thousand books." Nora said and smiled smugly to see his eyebrows lift in surprise. "Most of our books predate the barcode so it would take too long to individually list them on a computer programme."

"You should set up a system like Waterstones'." He walked towards the walkway that led further into the shop. "It would save your customers searching through *twenty seven thousand* books!"

Nora watched him disappear, her gaze sliding to Gilbert Keith Chesterton's ruddy face on the front of a biography displayed on a shelf.

"You would have had a witty but charitable reply to that, Gilbert." She told the photo on the book. "Mine isn't charitable so I'll bite my tongue."

The sound of a small fanfare announced the arrival of a Skype message from the other The Secondhand Bookworm in Seatown.

'Mr Hill is here.' The message flashed, accompanied by a horror-struck emoji.

Nora gasped and then grimaced.

Mr Hill was The Secondhand Bookworm's most eccentric customer who had fortunately started off the day at their Seatown branch, thus sparing Nora a morning of trauma. Her mouse pointer hovered over a smug emoji but she changed her mind and sent back a sympathising face instead.

The door opened again, letting in a waft of cold air and the loud drone of an engine as a car passed by. A woman marched in, tailed by her husband.

"I want a microwave cookery book." She said, blue eyes snapping. She stopped at the counter and dropped a large leather handbag onto the surface, knocking over a holder of business cards.

Nora blinked.

"Do you have one? My daughter bought me a microwave and I want a cookery book for it. I'm not just going to use it to reheat tea. I want to put it to its full potential."

Nora started to pick up the cards.

"We have a cookery section but to be honest I haven't seen any microwave cookery books in stock for a long time. I don't think we do."

"Can you check your computer?"

"Unfortunately we don't have our titles listed on our computer. They're all secondhand so they come and go from the shelves quite regularly." She moved aside the bag to collect a few more spilt cards and return them to the holder. "You're welcome to go up to the section and browse through it just in case, but I can't leave the till and our cookery section is on the next floor."

"I don't do stairs. You go up dear." She turned and prodded her husband.

"What?" He seemed to return from a trance and stared at his wife.

"*Mi-cro-wave* cookery books." She shook her head patronisingly. "For the microwave Louise gave us. They're upstairs."

"Well, I'm quite certain there aren't any there at the moment really." Nora hastened to say, fearing a marital dispute coming on.

"Humph." The woman snatched up her bag, sounding like a Borneo pygmy elephant (Nora had watched a documentary about them the night before while moping about her old bedroom dreaming about her boss's brother, Humphrey). "If you had your books listed you would know for certain!"

Nora paused.

"Yes, that would help," she agreed, side-glancing the Chesterton biography. She watched them stalk out of the shop, where they stood aside to allow a man wearing a bright blue bobble hat to enter. He stepped down, stood on the mat and was about to speak when he was distracted by the walls of books surrounding him.

5

"Wow! Look at all these books!" He exclaimed, amazed.

The phone started to ring so Nora grabbed the receiver quickly.

"Good morning, The Secondhand Bookworm." She greeted the caller, watching as the man stepped further inside and started to browse, mumbling the word 'wow', over and over.

"It's true! He's here!" Cara whispered hard.

Nora smiled at the sound of her colleague's voice from The Secondhand Bookworm in Seatown. Cara and Nora often worked together and were the best of friends. Sometimes they had arguments, and once Cara had thrown a book at Nora's head, but such events between them were rare.

"Well, I have to confess I'm glad you've got him and not me." Nora told Cara, watching the man in the bobble hat rummage noisily through the Folio Society section.

"Mr Hill has given up on Castletown. You keep sending him here."

"That's because I refuse to play his insane weekly book game." Nora pointed out. "Buying and then selling. Buying and then selling. There's only a certain amount of craziness I can take. Is he buying or selling today? I've lost track."

"Buying. Then selling I guess. Grrr."

"You could hide his books and tell him we sold them all to someone else."

"Georgina said she tried that once and he fainted right in front of her on the carpet," Cara recalled, referring to their boss and Nora's good friend, Georgina Pickering who owned the two branches of The Secondhand Bookworm.

Nora bit back a horrified laugh.

"Oh dear."

"Besides, only he is mad enough to buy his books. They're all so ancient and greasy."

"I'm well aware." Nora grimaced.

"Do you have any customers?"

Nora glanced at the man in the blue bobble hat who was now studying a copy of The Seven Pillars of Wisdom, still muttering, 'wow'.

"One or two."

"We've sold some motoring books and a few postcards so far. How did the flat hunting go at the weekend?"

"Oh…er…"

"Did you just mope about your old bedroom in your mum and dads house again, dreaming about Humphrey?"

Nora gasped.

"I don't sit about dreaming about Humphrey!" She denied loudly, blushing red.

The man in the blue bobble hat glanced at her, wide-eyed. Nora cleared her throat, flashed a polite smile and span around in the swivel chair to face the case of rare and antiquarian books with her back to him.

"You need to sort out a new flat soon." Cara pointed out with a knowing smile in her voice. "You can't stay in your old bedroom for the rest of your life. You're twenty seven years old."

"Hmm, well, I can't help it if my landlady threw me out because her whole building was subsiding."

"Still, you should sort out a nice new flat."

"I know. And I will." Nora agreed, running a fingertip carefully along the spines of a row of First Editions. "One in Castletown would be lovely and convenient. And it would probably come with a lot of history, you know, like having been built on the site of a monastery where Thomas Cromwell hanged all the monks for refusing to take the Oath of Supremacy. I might inherit some pious ghosts. Or it could have a secret room in the walls and I'll discover some ancient old books, perfectly preserved, like an early copy of Margery Kempe's autobiography or an original Shakespeare manuscript. Even better, it could have a tunnel to the ruins of the castle and I'll discover the handsome Duke of Cole there, holed up in one of the turrets on a secret archaeological camping weekend."

Cara giggled. Nora often had whimsical fantasies like that.

"Oh drat. Mr Hill is coming back. I'd better go and deal with him." Cara groaned in a whisper. "Speak to you soon, Nora."

"Bye, Cara." Nora smiled, reluctantly hanging up as she heard the man in the blue bobble hat walk over to the counter holding a Folio Society book.

Nora spun slowly around to face him.

"Is this in English?" He asked.

Nora stared.

"Yes."

"How can you tell?"

"Well, erm…if you take it out the slip case and open it you'll see."

"Oh! It opens?" The man exclaimed and turned the book box upside down. "How much does it cost?"

"There will be a price pencilled on the front page." Nora explained warily.

"Numerically?"

Nora wondered if she was suddenly in the Twilight Zone.

"Yes." Quickly she grabbed the book box, slipped out the fancy tome, turned it the right way up and opened the cover. "It's fifteen pounds."

"Wow!" The man exclaimed. "I'll leave it."

"Okay." Nora smiled politely.

"Is there an internet café around here?" He asked.

"I'm afraid not. You could try Seatown; it's ten miles west."

"Thanks for your help," he said and headed off out of the shop.

Nora watched him head off across the cobbled square, wondering if she should start a bobble hat tally chart (she kept several tally charts, including an '*it's warm in here*' comment tally chart for anger therapy), when a familiar voice interrupted her thoughts.

"Morning, Nora."

A man stood in the doorway, his shoulder-length pure white hair gleaming like a halo in the sunlight, his long black coat billowing about him like a vampire's cloak. His name was Spencer Brown and he lived at the top of the hill by the castle walls in a gothic house with a tower.

"Anything new come in for me over the weekend?" Spencer Brown asked.

Nora watched him step down into The Secondhand Bookworm.

"Morning, Mr Brown. Let me see." She eased back her chair to check under the counter where the reserved books for customers were kept.

"I haven't seen Georgina for ages." Spencer said. He picked up a book about letterboxes from the counter top. "Did you thank her for the latest books she put by for me?"

"Yes." Nora's strained voice assured, "She was pleased you bought them all."

She moved aside several comics the Saturday staff had bought from the local newsagents, her Kindle and a packet of biscuits she was enjoying and then hunted out a bag of heavy books, placing them before him.

Spencer Brown was an avid collector of occult books. He insisted that he used them for research, contributing articles to esoteric magazines and writing his own books

about the occult history of Castletown, but Nora
suspected he ran his own cult in the woods behind the
castle ruins and sacrificed people at the top of his tower.
He was a tall, thin man with piercing blue eyes and
especially long canine teeth which flashed like Dracula's
when he smiled. Once, Nora had seen a bat flapping
above her all the way to her car at the top of the hill and
had been convinced it was Spencer Brown.

Quickly, Nora removed the slip of paper inside the
plastic bag of books which said '*For the local
Ghostbuster*'.

She slid the pile towards him.

"Already have that one." Spencer said straightaway.
He then frowned in concentration as he began to browse
through them.

Nora threw the piece of paper over her shoulder
where it landed in the small waste paper bin behind her,
leaving Spencer to ponder the books. Another customer
arrived, said a polite hello and disappeared into the back
of the shop, so Nora checked the emails. There was one
from a lady looking to sell her father's collection of
fishing books, so she forwarded it on to the Seatown
branch for Georgina to deal with.

The customer returned from the back room and stood
looking perplexed.

"Do you have your books listed on your computer?"

Spencer burst out laughing.

"Everyone asks her that," he said, flicking through
the leaves of a book about County of Cole poltergeists
and banshees.

"I'm sorry, we don't." Nora replied.

"I've looked in your railway section for a specific
title but I didn't come across it. Is that the only place it
would be?" The customer ignored Spencer.

"Yes. We have rare books which we keep back here
in these special cases, but there aren't any antiquarian

books about railways or trains in stock at the moment. We can take your name and number and keep an eye out for the book for you." She suggested.

"I'm not local so I don't think that's necessary." He began to walk away. "Thanks though. Great shop."

"Thank you. Bye." Nora smiled.

Spencer nudged a pile of books towards Nora.

"I definitely have those already so they can go back onto your shelves. Can you write these other ones down for me and keep them by? I'll check if I have them back at home. The publishers change the covers when they reprint them and I've got so many now I lose track. I once ended up with eight copies of 'The Headless Hog of Hill Town'."

Nora nodded.

"No problem."

She took a pen out of a broken mug beside the computer monitor while Spencer stared at her steadily, almost as if poised to lunge for her neck. Nora edged back warily.

"Do you need me to read out the titles?" He asked.

"No, I can manage." She assured.

Spencer watched her write down the first one.

"I'll have to get back to you sometime next week because I'm going to a UFO convention at the weekend and I have to prepare for that. I doubt I'll have a chance to come down before then."

Nora nearly dropped her pen.

"A what?"

"A UFO convention."

"Do they have those in England then? I thought they just took place in the USA."

"Of course they have them in England!"

"Will there be aliens there?" Nora asked mildly.

"You never know." His round blue eyes shone hopefully. "It's really good; my wife Sal and I have been before. Last year I gave a three hour long testimony about my abduction from Castletown Park. The audience was riveted."

"I didn't know you were abducted."

"It happened in the seventies when I first moved to Castletown. I was picking toadstools while following a gnome trail and several blue and white bright lights descended upon me. I went on a trip to the mother ship, it was cloaked above the town, and I was experimented upon, finally waking up eight hours later face down in a puddle."

"Are you sure you didn't accidently pick some magic mushrooms?" Nora teased.

"No. It was a real experience." Spencer assured her. "We're also going to stay in a haunted hotel. Last time we stayed there we felt something sit on the end of our bed. It was the ghost of a cat that had been squashed by a bookcase falling on it in 1885."

Nora stared at him.

"We're also visiting a village that's supposed to be plagued by the violent ghost of a horse. There's even a book written about it. I've got it already so I don't need it from you."

"That all sounds very lovely." Nora replied politely, hastily scribbling down the rest of the titles and authors and handing the piece of paper to him.

"Thanks, Nora." Spencer said appreciatively. "I'm writing a book about the spirit that haunts the town square. If you ever notice anything unusual out there, let me know."

"Like what?"

"The spectre of a highway man who was hanged right in the middle in 1777. He stands and stares into shop windows."

"I'll be sure to keep an eye out," Nora said.

"Thanks. And thank Georgina for the books for me. Bye Nora."

"Bye, Mr Brown."

The sound of footsteps on the staircase in the hallway beyond the front room finally signalled the return of Nora's Patrick O'Brian customer descending from the attic room. He was breathing heavily when he reappeared. Two novels were clasped in his left hand.

"Well you had it so it was worth the bleeding climb." He slammed the two paperbacks onto the counter beside the occult books Spencer Brown had left and then proceeded to shove his hands in the pockets of his corduroy trousers and his fleece jacket, searching for his wallet. "It feels like I was up there for hours. You might think about putting an espresso machine up there. And some sofas. Just for your information, in case someone asks you in the future, the fifth Patrick O'Brian novel is called 'Desolation Island'. I found it up there too. So I'll take them both."

Nora drew the paperbacks towards her. 'The Mauritius Command' had been priced at two pounds fifty and 'Desolation Island' at two pounds. Nora tapped the prices into the till.

"Four pounds fifty please, sir."

"Why is one priced at two fifty and the other only at two? They look the same to me." He asked, opening his wallet.

"Probably the earlier one is fifty pence more because it's harder to find."

"I found it. It wasn't that hard."

"It probably wasn't hard to locate it on the shelf." Nora agreed. "But it may be hard to come by for stock."

The man glared at her.

"How about both of them for four quid?"

"Unfortunately I can't change the prices."

"They're a rip off if you ask me."

He sighed and counted out four pound coins, two twenty pence pieces and a ten pence piece. He dumped them unceremoniously on top of the cash book.

"Thank you." Nora smiled.

He watched her deposit the money in the till.

"Do you need a bag?"

"No!" He picked up the books, shoved them in an inside pocket of his jacket and turned. "Good day."

"Goodbye." Nora smiled and watched him stomp across the carpet and the flagstones to the door.

She picked up her pen.

"First official sale of the day." She cheered and wrote it down in the cash book.

The cash book was a methodically kept record of all sales and expenditures in The Secondhand Bookworm. It was a long, thin ledger. Nora wrote the sales down the right hand side of each page and any expenditure down the left. Sometimes she was specific such as writing down 'Patrick O'Brian novels' or '*The History of Castletown*'; at other times she was less detailed and simply wrote '*fiction*' or '*something old and smelly*'. Georgina kept the daily records to glean an idea as to what topics were more popular with her customers and also to see what Nora spent the till money on. Mainly books that were brought in for sale. Sometimes sausage rolls.

The town postman suddenly appeared at the window, staring at Nora like the spectre of the highwayman Spencer had told her about.

"Post for you." He mouthed.

Nora wondered why he wasn't pushing the letters through the letter box or bringing them in to her so she sighed and walked around the front of the desk, opening the door

"Hiya, Nora. How are you?" Phil greeted her cheerfully.

In his early thirties, Phil was one of the regular faces in Castletown. He led a double life as a waiter in 'The Duke's Pie', a crumbling but popular restaurant close to the top castle gates. As a postman and a waiter he lately prided himself on being the biggest gossip. Several old ladies now went to him for information.

Phil passed Nora a pile of letters, bills and catalogues.

"I heard your brother Seymour inherited a theatre." Phil revealed.

"Wow. You really are the town gossip." Nora teased.

Phil grinned proudly.

"Thanks."

"Seymour did inherit a theatre. He's in the process of doing it up and hopes to have it open for Christmas productions."

"A lot of debris was washed up on Littlesea beach during that storm last night. You should let Seymour know." Phil suggested.

"Why would I do that?"

"I expect he'll want some stock for the theatre before he reopens it. You never know what's been washed up. Maybe some great props like old sea chests, wooden legs, dinosaur eggs, a cannon or two, things like that? Once, Jimmy from the coin shop found a whole box of machine guns. He sold them from under the counter for years."

Nora stared.

"I'll send Seymour a text message," she promised warily.

"Mr Sykes said he saw you leave The Secondhand Bookworm with Georgina's brother last weekend. Are you dating Humphrey Pickering, then?"

Nora sputtered.

"That's not really anyone else's business. Do you actually run the Castletown spy network?" She asked, frowning.

Phil grinned.

"Just interested in the ins and outs of the town." He shrugged, then swung a leg over his bike. "Have a good day." He winked and peddled off up the hill, leaving Nora standing in the bookshop doorway.

"NORA!" A booming voice carried across the cobbled square making her jump. Nora saw Billy from one of the antique shops waving frantically. "I'VE GOT SOME BOOKS I WANT TO SELL. I'LL BRING THEM DOWN LATER." He yelled.

Nora stuck her thumb up, wincing inside as she wondered what horrors Billy would have discovered to try and sell her this time. He adamantly believed that The Secondhand Bookworm traded in falling apart odd volumes of law or tax manuals he found in house clearances, usually riddled with worm.

Nora insisted the word 'bookworm' in the shop's name referred to someone who loves to read and that they didn't actually provide books full of paper lice, boring beetles or termites. Billy usually just laughed patronisingly at that.

She was about to turn back into the shop to make another cup of tea when, with a sudden jolt of horror, Nora noticed two ladies waiting to cross the road from over the other side of the square, their beady bird-eyes fixed on the bookshop. Quickly Nora ran inside and closed the door, leaning against it.

"Oh lovely. The Ravens." She sighed and headed back to the desk.

For a moment the bookshop was lovely and peaceful, the sun streaming in between the shelves in the bay window, illuminating a set of gold edged Rudyard

Kipling novels which Georgina had purchased from a pleasant man in Seatown last week.

Crows and rooks from the huge ruined castle behind the bookshop could be heard squawking; pigeons cooed down the chimney pot that was boarded up behind the antiquarian shelves; the gleam and glitter of dust motes floated lazily in the air; three woodlice sat as if staring at her from the carpet.

And then the Ravens cast open the door and entered the shop whispering.

Nora pretended she hadn't noticed them.

"Ask her if…ask her if she'll do it for…ask her if…ask her…." The elder lady, Mrs Raven, was whispering.

"I will poppet!" The younger lady, Miss Raven, whispered back hard.

Aware she was being stared at, Nora turned slowly from the computer screen to smile politely.

Mrs Raven hung back while her middle-aged daughter smiled in a sinister way and glided toward the counter. She wore a large coat, a long white scarf, a deerstalker hat with flaps either side of her ears and big flannelette shorts with knee high white socks and white plimsolls.

"Hellooooo." She greeted in a sweet, high voice.

"Hello, how are you?" Nora welcomed her.

"I'm fine, fine. How are you?" Before Nora could answer, Miss Raven glared at her. "You have a book in your window. Can we have a look, please?"

Nora edged back her chair.

"Yes, certainly."

"And we're going to look upstairs; can we leave our bags here?" She asked with her dark eyebrows lowered and a set smile, almost daring Nora to refuse.

"Er…yes, of course." Nora knew better than to argue.

Mrs Raven scurried forward with four carrier bags, a shopping trolley and a black sack. With much rustling she arranged the bags behind the counter and when finished stared at Nora who stepped over them to go to the window.

"It's the ladybird book about 'The Workman'. In the front for two pounds." Miss Raven indicated airily.

Nora moved aside a costume book and a 'Jowett Javelin and Jupiter' tome to reach in the front for the book.

"Ask her if…ask her…" Mrs Raven whispered from behind.

"I WILL," Miss Raven whispered hard and when Nora turned she beamed. "Thank you." She took it and the two women bent their heads together over the book, whispering.

Nora walked back to the desk, sat down and brought up the Skype chat.

'You think you've got it bad with Mr Hill? I have the Ravens.' She wrote with a smirk just as the telephone started to ring.

Leaving the Ravens to their in-depth discussion, Nora picked up the receiver.

"I saw your advert in the Yellow Pages that you buy old books." The man at the end of the line said, sounding small and distant. "We're down-sizing and have cleared out some bookshelves and I have some books I want to get rid of. These are old, from the nineteen fifties. I have a set of Children's Encyclopaedias and a set of General Knowledge and some story books. How much will you give me for them?"

Nora leaned back in the chair, observing the Ravens.

"Unfortunately the Encyclopaedias and General Knowledge books wouldn't be for us."

"Your advert says you buy old books!" He objected indignantly.

"We find the ones you mentioned very difficult to sell on. What story books do you have?" Nora asked hastily.

"Fairy tales, nursery rhymes…."

"Are they illustrated?"

"They've got pictures, yeah," he replied suspiciously.

"Well if they are illustrated by Arthur Rackham or Edmund Dulac or Mabel Lucie Attwell or…"

"Yeah 'Grimm's Tales' is illustrated by Arthur Rackham," he interrupted, excited.

Mrs and Miss Raven moved towards the counter, staring at Nora.

"What sort of book is it? Is it large and with a dust wrapper?" Nora inquired.

"No it don't have a wrapper but it's blue cloth and has gold writing and the other one, the Nursery Rhymes, has a glossy wrapper but it has the ring of a coffee mug stained across the face of the Cow that jumped over the moon on the front."

Nora smiled at Miss Raven who was staring pointedly at her, grasping the ladybird book with both hands.

"Probably the Arthur Rackham illustrated book would be worth us looking at…"

"The back cover is missing and some of the back pages have gone; it's hanging apart a bit, would that make a difference to the price?" he interrupted.

Nora paused.

"Yes." She said quietly.

"Oh, I thought I'd try before I threw them in the bin." He seemed to shrug at the other end of the line. "The pictures inside might be worth tearing out then for this Arthur *Rack-man* chap?"

"You might like to keep them," Nora nodded with a sigh.

"I could try and sell them on EBay. Thanks mate." The phone clicked as he rang off.

Nora took a deep breath, returning the receiver to its cradle.

"Yes, we'd like this one but we'd like to go upstairs." Miss Raven explained, her voice even higher than before. "Can we leave it here while we go and have a look in the children's room?"

"That's fine." Nora assured her.

"Come on, poppet." Miss Raven whispered to her mother and they shuffled off.

Nora watched them go.

Turning back to the computer monitor Nora noticed the word *'AAAAAAARGH'* spelt out on the Skype Chat by Cara in reply to her comment that the Ravens had arrived. She chuckled, feeling better, and set about sifting through the post.

Monday mornings were often so quiet in The Secondhand Bookworm that Georgina rarely put anyone else to work with Nora, unless it was summer when the town became overrun by tourists and visitors, many of whom liked to clamber over the ancient stones and wander around the huge hollow rooms that gave Castletown its name.

The large castle ruins behind the shops belonged to a Duke who was ignored by the national press because the media considered him to be a bit of a bore. He was never seen in social circles, had never caused a scandal, was a thirty-something bachelor and spent his time wading lakes, undertaking restorations of abandoned old ruins into stunning properties and giving talks about conservation and rewilding while running an international architectural business from behind the scenes and living alone on the Scottish borders.

Rumours recently abounded that the Duke of Cole was thinking about rebuilding his family castle behind the bookshop. A town meeting had been called to discuss if businesses would be affected and whether or not rioting should be organised in protest. The old mayor had passionately convinced everyone that a restored castle would be more of a tourist attraction for the town than a pile of old stones and crumbling empty rooms filled with crow and rook droppings and Nora thought so too.

Nora was lost in thoughts about Dukes and castles when The Secondhand Bookworm door opened and a middle-aged man stepped down.

"Good morning." He greeted cheerfully with a tip of his hat, closing the door behind him.

The man was dressed smartly in a brown tweed suit, waistcoat, white linen shirt, fancy tie, boater hat, round glasses and white gloves. Nora watched him roll on his heels, hands linked behind his back as he perused the shelves of art books before he tipped his hat at her again.

"Do you have any books about etiquette, madam?" He asked politely.

"Yes. In the back room." Nora replied warily.

"Many thanks, madam." He tipped his hat once more and headed deeper into the shop.

Nora leaned forward to stare after him dubiously.

Last week he had cornered her in the gardening section dressed in bell bottom jeans and a denim shirt covered with embroidered flowers, to lecture her about the benefits of human waste compost and veganism. When he asked if she'd like to go on a date with him to the local chilli festival Nora had refused and run hastily away.

The week before that he had arrived dressed as a Victorian gentleman and given Nora hiccups by making her jump when he had prodded her with his cobra headed cane, saying she looked pale and that he would recommend arsenic for anaemia. Nora began to wonder

21

if he wanted to poison her when he next offered to fetch her some chloroform to cure her hiccups, explaining that that was how it was done in Victorian England. She thought about getting him put on Georgina's 'banned customer' list so decided to keep an eye on him for any other odd behaviours today.

The front door opened once more.

"Hello. I'm probably in the wrong shop but do you sell printer paper?" An elderly man asked.

"No we don't, this is a bookshop."

"Where can I get some?"

"There's a computer shop down Market Street. The only *modern* establishment in town." Nora added for her own amusement.

"Oh. I must have missed it. Do you sell set squares?"

Nora looked blank.

"Set squares?"

He looked around.

"No, it doesn't look like you do." He decided.

"We only sell books." Nora explained.

"Oh. Do you sell newspapers?"

"No, only books." Nora stressed.

"Oh. Where is there a newspaper shop?" He asked.

"Down the road next to the post office." Nora indicated

"Do you sell jam pots?"

"No!"

"Thanks for nothing," the man said rudely and left.

Nora groaned when she heard heavy footfalls descending the staircase in the next room. The sound of intense whispering preceded the Ravens. They returned to the front with a Disney book and three more Ladybird books.

"Ah yes, we'd like these please." Miss Raven said, walking around and placing them on the counter top.

"Ask her if she'd…" Mrs Raven whispered but her daughter pointedly ignored her.

"We'd like to pay for these four Ladybirds now but can you keep this one by for us please?" She handed Nora the Disney book. "And can you do the usual on those?" Her eyes darkened threateningly, poised for Nora's answer.

"Yes, of course, I can give you ten percent off because you're regulars." Nora assured her quickly.

Miss Raven's face relaxed and she smiled sweetly.

"You're so kind."

Mrs Raven pulled a little bank bag from her pocket which was full of coins.

"Are you going to pay for them?" Miss Raven asked her.

"We discussed it." Mrs Raven whispered. "Yes, yes, I've got it." She emptied the whole bag on the counter so that coins rolled and skidded in all directions. There was a whispered argument as Nora ran the prices through the till, taking ten percent off, while trying to keep a straight face. Mrs Raven counted out numerous five pence pieces.

"That's four pounds."

"No, that's three pounds ninety-five."

"Count them all out again!"

"I'm not senile."

"We don't want to pay too much."

"Make sure it's enough."

"IT IS!"

Nora carefully took the handful of coins.

"It's all correct." Miss Raven assured pleasantly.

"Thank you." Nora nodded but counted out the five pence pieces anyway as she dropped them into the till, secretly hoping it would annoy the Ravens so they would stop paying only in small change. It never did. They just waited patiently, glaring.

"And can we have a bag please?" Miss Raven asked sweetly once Nora had closed the till.

"Sure."

"Can you double it please into two bags?"

"Erm…." Nora looked at the tiny pile of books.

"We're going home by taxi and it has to be strong!" Miss Raven snapped, blue eyes flashing.

"Okay." Nora grabbed a bag, biting her tongue against mentioning her colleague's recent comment about the Ravens' carbon footprint due to their obsession with bags.

"I bet the Ravens line their walls with our blue carriers." Terri had said last week.

Nora smirked again when she thought of it.

"We're getting cotton and jute bags soon." She couldn't resist saying.

Miss Raven just smiled sweetly.

Nora cleared her throat, bagging the books and then holding them out.

"Ask her if she can hold on to it," Mrs Raven whispered, nudging her daughter.

"Ah, would it be possible to leave them here while we go and walk around the town?" Miss Raven asked.

Nora withdrew the bag.

"No problem."

"Ask her if…"

"I know poppet!" Miss Raven snapped and smiled broadly at Nora who knew what was coming. "Ah, could we leave all of our bags here? While we walk around the town? As we bought some books today?"

Nora glanced at the pile.

"Well, I suppose you can, seeing as there aren't any books on the floor at the moment waiting to be put away. Alright, that would be..."

"We won't be long!" Miss Raven interrupted, grabbed her mother's arm and they bolted for the door.

"Don't you need your gloves?" Mrs Raven whispered hard.

"I'm fine, poppet." Miss Raven assured her and they almost wedged one another in the doorway, fighting to leave the shop as quickly as possible before Nora changed her mind.

Nora dropped the bag with the others and was about to growl when she noticed Billy bowing low to the Ravens outside the door.

"Good morning, ladies."

"Ugh." Miss Raven exclaimed, dragging her mother up the street.

Billy stuck his head into the shop.

"I'll bring those books in another day, Nora!" He said loudly. "Someone's coming to see my Nazi daggers so I want to polish them up."

"Okay." Nora said, trying not to sound too relieved.

"He said his name was Göring. Could be a relative of the man himself." Billy added hopefully.

Nora stared.

The man who changed his fashion drifted in from the back room, paused to tip his hat and then left silently, closing the door behind him. Nora decided he didn't need to be banned. The door had been closed for less than five seconds when it flew open once more.

A man stepped inside and shut the door so hard behind him that the windows rattled.

"Sorry about that." He said, not sounding sorry. "Got any books about the Minoans?"

"The Minoans?" Nora's gaze scanned the Folio Society section beside the window before jumping to the doorway that led further into the shop. "Possibly in the back room." She indicated.

"I'll have a look." He said, heading that way.

A Skype message arrived.

'Just spoke to Georgina because a man wanted to sell a rare book bound in badger skin of all things! I wasn't sure what to do so I phoned her. She's currently having a filling at the dentist so she was hard to understand, but she told me to tidy up our art section and asked me to remind you to tidy up the Ordnance Survey maps there. Apparently the 'Map-Boy' came in again at the weekend so they will be messy. Xxx'

Nora grimaced.

'Okay. Erm…what was the conclusion about the book bound in badger skin?'

Nora watched the little pencil start moving as Cara wrote a reply.

'Several disgusted comments but I couldn't really understand because she's had a numbing injection for her filling. I deduced that she didn't want it and said the man trying to sell it should be arrested.'

'Did he bind it himself?'

'No. But the fact he had it annoyed Georgina. You know how she loves badgers.'

Nora giggled to herself and was about to stand up and climb over the Ravens' bags to set about re-sorting the Ordnance Survey maps, located in the small room behind her where the start of the staircase was located, when another customer arrived. She was a tall lady with silvery hair in a bun, a blue ankle length coat and lilac shaded sunglasses.

"I would like this book ordered." She announced, waving a slip of paper like a handkerchief.

"We don't order books I'm afraid." Nora explained.

"Oh. But you sell books." She planted her feet firmly on the ground with two small stamps.

Nora edged back behind the counter, almost tripping over the Ravens' bags.

"All of our books are bought into stock secondhand. We have a few local new ones but we never order in new releases."

"Can you order me a secondhand copy then?" The lady asked.

"We can't place specific orders. We just buy what is brought in by people who want to sell them to us."

"Can you check on your computer to see if you have it in stock?"

Nora felt her temperature rise.

"We don't have our books listed. They're organised throughout the shop in sections of subject."

The slip of paper was offered to Nora aloofly.

"This one has just come out." She said gravely. "Last week."

"Okay. It's possible someone sold it to us without reading it themselves. What kind of a book is it?" Nora attempted to take the slip but the lady held on firmly.

"It's big and it's a paperback." She kept hold of the slip. Nora decided to let go.

"Is it a history book or an art book…or….?" Nora prompted.

"No, I'm not looking for an art book or a history book!" She was severe.

"What's the subject?" Nora asked patiently.

"It's a novel."

"Well, all our fiction is in the attic room…" Nora started to indicate.

"Oh I don't do stairs!" The woman announced and returned the slip of paper to her handbag. "I'll look in Waterstones. Good day."

"Bye." Nora said wearily and dropped into the chair.

The Minoan man came out of the back room.

"Nope. Nothing on the Minoans. By the way, I saw a book in the wrong place. It was a submarine book and it was in the section next to it containing books about ancient civilizations."

Nora stared at him as he began for the door.

"Oh dear. Maybe a customer put it back wrong."

"Or you need to do some organisation." He shrugged. "It would be a lot more helpful for customers if your books were organised. Don't you think?"

"Yes, that's a good idea." Nora agreed politely.

"You might consider listing all your titles on your computer too. And your Ordnance Survey maps are all over the place. You might want to think about sorting those out as well."

He gave her a belittling look and left, shutting the door again so hard that the windows shook.

"This is NOT a typical Monday!" Nora exclaimed, propelled herself out of the chair and set about with determination to tidy up the maps.

2 MR TWO STICKS

"How much for cash?" A man asked, dropping a book on the counter before Nora's fourth steaming cup of tea.

Nora looked up from placing a book about misericords on the reservation shelf under the counter for the local vicar who had just left. She straightened up and pondered the customer as his watch beeped midday.

"Hello. It's not my shop so I'm unable to change the prices." Nora explained.

"Oh." He lost some of his attitude and reached for his wallet.

"I don't do all of the buying so I'm not allowed to knock money off as I'm not always sure what the owner paid for the books." Nora added insistently.

"Yeah, no problem, I had to ask though." He laughed it off. He was carrying a large, partly wrapped stuffed squirrel, the glass eyes of which stared at Nora. The man placed the squirrel onto the counter, pulling out a twenty pound note. "It says twelve pounds."

"Twelve fifty." Nora read.

"Is it? Oh." The man shrugged and thrust the twenty pound note at her.

"Excuse me." A woman in a huge fur coat appeared from the back room, knocking the ground loudly with her cane.

"How can I help?" Nora smiled, pressing buttons on the till as the man shoved the book in his pocket.

"Where are your books about needlecrafts?" She wanted to know.

"Mum, they're upstairs." A voice called from the back where the list of locations of subjects had been tacked to the wall at the bottom of the first staircase.

"Oh. Thank you." She peered disdainfully at the stuffed animal before walking away.

"Can you recommend a nice place for a cup of tea around here?" The man asked.

Nora was distracted by the front door opening and a man stopping on the threshold. He was mostly hidden behind the large pile of boxes he was holding but Nora recognised his fancy suit and his dark, swept back hair above the top box of books.

"The Flowery Teacup is nice, down Market Street." Nora told her customer, pondering the new arrival with a small smile.

"Do they sell cakes?"

"Yes."

"Rock cakes?"

"I expect they sell all types."

"It's not a café just for women is it? With a name like that?"

"No. I'm pretty sure they sell to all genders. Even the gender free." She teased.

Nora heard Humphrey's muffled laugh as he remained on the doorstep while listening to her conversation.

"Oh." The customer glanced at his squirrel while Nora walked around the desk to relieve Humphrey of one of the boxes.

Humphrey was a few years older than Nora and had recently moved back down to the County of Cole from London after having run a highly successful international business for eight years. He had decided that living the high life and keeping such long, stressful business hours would kill him before long and so had sold his share in the company and was now looking for a change in his life.

While he was sorting out his own place, Humphrey was staying with Georgina so his sister had him doing maintenance work for her about the house or the bookshops, something Humphrey welcomed and enjoyed. She also cooked for him and cleaned his clothes so he was having a lovely time.

Nora had met Humphrey on several occasions over the past few years and he had always shown a friendly interest in her, but over the last several weeks she had worked with him a few times in The Secondhand Bookworm and they had become firm friends.

Last weekend, Humphrey had repaired several things that needed mending around the shop. Nora had shown him the third from top wobbly step by the attic room, the window that wouldn't open in the top floor front room, the shelf that had cracked in half in the equestrian section and three broken lights in the ground floor back room. He had rolled up his expensive shirt sleeves, unbuttoned his waistcoat and stayed and fixed everything well past closing time. When finished he had asked Nora to join him for fish and chips, ice-creams and a ride in the observation wheel on Piertown seafront promenade not far from Nora's village, so Nora had agreed and had had a wonderful time, although they had settled on delicious pizzas and calzones instead.

"Hello again." He greeted.

"Hello again." She smiled.

"These are for you."

"That's very nice of you."

"My pleasure."

"Would you like to come in?"

"Thanks." Humphrey followed Nora into the shop with a nod at the customer, who left with his stuffed squirrel.

"I didn't know we had a delivery of new stock due." Nora admitted, placing the box on the floor.

Humphrey put the last two boxes beside hers and straightened up, rotating his left shoulder.

"Georgina took me on a call at the weekend where she bought an entire library." Humphrey explained, slipping off his sunglasses. "I helped her load up the van this morning and offered to deliver them to you because she's been to the dentist."

"Thanks." Nora smiled.

"You're welcome." Humphrey smiled back, watching Nora turn to examine the books and pick up a bright, crisp, early Wisden's Cricketers' Almanac.

"Georgina said there are some special books in these boxes, some of them quite expensive. I'm here to cover your lunch so you don't have to eat while sitting behind the counter serving customers."

"That's nice of you."

"I can stay until two o'clock."

"I'll go for lunch at one o'clock if that's alright." Nora replied, loading her arms with a selection of leather bound volumes from her box.

"Why. Do you have a lunch date?" Humphrey asked quickly.

Nora glanced at him.

"Only with a couple of swans I expect."

Humphrey grinned

"There's one more box in the van. I'll bring it in and then help unpack." He decided, heading out the door while looking back at her. "See you in a minute."

Nora watched him go, smiling to herself.

A man in a dark brown suit arrived as Humphrey walked past the window smiling at Nora. He was tall and handsome with rich black hair and a pleasant smile.

"Hi. Is this your shop?" He asked.

"No, I'm the manager here."

"I just bought the Indian restaurant behind here in Tree Lane. It overlooks your back yard."

"Oh, hello! We heard it was under new ownership."

"I'm Max." He stuck his hand out and Nora shook it.

"I'm Nora."

"A pleasure, Nora. I moved in last week. I'm keeping it as an Indian Restaurant with the same interior layout but I thought about choosing a new name for a fresh start. It's a massive property with loads of rooms. I'll have to give you a tour one day."

"Well, welcome to Castletown." Nora smiled. "Did you also hear about our previous trouble with your predecessor and the blocked drains?" Nora then asked.

He grimaced.

"I did. Don't worry; I won't be pouring cooking oil down the sinks."

"Best not." Nora chuckled.

"Did it cause a lot of problems?"

"Several. All the drains from the other nearby shops and the flats back up into our yard when blocked. It's most unpleasant. Georgina, the owner of this shop, had to pay for a company to unblock the main drain that runs alongside all of our properties and the cause was a build-up of cooking oil."

Max winced. His iPhone then started to ring.

"Oh excuse me, Nora; I have the builders coming in this week. Good to meet you."

"You too." Nora smiled.

He answered his phone with a wink at Nora, heading off as Humphrey returned carrying his final box, speaking to a large man who was strolling with him.

"We're on a mystery coach tour." The man was saying, trailed by two elderly ladies clasping postcards.

"We've no idea where we're going." One lady beamed.

"We're hoping it's the sea, else there'll be a riot; we're from Buckinghamshire." The other added.

"You should see the sea while you're down here." Humphrey agreed.

"Two postcards?" Nora smiled, taking the cards from the lady.

"Thank you dear. Do you sell stamps?"

"I'm afraid we don't. Maybe one day."

"Do you have any non-fiction?" The man asked.

Humphrey gave Nora a look and headed for the kitchen to make himself a cup of tea.

"Erm…well actually they're all non-fiction except upstairs where all the fiction is kept." Nora replied to the customer.

"Do you have any Danielle Steele?" The lady with the postcards asked, passing Nora a handful of two pence coins.

"There were some Danielle Steele paperbacks in the charity shop, Mavis. They'd be cheaper than in here." Her friend explained.

"I'm looking for a book. It's old. Would you have it?" The man next asked, picking up a business card and reading it.

"It depends what it is." Nora said, slipping the postcards into a paper bag.

"Well, it's green." He peered at Nora and smirked. "You probably haven't."

Nora stared at him.

"We'd better get back to the coach" Mavis said, returning her purse to her handbag. "Thank you dear."

A man with two walking sticks was attempting to enter the shop. Nora watched as the coach party grew impatient and Mavis attempted to squash past him.

"I CAN'T GET IN!" The man cried. With much huffing, puffing and complaining he manoeuvred his two sticks first and almost swung in. He scowled at the coach party and remained blocking the door, breathing hard while mopping his forehead.

"Are you alright there?" Nora asked tentatively.

The man grinned, showing enormous yellow tombstone-like teeth with a few gaps between them. He had a huge white beard and his woollen jumper was stained with food. He shuffled in, his sticks slamming on the flagstones and then on the carpet.

"One postcard." He announced and slammed it onto the desk. "They're after me. That helicopter out there, it's looking for me."

Nora took the card.

"What did you do?" She bit back a smile.

"If I told you that I'd have to KILL YOU!" He shouted dramatically and started coughing and spluttering and hacking so that Nora backed away.

Humphrey practically ran into the front room, spilling the freshly made tea he was holding, having heard the shouting and banging. He stopped in the walkway, glancing from Nora to her customer, who looked at him suspiciously.

"Do you have a stamp?" The man demanded, banging one of his sticks on the floor and then dropping the other. "Blast and damnation. I can't pick that up. Someone help me!"

"It's fine, I'll get it sir." Humphrey offered, putting his mug down next to Nora's and placing a book across both of them to protect them against the man's spittle.

"Don't split it! It's always splitting and I fall flat on my face in the gutter." He cried.

Nora saw Humphrey's shoulders shaking with silent laughter.

"Can you write it for me? I can't write." He asked, his blue eyes wild.

Humphrey walked around the desk to pick up a pen.

"What do you want written?" He offered.

"Dear John." The man bellowed, ignoring two people who came into the front from the back of the shop, looking alarmed at the commotion. They were carrying books to buy.

"Shall I take those for you?" Nora asked.

"One of them is more expensive than the original price." The man pointed out.

"Ignore the original prices, sir." Humphrey cut in, drawing the postcard towards him. "We won't ever charge you seven and six and that's what you'll find is the original price on some of the books in here."

The man looked embarrassed.

"Dear John, they've taken my sheets." The man with the two sticks continued, rapping them together for attention.

"Excuse me!" A woman in the doorway called.

Nora looked up from the till.

"Which way to the castle ruins?" She asked.

"Follow the road left and it's opposite the coach car parks." Nora explained. "Would you like a bag for these?"

"Please." Her customer nodded.

"When are you coming to visit me? I'm sure they're going to poison my stew, John. Phone me soon and visit. From Ted." The man in front of Humphrey concluded. "And a stamp."

Humphrey dug out his wallet and Nora watched him stick one of his own stamps onto the postcard. While she finished serving her customers, Humphrey wrote down the address that was loudly dictated to him and handed the card back to the man.

"Where is there a bank here?" He demanded.

"What bank do you want?" Humphrey asked, walking around to help him.

"Gumfoundles man, a bank. A bank to change some money!"

"Up the road." Humphrey grinned, walking with him to the door. There was a struggle to get up the step and much shouting of 'I CAN'T GET OUT' until he finally left.

Nora finally handed Humphrey his tea.

"You gave him a free stamp."

He took the mug with a dashing grin.

"I thought it would impress you."

"He didn't pay for the card either you know." Nora added as he took a sip of tea.

Humphrey choked.

"Didn't he?"

Nora chuckled.

"Best not tell Georgina." She suggested, slapping his back as he coughed.

They unpacked more of the new stock and finished their tea until Nora noticed the time on the clock above the shop alarm.

"I'll go and grab some lunch." She said, unhooking her coat from where it hung behind them in the small walkway leading to beneath the stairs.

"See you in a bit." Humphrey smiled.

Nora smiled back and set off out of The Secondhand Bookworm, closing the door behind her.

The sun was shining across the cobbled square where the community policewoman was writing a ticket for a Volvo parked next to the war memorial, with a look of smugness. There was a cold wind so Nora pulled her collar tight, shoved her hands in her pockets and waited for a stream of cars to pass by before crossing the road to head into the delicatessen. The bell rang above the door as Nora stepped down the sunken stone step.

"Afternoon," The owner, Philip, greeted her, wiping his hands on his apron, almost hidden behind a delivery of organic cheese wheels.

"Hello." Nora waved.

"Busy in the bookshop?"

"Not bad for a Monday."

"It's been dead in here." Alice called from the kitchen where she was making sandwiches. "Although someone bought our entire supply of roasted hog."

Nora grimaced, browsing an arrangement of stuffed olives next to heaps of newly baked bread before moving to ponder the rows of freshly made sandwiches and baguettes in the fridge.

"I saw the new Indian Restaurant owner just pop in to visit you." Alice said, stepping out of the kitchen while mixing a bowl of tuna and mayonnaise with sweetcorn.

Nora nodded.

"Yes, he seems nice. Mackerel pate and salad sandwich, artichoke heart and grilled pepper baguette, peanut butter, creamed cheese and celery barm." She read aloud.

"I'm making Brie and grape rolls with flaked almonds and basil back here." Alice called over her shoulder as she returned to the kitchen.

Nora smiled politely, chose a simple cheese and salad in granary bread, paid for it, bid Philip and Alice goodbye and left the shop quickly, as a lady in a bright yellow bobble hat entered pondering her grocery list.

Holding her neatly wrapped sandwich, Nora walked past the butchers where Tim winked at her as he pulled out a tray of chipolatas.

She stepped across the small road and stood before a row of jewellery shops, a traditional sweet shop, an antique shop, a clothes shop and a furniture shop, choosing to go to her favourite garden to eat her lunch in peace.

A sightseeing boat was moored on the river edge where people sat eating cream teas or feeding the ducks that stood along the top of the wall amidst black-headed gulls. It was almost deserted down the little road that ran along the river, where Nora walked past a car park followed by the old converted salt factories which had been in use back when Castletown was a port.

The first public garden was full of flowers, shrubs and trees with a circle of empty benches, low walls, a great magnolia tree in bloom and a bench up some steps overlooking the river. Nora noticed Tobey from the bank feeding two swans and some ducks with Imogene from the organic greengrocer shop, so she opened the gate and stepped up to the wall by the fast flowing watercourse.

Imogene turned and grinned. She was petite and pretty with a blond pixie cut and enormous green eyes.

"Hey, Nora."

"Hi, Imogene."

"Hi, Nora." Tobey smiled, throwing a handful of crisps for the birds.

"Hello." She greeted, opening her sandwich packet.

"How's the bookshop been this morning?" Imogene asked.

Leaning against the wall Nora bit into a half of her sandwich, contemplating the view of the tall town houses across the river while one of the swans looked eagerly at her lunch.

"Strangely busy." Nora replied. "I left Humphrey unpacking a delivery of books Georgina marked up this morning."

Imogene looked interested.

"Oh, he's the owner's brother, isn't he?"

"Yes." Nora nodded.

"Is he dating anyone at the moment?"

Nora gave her a look.

"I don't think so."

"Is he working at the bookshop now?"

"No. He just helps out a bit. He's in between jobs."

"I heard he was a successful businessman up in London."

"He was. He wants a change from the fast pace up there."

"So, he's into books?"

"Not really. But he knows a lot about them."

"Where *do* all your books come from?" Tobey asked. He had only been working in Castletown for a couple of months and had yet to visit the bookshop.

Nora pondered the path alongside the river to where the road to and from the town arched over the water. A little motor boat was casting off from the café on the water's edge.

"They're all bought from various customers who have clear-outs or inherit a library or are downsizing." She explained, watching a robin hop down from the magnolia tree onto the wall not far from them. "People either bring them in to us or we call out to them in our little bookshop van."

"Nora knows every book she has in stock." Imogene told Tobey, sipping her coffee.

"Roughly." Nora amended modestly.

"Awesome. And do you know every fruit and vegetable on your shelves too?" Tobey teased.

"Pretty much." Imogene winked.

Nora laughed, watching Imogene nudge his arm with a grin and a flutter of her eyelashes.

The sun grew stronger as wispy clouds sped across the sky and disappeared, revealing a blue hue above. The air was warm so Nora removed her coat, enjoying the feel of it and longing for summer. She stood at the wall with Tobey and Imogene for almost half an hour, talking about events in the town and their various customers.

Imogene left first to return to the greengrocers, although Nora suspected she was going to go and see Humphrey. Five minutes later Tobey and Nora collected their rubbish, popped it into the bin outside the garden and made their way back to the town centre.

"Are you working all week?" Tobey asked, slipping his sunglasses on, looking at Nora beside him.

"All week including Saturday." She replied.

"Lucky you. Any plans for the weekend?"

"Not yet. I'm sure something will come along."

"Do you know if Imogene is dating anyone?"

"I don't think there's anyone serious." Nora assured him.

He looked interested and thoughtful as they walked past the riverside houses and back to the square. Tobey saw Nora attentively across the road to the traditional sweetshop where they peered through the window discussing the retro sweets, fudges and drinks.

"How long have you known Imogene then?" He asked casually.

Nora smiled.

"She opened her organic greengrocer shop three months ago in Castletown, but she doesn't live here. She's over in Seatown I think. If you're interested in her ask her for a drink in the Black Hart after work. She closes her shop up at five."

"I think I will." Tobey decided with a determined look.

"Great." She chuckled. "Have a nice afternoon in the bank. I'd better relieve Humphrey."

"I might buy some of those rhubarb and custards for Imogene." Tobey decided and headed for the door.

41

Smiling, Nora continued towards the bookshop where she almost bumped into a six foot tall skeleton holding a banner advertising the town Ghost Hunt. Nora gave a small squeal. The skeleton laughed hysterically.

"Wow, Nora. Every time." Ian mocked.

"Very funny, Ian." Nora sighed and left him to chase three screaming Japanese tourists up the road while she returned to the shop.

Humphrey made Nora a fresh cup of tea, making sure she had everything she needed for the rest of the afternoon alone.

"Anything interesting happen while I was at lunch?" Nora asked innocently, returning the keys to a little hook above the radiator after having used them to unlock the upstairs loo.

"No." Humphrey assured her, straightening his tie.

"Any interesting visitors?"

"A man who was looking for books about highland cattle keeping. And that small woman from the organic greengrocer shop popped in, the one who looks like a pixie."

"Imogene."

"Oh, was that her name? I think she was trying to sell me organic bananas or something. Anyway, she soon left."

Nora smiled to herself.

"You took a few sales." She examined the cash book, admiring Humphrey's neat penmanship.

"A couple of paperbacks and an art book. It was pretty quiet."

Nora watched him lift up the empty boxes which he had collapsed into a small pile, slip on his sunglasses and smile at her.

"See you soon. Have a good afternoon."

"See you soon." Nora bade and watched him leave, grinning as he passed the bay window still staring at her.

The post-lunchtime lull allowed Nora to rearrange several shelves of stock behind the counter where the leather bound books and first editions were situated. She was interrupted three times in the hour after Humphrey had left to sign for a delivery of new local books Cara had ordered the previous week, to help the Ravens gather their mound of bags and to retrieve a volume from the window about lacemaking which an excited customer bought.

The sun moved around to stream in the right hand side of the bay window, casting its light pleasingly on the beige carpet of the front room. Once the leathers were arranged, some early P G Wodehouse's displayed, three piles organised for Nora and Jane to put away the following day, and a sign typed, printed, cut out, glued onto card and placed before a big tome about Spanish dresses in the window, Nora unpacked the new local books and sat down to price them inside in pencil.

The telephone rang, making her jump in the disturbed silence.

"The Secondhand Bookworm." She greeted cheerfully.

"Hi Nora, it's Georgina." The friendly voice returned.

"Ah, hello! How are things?"

"Oh, I'm so bored of paperwork. Fluffy, get off my keyboard!! Sorry, he's been running up the curtains this morning."

"Oh dear. How are your teeth?"

"Humph. Fine, I guess. How's it going over there?"

"Surprisingly busy this morning but a little bit quiet at the moment. We're on…." Nora's gaze scanned down the cash book page of written sales. "…two hundred and four pounds."

"That's good for a Monday. Humphrey's just walked in."

"Ah. He was great with our customer 'Two-Sticks'." Nora said.

Georgina laughed.

"He can tell me all about it. Did you see the book in one of the boxes for the Cat-Man?"

"I saw some under the counter that Humphrey put aside for him." Nora leaned back to consider them again.

The Cat-Man was one of The Secondhand Bookworm regulars. He had bright blue hair and always smelt strongly of whisky. He collected books about cats, even special ones, and didn't blink an eye at the price of rare or collectable editions such as any early Louis Wain books which sometimes reached several hundred pounds.

"I left a message to say we had that one aside for him." Georgina explained. "He may already have it but the dust wrapper is so yummy. It's rare to get it in such good condition. Oh, tomorrow, Jane won't be able to come in to work. She just texted me so say that her son has a stomach bug so she thinks he'll be off school so, let me see…" There was the sound of shuffling as Georgina consulted her shop rosters. "I thought I'd split Roger over both branches so he can start the morning in Seatown and then come to you to cover your lunch and spend the afternoon with you there. I've got a hair appointment in the morning and then I'll do the afternoon in Seatown as I need to complete this paperwork in the office upstairs in the shop."

"Okay, that all sounds good."

"Fluffy! Leave Humphrey's shoelaces alone!"

Nora giggled.

"I heard there might be a lot of rain tomorrow throughout the County of Cole so hopefully you'll have a few customers over there despite any downpours."

"Yes, I'm sure some eager bookworms will brave the weather for their reading material." Nora straightened up. "I have a customer coming downstairs. I'd better go."

"Okay, I'll catch up with you tomorrow. Bye." She rang off and Nora hung up just as a tall man wearing a cowboy hat came into the front room from the back and dropped a book on the counter with a furrowed brow. He had enormous white sideburns and a scar in the shape of a banana on his right cheek.

"This book is marked too high. The dust wrapper is torn. I'll give you five pounds for it" He proposed dryly.

Nora drew the book towards her and picked it up.

"Oh dear. I see it has a little rip but I can't change the price." She said, examining the book which had a small tear on the back wrapper.

"It's in used condition." He pointed a finger at the tear. "I'd buy it for a fiver but no more."

Nora opened the book.

"It's in used condition because it was previously owned and read by someone else. This is a secondhand bookshop." She arched an eyebrow. "It's priced at ten pounds so I certainly couldn't knock five pounds off. I can't do it for half price for you."

"You'll never sell it for ten pounds." He almost sang, glaring at her.

Nora leaned back so as to put it on a pile of books tottering on the floor behind her, waiting to go away on the shelves in the upper rooms when Roger was with her tomorrow afternoon.

"Well, if you don't want to purchase it then I'm sure someone else will buy it." She shrugged.

The cowboy's stare trailed after the book.

"Let me look at it again!" He lunged at it, making Nora scream silently. Quickly she handed it back to him, watching warily as he examined every inch of it. He tutted at the tear.

"I'll take it for eight pounds but no more." He said.

Nora smiled apologetically.

"I'm so sorry; it's a good book about horse riding so it'll retain its price despite the damaged dust wrapper." She knew.

He screwed up his face so his banana scar resembled a bright red angry dolphin, then he reached for his wallet.

"I'll take it but I think it's priced too high." He grumbled.

"Okay, I'm sure you'll enjoy reading it. Would you like a bag for it?" Nora stood up to work the till.

"No. But I'll have a receipt." He glowered.

As Nora took his ten pound note the door opened.

"The last of the big spenders." A lady's voice sailed in.

Nora looked up to see a large woman wearing a figure hugging floral dress step down into the shop, waving a single postcard.

"Oh! My corns." She winced, padding towards the counter.

The cowboy glared at her, and then at Nora, and then at the new arrival once more before leaving with his book and little paper till receipt.

"Hello." Nora greeted politely.

She leaned back for a small paper postcard bag while the woman placed her handbag on the counter.

Georgina had decided to stock postcards in The Secondhand Bookworm last summer when Nora had been plagued by tourists asking where they could purchase them one too many times. Rather than constantly send them to the souvenir shop, Georgina had ordered her own stock in and was now doing a roaring trade. Nora suspected another spinner would be ordered in the near future and she'd have to drag that up the step and out onto the pavement every day too. She hoped the people at the souvenir shop weren't too angry.

"Thank you dear." The lady said when Nora placed the postcard into the small paper bag. She rummaged for her purse and was joined by her husband who looked keenly around the front room.

"You could get lost in here." He decided.

"Oh, yes. We have a lot of books and rooms." Nora smiled.

"Here you are, dear." The lady offered Nora a ten pound note.

"Do you have any change?" Nora asked.

"No." She assured her.

Nora took the note while the lady placed the twenty pence card in her bag.

"Where is a good place for a cup of tea?" she asked while Nora counted out her change.

"There are several nice cafes here in Castletown." Nora explained. "I know all of the owners so I don't favour one in particular. They are all lovely."

"What would you recommend though, sweetheart?" The husband asked with a wink.

"Well, you can sit outside by the river down at Riverside Café or there's The Flowery Teacup which does very good fruit cake." She proposed.

"I don't want a cake, just a cup of tea!" The lady was adamant.

"Oh. Well, they all do tea anyway." Nora closed the till.

"Thank you dear." The lady smiled.

As they walked away, a couple come through from the back room.

"You've spelt *Bodleian* wrong." The man said severely.

Nora blinked.

"Pardon?"

"On your sign for the run of books about the *Bodleian* Library back there." He looked at her as if she was an idiot. "You spelt it wrong!"

"Oh, I'm very sorry." Nora apologised, thinking of Terri who had done the sign at the weekend. "Oh dear. Well, at least we all know what it's meant to say."

The woman with him clicked her tongue, shaking her head while looking Nora up and down.

"You need to change it!"

"Yes, change it right away!"

"Erm, okay, I will." Nora assured warily.

They walked off and as the man opened the door he looked back at Nora.

"It says a lot for English education!" He almost shouted in disgust.

Nora flinched when the door slammed. The couple walked along a few steps, peered in through the window at her and the man shook his fist. He then mouthed the word '*Bodleian*' and shook his head.

Nora sighed and reached for her cup of tea.

"Are you closing up now?" A man asked, watching Nora hoist up a box from the pavement to take into the shop. It was almost five o'clock and the town was empty, expect for a gypsy walking up and down knocking on the shop doors with a small box of lucky heather, and the large man standing in front of her. Nora hoped she'd get away before the gypsy reached The Secondhand Bookworm.

"Yes." She nodded. "We're closed now."

"Okay, I won't be long." He made to enter the shop, squashing Nora against the door frame.

"Excuse me!" Nora grimaced as he popped through the opening between her, her box and the opposite door frame with a loud grunt. "I'm afraid we're closing."

"Yes. I won't be long."

Nora stared after him baffled. She placed a box of cheap pavement books she was holding next to the postcard spinner she had already brought inside.

"Is there anything particular you're looking for? I have to cash up." She called.

"A specific novel, yes." He said, continuing across the room.

"Our novels are in the attic room. You'll have to be quick." Nora glowered.

"Yes, yes. I won't be long. It's unlikely you'll have it but my bus doesn't come for ten minutes so I thought I'd kill some time."

Nora growled like a gremlin as he stomped off up the stairs.

"Hello, Nora." A well-spoken voice greeted.

Nora looked aside to see a tall, plump man approaching the bookshop wearing a faded green velvet jacket.

"Oh hello, Mr Rutler." She greeted fondly.

"Any new theatre books in stock?"

"I'm not sure. You're welcome to have a look." She offered and he followed her inside.

"I've just been to the new organics shop. Bally good stuff in there." He said, rustling a brown bag stuffed full of vegetables that emitted a strong smell of leeks.

"I heard it's meant to be nice."

"Yes it is, it is." He agreed vigorously, pausing by the architecture section. "Hmm, that's new. Oh, what a wonderful book! I don't have anything on Cistercian Abbeys. I'll have that." He decided keenly.

He passed it to Nora who popped it onto the desk top, leaving him to browse intently along several shelves while she continued bringing the things in from outside. Once finished, Nora turned the sign to CLOSED and popped her key in the lock, turning it.

"You're closing. I've finished I think. Just the Cistercian abbeys today." Mr Rutler said, pleased. He dug out his wallet.

"It is a lovely book. Twenty pounds." She punched the priced into the till and then pressed the ten percent discount. "Eighteen to you."

"Ah! You're very kind. So kind." He passed Nora a crisp twenty pound note. "I've hundreds of your bags, I must bring some back. Thank you. I shall read that tonight."

"And enjoy your leeks." Nora smiled, walking round to see him out.

He laughed heartily and tipped his hat at her.

"Cheerio, Miss Jolly." He bowed and Nora closed the door.

The man browsing as he waited for his bus returned empty handed and left without saying anything, so Nora locked up, pleased to see the gypsy heading off away from the shop.

Once she was finally alone, Nora banked the PDQ machine and cashed up the till, turned off the computer, ran around and checked that everyone was truly out of the shop, turned off the back lights, locked the kitchen up and shrugged into her coat.

"At last." She sighed, happily.

Grabbing her bag Nora switched off the front lights, put in the alarm code and left The Secondhand Bookshop, locking the door behind her. She had parked her car at the top of the hill by the Roman Catholic Church so she popped inside to light a candle and say a prayer of thanksgiving that she hadn't strangled a single rude customer that day before she jumped into her car at last and drove away, leaving Castletown in the fading light.

3 MORNING GLORY

"Young man! Do you sell national book tokens?"

The tiny woman stood on the doorstep of The Secondhand Bookworm the next morning, blowing her nose.

Nora turned around from where she was crouched straightening a row of new Ordnance Survey maps on the short bookshelves under the front of the counter.

"I'm a woman. And no, sorry we don't." She replied with a smile.

"Thanks a lot." The woman glowered, turning to leave. "Oh, sorry! I didn't see you there!"

Nora watched the woman leave quickly to admit a laughing French man and his black poodle that had been waiting to enter the shop. The poodle ran towards Nora.

"I hope you're not allergic to Princess." The man called after the woman with his strong French accent. "Ah *oui*, many people find Princess's perfume too delectable."

"Good morning, Henri." Nora greeted, almost bowled over by Princess. She winced to see the muddy pawprints and footprints all across the carpet, a regular occurrence when Henri was back in town.

"We've been for a swim in the river." Henri chuckled unrepentantly, looking over the Folio Society books in the case to the left of the bay window.

"I can see." Nora muttered, watching him continue to tread mud all over the clean carpet.

"Ah, is that us, Princess, with all the mud? Ah, sorry, Nora." He apologised, persisting in walking about regardless.

Nora remained silent, straightening up when Princess scurried off into the back rooms sniffing piles of books.

"How are you, Nora?" Henri asked cheerfully.

"Very well. Are you back in Castletown to stay?" Nora replied.

"Ah, *non*. Just to visit my family for a week or too. Then back home I go to France. Ah! You have a Graham Greene folio. Put it by for me; I will buy it next week!"

Nora took the book.

Princess ran out into the front of the shop and headed towards the door. Henri stuck his foot out to trap her lead and she stopped sharp.

"She's off! I shall try back next week for the Graham Greene and to browse and find some more good reading. *Au Revoir*." Henri announced, stooped to catch the lead between his fingers and strode off speaking to a hacking Princess in French.

Once he had left, Nora popped the Graham Greene folio under the counter and pondered the wet mud all over the carpet, deciding to leave it to dry and vacuum it up at the end of the day. She winced at it and then picked up the stock list she had needed to check for the postcard rack.

"I hope you're not going to put those postcards out today. A big risk. It's going to rain." Monica Blythe advised grandly, stepping into the shop.

Nora turned to see one of the castle ruins tour guides, an elderly lady who often popped in on her way past The Secondhand Bookworm. She was small and thin with bright red lipstick applied messily on small perpetually puckered lips. Her eyes were droopy and she always wore the same black rain coat and black velvet beret.

"Good morning, Monica." Nora greeted cheerfully.

"Any luck with 'The Lucius Fairy Tale' book yet, Nora?" Monica asked morbidly.

"No, no luck so far." Nora assured her.

"I remember it as a child. Great ferocious dragons, brave princesses, wonderful stories of chivalry and bravery. Not like the sex tales these days." She shook her head grimly.

"I'll keep an eye out for it. You never know, it could turn up."

"Thank you, dear. But I doubt it."

Monica looked at her watch.

"Oh, my duties start at eleven so I'd better go up to the castle. Watch out for rain, Nora. I'm sure it will be a terrible downpour." She waved grandly, leaving the shop.

Nora closed the door behind Monica, peering up at the sky through the large window above the letterbox until Max from the Indian Restaurant stood in front of her holding a steaming cup of coffee. She opened the door again.

"Hello, Max."

"Hello again, Nora. Selling lots of books today?" He asked, peering inside.

"Not yet. How's it going at the restaurant?"

"Good. The builders are here and we need to get into your yard out the back to survey the kitchen and flats. I noticed the wooden door. Mind if we use it?"

Nora nodded.

"No problem. Come through and I'll unbolt it for you." Nora offered, stepping back so he could enter the shop.

"Wonderful, Nora." Max appreciated gratefully.

He followed her as she dropped her postcard stock list onto the desk and grabbed the bunch of shop keys.

"You wouldn't believe how many rooms there are above the restaurant. I think I'll convert them into more flats. Need a place to live?"

"As a matter of fact I am looking for a new flat to rent." Nora admitted, unlocking the kitchen door.

The door to the back yard was in the kitchen. The yard was small and mossy and constantly steeped in shadows but it attracted a family of sparrows and one insane wagtail which Nora sometimes fed with crumbs from her sandwiches or stale biscuits.

The buildings surrounded it completely in a small square with a black door that led to a covered alley and then a second passage that went left to the high street or right to the rubbish bins and a car park behind the old town hotel, some more flats and the Indian Restaurant.

"Well, once I've renovated the building I'll give you first choice." Max said and pinched Nora's bottom.

Nora yelped and turned around to face him. He winked cheekily so she laughed falsely, hurrying ahead to the door.

"I'll bear that in mind." She said, deciding she would rather live in the outside loo than in one of Max's flats with him as her landlord.

"Great." Max grinned.

A box of mouldy paperbacks was waiting to be taken to the bins by the large black, bolted door. Nora stepped over the box, opened the door, let Max through and returned to the front of the shop where someone was calling.

"Is anyone here?" A man hailed. "Hello? Earth to person in charge? Do you hear me? Hellooooo?"

"Hello." Nora greeted, stepping through the walkway into the front room.

"Ah, good morning. Are you a bookshop?"

Nora stared at him as she hung up the shop keys. "Yes."

"That's nice to know. Do you buy books?"

Nora moved behind the counter.

"Yes, all of these books have been bought in secondhand." She explained.

"I've got some boxes in the car, full of books. Can I bring them in? They possibly won't be of any interest but you might want to take a look just in case." He asked, picking his nose.

Nora hid her revolted look.

"Yes, certainly. If you're happy to bring them in I'll go through and see what we can use." She agreed.

"I've parked my car on the cobbles opposite, is that okay?"

"Well, the wardens do have meltdowns when cars are left on the cobbles because it's part of the public highway but I haven't seen any about today, so if we keep an eye on it then it should be fine." Nora warned him.

"Grand. I'll be across with the books." He walked off as a customer came into the shop carrying a book from the cheap boxes outside.

"It says fifty pence." She pointed, handing a creased Agatha Christie paperback from the outside boxes to Nora. "What a bargain!"

"Thank you." Nora said cheerfully. "Would you like a bag?"

"No thanks. Do you buy books?"

"Yes we do." She took the pound coin.

"I inherited some from my godfather who died last month. They're all a dead bore; military books, some fiction, management and some science; a whole mixture. Can I take a business card?"

"Please do." Nora nodded, handing her the fifty pence change.

"Do you come out to look at books?"

"Yes, we have one or two calls days each week where we travel to look at books for sale. Give us a call when you're ready and we can arrange to come around."

"I will. Thanks!" She smiled.

Nora smiled politely, watching her leave with her book, reading the business card.

"Any Regimental Histories?" A man named Don asked loudly, walking in and heading for the back room.

"Not since Friday!" Nora assured her regular customer.

"I'll go and have a look anyway," he decided, walking past the counter towards the back.

"I'm pretty sure we don't."

"It's worth a look though."

"Is it?"

"You never know."

Nora rolled her eyes, never able to convince Don that regimental histories didn't come in for stock every day.

The man with the books for sale appeared on the doorstep holding a big blue crate.

"A large fat bloke with three chins told me I couldn't park there. He wasn't a warden so I told him he couldn't tell me what to do. But he looked like he was going to hunt one down so we'd best be quick!" He announced.

"Oh dear."

Nora walked around to meet him and he dropped the crate onto the floor.

"I've got a set like that in the car. In good nick." He said, pointing to a blue run of Dickens novels in the window. Nora looked up.

"If it's a complete set, sixteen volumes and in good condition, then we can use it but they are very common sets. We'd pay ten pounds for it."

"It's red."

"Yes, they published it in red cloth too, with gold lettering."

"Yes, that's it. I'll leave you to look through those and go and get the rest." He decided, striding off.

"Any Muffin the *Moo*?" A familiar voice called in.

Nora looked up to see a plump, balding man with his front teeth missing who showed up whenever there was a craft fair in the town hall or scout hut round by the entrance to the castle ruins. He sold small sculptures of mules and collected Muffin the Mule books but he referred to the later as a *moo* rather than a mule.

"No, I'm afraid not." Nora replied.

"Na, na, na, it's okay; I always ask when I'm here." He exclaimed. "They're very rare, very rare, Muffin the Moo books are. See you again."

He left Nora looking down at the books in the crate. There was a large selection of art books, one about Monet, which she knew they already had, a biography of Edward Hopper and a selection of books about various art movements.

Nora pulled some books about walking out of the crate, an interesting book about public hanging, some Shire albums and a set of 'The Spectator' rebound in clean red cloth. The rest was tatty fiction which Nora left with the Monet biography.

The man brought in a few more boxes with the bully and his three chins glaring in the window making phone calls, so Nora quickly pulled out a variety of others, including the complete set of Dicken's books, resulting in three stacks which she pondered thoughtfully, working out the pricing. Then she made him an offer which he cheerfully accepted.

"Do you know that bloke?" The man asked as Nora paid out the cash and wrote his details down in the cash book.

"The man with the three chins?"

"Yeah, him."

"No." Nora peered at the bright red, threatening face pressed against the glass of the bay window. His three flattened chins looked like three extra smiles. His real mouth was turned down in a scowl. She took out her iPhone and took a photo of him quickly, causing him to frown. "I'll ask the owner of The Secondhand Bookworm if she recognises him."

"He said he's called the police on me for parking on the cobbles."

"Oh dear. Sorry, I haven't seen him before."

"Are you sure about that? He must be a local."

"Maybe he's new." Nora grimaced. "But he could be a visitor."

"You might want to report him for harassing your customers." The man suggested, picking up the books she didn't want and his empty boxes too.

"Yes, I'll consider it." Nora agreed.

He then pulled open the door and left.

The man with the three chins shook his fist at Nora's customer and then followed the car down the road as he drove away. Nora hoped he wasn't a new resident.

The Secondhand Bookworm was quiet again at last.

After making a fresh cup of tea and sending the photo of the menacing new man to Georgina, Nora sat on a little stool by the bay window, marking up the new stock she had just purchased while glancing out at the street.

The town square was empty.

A solitary man in a red coat and red trousers stood reading the menu outside the Italian Restaurant opposite, while Gregory in the bakery placed a fresh basket of white chocolate and strawberry muffins in his window.

The weather was overcast. Tiny spots of rain dotted the windows. Nora had clipped the four black cheap paperback boxes to the walls outside. They lived either side of the door in two neat towers made of two boxes each, the large sizes on the bottom, the small sizes on the top. The bargain books inside were usually sheltered against any light rain, provided it wasn't windy enough to blow it against the insides, so Nora decided to leave them seeing as it was only spitting lightly.

Georgina replied to Nora's text photo.

'Who on earth is that supposed to be?!!'

Nora laughed.

'I wondered if you recognised him. He was harassing one of our customers for parking on the cobbles.'' Nora sent back.

A moment later:

'No I don't know him and I don't want to!'

'Hopefully he's not a new resident.'

'Hopefully not! I'll make sure Roger comes over to you in good time. I'm heading to the office in Seatown now xx'

'Okay, speak soon xx'

Nora had just finished marking up the Dickens set when the shop telephone began to ring.

"I hope that's not you Mr Hill." Nora warned, easing herself up with a groan and heading over to the phone carrying her mug of tea. She picked up the receiver warily.

"The Secondhand Bookworm." She greeted, leaning over the counter.

"It…is…*POURING*…here." Roger's annoyed voice told her from the Seatown branch.

"Really?" Nora walked back over to the window, peering up at the dark skies. "It's just started to rain lightly here but only a few spots."

"I reckon you'll have the tsunami in fifteen minutes. The wind is easterly." Roger said. "I managed to bring the penguin book deckchairs in from the pavement just in time. No. I wasn't sunbathing today."

"Are you sure you weren't." Nora teased. "It's a wonderful advertisement and Georgina's convinced that's why you sell so many over there. You make such an attractive male model."

"Har-har." Roger laughed falsely. "Georgina just phoned and told me to let you know when I'd be over. Have you been complaining about me?"

"No!" Nora assured, offended.

"That's alright then. I'm planning to leave here a little after one o'clock. Can you hold out that long? Just a moment. Hello sir, can I help?"

Nora waited for Roger to direct his customer to the nautical section. She sipped her tea which was lukewarm.

"As I was saying; I need to run some errands here on my lunch break. I'll get to you by one thirty. Is that convenient? Blimey, it's really tipping it down now."

"That's fine." Nora nodded. "Thanks for letting me know."

"As long as you don't fade away into nothingness."

"No. I have some biscuits under the counter."

"I had Mrs Bookbinder in for one whole hour earlier." Roger then shared flatly. "Cara left me stuck with her. The old bat wouldn't leave. She just stood in front of the counter telling me about all the books she's rebound and how she'll bind several of our books for us to increase their value. In the end I pretended I had to make a phone call."

"I do wish Georgina had given her a job when she asked." Nora teased. "You'd have a lovely time working together over there."

"What a pleasant female you are." Roger said sarcastically.

Nora laughed.

"Cripes, the road is flooding outside. I'd better go and stop Mr Logan from drowning. He's one of our best customers and I want my bonus this month." Roger then exclaimed.

"See you later." Nora chuckled and hung up.

Roger was in his early fifties and knew Georgina from an amateur orchestra they both played in ten years ago. Georgina had played the double bass and Roger the timpani drums. Georgina said Roger had played the timpani drums to pretend they were the faces of his ex-wives while going through his fourth divorce.

When he had been made redundant from his accounting firm a year ago he had turned up at The Secondhand Bookworm and asked Georgina if she had any jobs going. Georgina had offered Roger three full days a week, mainly in the Seatown branch, with the opportunity for bonus pay if the month's takings went over the projected targets, but she had forbidden him from playing timpani in the shops. Neither of them went to the amateur orchestra anymore and Roger wasn't angry with his ex-wives any longer either. Word was he occasionally dated two of them whenever he went to the theatre or cinema.

Max popped back to tell Nora they had finished in the yard so she slipped out through the kitchen, bolted up the big black door and was back just in time to receive a text message on her iPhone. She sat down on the swivel chair to read it.

'Read any good books lately?'

The message was from Humphrey.

'I haven't had the chance today. It's been quite busy.'
She sent back.

A moment later.

'Are you on your own?'

'Roger's due over at one thirty.'

'Good. It's been raining hard in London all day. I'm under an umbrella queuing for coffee.'

'Are you working up there again?'

'Not a chance. I've a few things to sort out. Will be back down in Piertown later this afternoon. Queue's finally moving. Speak to you soon.'

Nora smiled.

'Don't get too wet.'

'Will try not to.'

She swiped her phone screen, turned it off and popped it into the pocket of her jeans, still smiling to herself.

Nora had finished her postcard stock check, sent the list through to Seatown and was fixing a flyer about local teeth cleaning on the wall by the alarm pad when the door opened and a man stepped down.

"Greetings to you. I was in your Seatown branch earlier today." The thin man said slowly and precisely. "And the gentleman there told me that you have a lot of annuals here."

"Children's annuals?" Nora asked.

He stood in front of her, smiling blandly.

"Yes."

"We have some upstairs in the children's room."

His smile didn't falter.

"I've parked behind the shop. Is it your space I'm using?"

"No." Nora grimaced. "We don't have our own parking space. It belongs to the private flats by the old hotel car park. The person who owns it almost sued us because our large rubbish bin had wheeled onto their parking space during a storm. Probably best that you move your car as quickly as possible."

"Where can I park my car instead?" He smiled.

"Anywhere along the main street for an hour." Nora explained.

The tall, thin man remained smiling at her for a moment and then turned away.

"I'll go and move my car." He said, ignoring the door flying open and a burly man with facial tattoos stalking into the shop.

Nora shrunk back against the antiquarian book cases when she saw him.

"Any copies of 'Gruesome Cole Murders' in stock yet, darlin'?" Tattoo-Face asked roughly, referring to the title of a book about murders that had taken place in the County of Cole.

He was followed by a little scruffy friend who looked like a ferret.

"He's in the book." The Ferret announced proudly. "Because he killed a man."

"Yes, I heard." Nora nodded warily, keeping her distance.

"Has a whole chapter to himself he has." The Ferret told her. "We want a copy so he can autograph it for me."

"I didn't mean to kill the bloke. It was self-defence." The killer assured with a wicked grin. "But it was bloody and brutal."

"I remember you telling me before." Nora smiled politely, easing slowly around the antiquarian cases to the walkway that led under the stairs.

"Is your true crime section still on the top floor, then darlin'?" The killer asked

"Yes, but I haven't seen any copies of that book come in for a long time." Nora assured, peering at him from around the corner of the case.

"Ah, no harm in looking though." The killer shrugged, leading the way with the Ferret following closely. "I spoke to your boss at the weekend. She said she gets them in occasionally."

When they were safely climbing the staircase, Nora relaxed with a sigh.

"Thanks very much Georgina." She grumbled, shaking her head. "More tea I think." She decided and slipped out into the kitchen.

4 TORRENTIAL RAIN, SANDWICHES AND SANDBAGS

Nora was unclipping the black boxes of books that stood either side of the door as the rain pelted down. She was suddenly aware of a lull in the downpour so looked up to see a large golf umbrella in the shape of a pink pig's head over her. Holding the sides of the boxes she turned and met a pair of bright green eyes.

"Oh, thank you!" Nora smiled at Sam from the butchers.

"Hold the umbrella and I'll take those inside for you. They look heavy." Sam offered, considering the wooden contraptions she was struggling with.

"It's fine, really. I've built up my muscles over the last few years." Nora assured him and lifted the top one off, stepping down into the shop. Sam closed the umbrella and unclipped the last box positioned beneath, following Nora inside with it.

"The rain is getting so heavy that the paperbacks are starting to get soggy." She said with a sigh.

Sam placed the box he was carrying next to hers on the small area of flagstones.

"You were getting soggy too." He had noticed.

Nora laughed.

"Yes, a little bit."

"Need me to help you dry off?"

Nora stared.

"I'm sure I'll be fine." She refused.

"Okay then, I'd best get back." Sam said, stepping back out into the rain and opening his piggy umbrella. "I'll be chopping up turkeys until closing time."

"That's…er…good to know."

"Bye Nora." Sam smiled.

"Thanks for the shelter."

Sam winked.

"Anytime."

The phone began to ring so Nora walked around the counter to answer it. Sam saluted a goodbye from the doorway, running back to the butcher shop with the umbrella back up against the downpour like a half human-half pig and she watched him go, frowning.

"The Secondhand Bookworm." Nora greeted cheerfully.

"Hello. I was in last week looking at a Chagall book. Do you remember me?" The lady on the other end asked.

Nora sat down, noticing the Skype chat flashing on the computer screen.

"Erm…"

"You probably get lots of customers in so maybe not. I was in with my sister and it was a book about the artist priced at seventeen pounds fifty. I'd like it after all! Can you put it by for me?"

Nora stood up again, walking to the art section by the window.

"I'll have a look and see if it's still here." She nodded, distracted slightly by the torrential rain outside which appeared to be falling harder.

"It's in the art section which is beside the window in the front room." The lady directed.

Nora smiled.

"Found it."

"I knew it would be there. I have intuitions. Well, you don't need to know about my psychic abilities I expect, but I have to just tell you that I had a vision of you locating it and me buying it. I inherited that ability from my grandmother. I wanted the book when I was there but my sister said I shouldn't be materialistic. She was always throwing away my things as a child. I think she's a Puritan. However, Chagall has been haunting my dreams in the form of his little goat playing a violin, so I knew I simply had to buy it. Can I pay for it now and my sister will collect it tomorrow? Do you take payment over the phone?"

While the woman had been blithering Nora had been distracted by the immense downpour of rain that seemed to be pummelling the whole street outside.

"Yes, you can pay for it now but would you just hold on one moment, please?" Nora asked and walked over to the door with the phone. She stared out into the road only a few feet beyond the sidewalk and caught her breath. A lake of water was forming and the drain outside was bubbling up, seemingly blocked. Where the road narrowed between the kerb and the side of the delicatessen on the corner opposite, the water was lapping up over the verges, pouring in torrents off of the roofs and creating a lagoon.

"Yikes!" Nora breathed.

"Hello?"

"Can I call you back, madam? We're about to have a flood in here I think. If I take your name and number I'll call you a bit later." Nora asked hastily, grabbing a pen and dropping the Chagall book onto the counter.

"Of course, no problem. How amazing. I had a premonition about a flood; it was in a town and several people drowned. I hope you weren't one of them, dear."

"Your name and number?" Nora prompted urgently.

"Oh yes, of course."

Nora took the woman's name and number and then turned as a lorry sped through the lake outside the shop and a wave of water hit the entire door with a crash. Nora winced when she saw a large slosh of water lap under the door, pour over the step, down onto the floor and start to spread slowly towards the carpet across the flagstones.

"That's not good." She said and looked around for a means of stopping it.

Another car whooshed past the shop through the submerged road so that a second wave hit the door window, making Nora flinch. More water poured in and Nora attempted pathetically to catch it with her hands.

"Flippin' heck. Is it monsoon season?" A man's voice came from behind her.

"Yes!" Nora decided, stepping back as the water poured inside. "Oh dear. This has never happened before. I think the cooking oil from that blasted Indian restaurant has lodged further down and the drains can't cope with the downpour."

"Have you got any sandbags?" The customer suggested.

"No."

They stepped back automatically as a bus went past. It slowed slightly but still created a wave which hit the window with another loud crash and lapped like overflowing bath water under the door and into the shop. Nora watched helplessly. The phone behind her began to ring.

"There's my taxi." The man spotted, opened the door and ran for it, swearing as the rain soaked him, still falling heavily.

"Thanks." Nora muttered, grimacing as the carpet started to change colour and the water began to spread.

She grabbed the phone and greeted the caller breathlessly.

"I'M STUCK!" Roger's dry, unimpressed voice was on the other end.

"We're being flooded!" Nora yelped back.

"Eh?"

"Really. It's flooded and pouring into the bookshop!"

"I'm in the van in the car park by the castle ruins."

"Can you come and help me?"

"I can't come out in this!"

"Oh no." Nora gaped at another wave of water sloshing under the door and picked up a book about Cole maps that was on the floor. "I'd better ask Georgina what to do." She decided and hung up on Roger. She phoned the Seatown shop, grimacing as another car passing by caused yet another breaker. Georgina was chuckling as she answered the telephone.

"Take care, Mr Sawyer. Goodbye. The Secondhand Bookworm." She greeted.

"Georgina it's me! We're being flooded. The drains are blocked outside and the water is pouring in under the door." Nora explained breathlessly.

"What?" Georgina was always calm in a crisis although her tone was edged with alarm. "How?"

"The traffic is speeding through the water and creating waves." Nora explained, wincing as the water continued to spread across the carpet.

"Where's Roger?" Georgina asked.

"In the van in the car park. Oh dear, another wave just poured in. I can't think what to do." She gasped.

"I'll phone the van and get Roger to come and help you. I don't care if he gets wet!" She decided. "Try and block up the bottom of the door. Call me back and let me know what's happening. Bye."

"Okay, bye." Nora rang off and looked around the room. "Ah-ha." She spotted the little box of free local area maps that usually stood outside, turned it upside down and poured about two hundred over the whole floor.

The free maps were the bane of Nora's life because the map of Castletown was so small and was folded up on the reverse side of a large map about Seatown that most people couldn't find it. People often came in asking for the map of Castletown and Nora had to tell them to unfold the sheet and it would be found inside.

Georgina insisted on stocking them because they were given to them free and there was a tiny square advert for The Secondhand Bookworm around the edge of the Seatown map with fifty other local businesses. They were usually given four or five boxes to get through a month.

Nora spread the free maps about the entire carpet and then the flagstone area. Some of them started to float. Then she piled up rows and rows of cheap paperbacks from the black boxes in front of the door, attempting to block up the little gap between the worn-down step and the bottom of the barrier. She stood back hesitant, and the door flew open, sending them flying.

Roger stood in the doorway like a drowned rat and swore loudly.

"Oh dear." Nora almost laughed.

His hair was stuck to his balding head, his glasses were steamed up and his jumper and trousers clung tightly to his body.

"Georgina told me to come and help you."

"Look out!" Nora ran to grab his arm as the sound of an approaching vehicle competed with the pelt of heavy rain.

Roger skidded and tripped over the piles of paperbacks and maps in his path and Nora slammed the door just as another wave met it. There was a splashing sound and a slosh as more water came in.

"What the hell?" Roger watched it and shook his head, starting to shiver.

Some paperbacks were sent moving towards Nora's feet. She pushed them back and began to heap them up in front of the door.

"Looks like they're ruined." Roger said glumly.

"Help me pile them up. It might work and stop it coming in."

"I need to dry off." There was a huge sucking noise as Roger pulled his jumper away from where it clung to his chest. "Look at the time. What about our lunches? I didn't get a chance to eat because I was running errands."

"Roger! We need to stop the water coming in before we think about lunch. Pass me some paperbacks."

Reluctantly Roger tipped over a black box and send forty or more paperbacks hurtling to the floor. His footsteps sloshed noisily as he helped Nora pile them up before the door and then she stood back, noticing the rain easing off.

"I can't believe we don't have any sandbags." Roger shook his head, sending water droplets everywhere. "Yuk! I need some paper towels."

Nora studied their barricade as he slopped off, his teeth chattering.

"I think that'll work." She decided, watching an approaching lorry.

A little trickle came under the door at about five different places between the paperbacks. Nora smiled, relieved. She then looked about her in dismay.

The front of the shop looked appalling. Hundreds of maps, some submerged in the water on the flagstones, covered the whole floor amidst paperbacks that were desperately attempting to suck up the flood. The whole carpet had absorbed a lot of the water like ink on blotting paper so that the entire floor was soggy and ruined.

As the rain eased off Nora looked out at the submerged road and pavement. The water was level with the kerb. It was mainly the traffic that was causing it to wash up across the pavement and create waves but at the moment it didn't appear to have anywhere to go. Nora arranged more paperbacks tightly against the door, turned the sign to 'CLOSED' and put her key in the lock, turning it.

"Want a cup of tea?" Roger asked, appearing in the doorway to the back room, rubbing paper towels over his head.

Nora stared at him.

"It'll dry out." He shrugged, grimacing at the feel of his wet jumper. "I'll wheel the heater through from the kitchen. Kettle's boiling."

"This is a hideous nightmare." Nora exclaimed.

"Yeah, I need a change of clothes. I'm soaked. And I'm starving."

"I'd better phone Georgina." Nora decided.

"I'll make some tea and we can have our sandwiches." Roger said, turning and heading back to the kitchen.

Nora grabbed the phone, watching him go.

"How is it?" Georgina asked.

"You don't want to see it." Nora sighed. "The rain's eased off for the moment but…" She looked out onto the road, "…the lake is still there. I stopped it coming in by destroying all the outside paperbacks though. And the free maps."

"Oh that doesn't matter. Right, I think you should close the shop and you and Roger go and buy some sandbags from the warehouse next to the train station. They sell them there. Cara just looked them up on her phone."

"Hallooooo." Cara's distant voice sang.

"Get Roger to drive the van and buy lots because the forecast is for heavy rain all day and it would be sensible to have a supply after that event!"

"Good idea." Nora agreed. "Then I'll bag all these wet books and maps into black sacks, fill up the large bin behind the shop and we'll need some heaters."

"I like your positive attitude."

"It will be more positive when we have sandbags." Nora decided.

By the time Roger came back with two cups of tea, Nora had danced around on all the maps to soak up some of the water and taped a sign up on the door window saying *'Due to flooding we are CLOSED'*.

"What are you doing? Irish dancing?" Roger frowned, placing the mugs of tea onto the counter.

"It's soaking it all up. And it's good exercise." Nora assured. "We need to go and get some sandbags from the warehouse down by the train station before it pours with rain again."

"We'd better have lunch first then." Roger decided.

Nora watched him bring a stool into the midst of the maps and sit down with his packet of sandwiches.

"I may as well eat mine then." She said and almost skidded on the maps as she crossed the room.

A man peered in to examine the damage inside and Roger glared as he bit into his sandwich.

"I need a change of clothes." He said with a sip of his tea.

"Pop into the charity shop." Nora suggested. "Oh, I just remembered I've got a painting shirt hanging up on the back of the kitchen door."

"I'll borrow that. I'm soaked."

Nora smiled slightly, shaking her head as she examined the mess. They ate their lunch, reminiscing about the downpour and planning to bag up all the maps and sodden paperbacks, until Nora decided they needed to go and get the sandbags before it rained again.

"The van is in the car park in front of the castle ruins." Roger said, digging in his pockets for his van key. He had changed into a large blue and white shirt covered with white paint from when Nora and Cara had decorated the ceiling of the children's room upstairs. It looked like a dress. His trousers were still wet and he had irritably refused to wear Georgina's gym leggings which she had left under the stairs in her gym bag.

Roger draped his wet clothes over the oil heater in the kitchen and then Nora shoved two twenty pound notes into her pocket from the till. They climbed over the pile of paperbacks and dragged open the door, stepping out into the street.

"Did you have a flood?" A man asked, trying to peer inside the shop as they stepped out.

Nora shot a look at Roger who had the beginnings of a sarcastic expression.

"Yes. Sad isn't it. We're off to get sandbags before the next deluge." She nodded, glancing up at the sky which looked dark and stormy.

"Are your books wet?" A woman was stepping through the slowly draining puddle holding up her trousers from her ankles.

"No. All fine." Nora assured, hurrying down the street.

"Due to flooding we are closed." They heard someone read the sign and Nora dragged Roger across the road.

"Have you ever been to this warehouse by the station?" Roger asked incredulously.

They passed the little barber shop on the corner, the dolls shop and then the charity shop where Simon and Annabel were outside drying off some boxes of clothes someone had donated.

"No." Nora admitted.

"I hope it's not flooded. The van might get stuck." He pondered.

"I'll get out and push." Nora offered with a smile and Roger's lips twitched.

They turned left at the end of the street, crossing vast puddles and passing soaked people before they finally reached the car park. The van steamed up as they sat inside. Roger turned the heater on full blast.

"This isn't one way is it?" He frowned as a car beeped him and someone glowered, reversing backwards to let him through as he drove out of the entrance. "Why don't they make the signs clearer?!"

They travelled the short distance over the bridge that crossed the swollen river, out of the town and to the train station. A wooden sign directed them to Howards Warehouses and down a small muddy lane which was like a river. Roger muttered and spun the wheels of the van a few times, finally drawing up before a deserted building which had great heaps of wet sand outside.

"This is an adventure." Nora decided.

Roger gave her an amused look and they stepped out onto the gravel, Nora's foot sinking up to her ankle in a puddle. Two young men were leaning on the counter inside the building, watching them silently. The radio was playing a 1980's song in the background.

"We'd like some sandbags." Roger said, looking around.

"Yeah." One of them replied and gestured his head to his left.

"How many?" His colleague asked.

"How many do you think?" Roger asked Nora.

"Erm. Five?"

"Why not. Five please."

He punched in some figures on his till.

"Fifteen pounds and eighty nine pence." He said.

"Can I have a receipt?" Nora asked, handing him a twenty pound note.

"Where are the sandbags?" Roger inquired.

"The sacks are there. The sand's outside in the yard."

Roger and Nora stared at the men and then their gazes slid to a barrel of sacks.

"Can you fill them up for us?"

"No." They replied in unison.

"No." Roger repeated blankly.

"You buy the sacks and fill 'em up." The man on the till said as if it was obvious.

Nora bit her lip and Roger looked thunderous.

"Have you ever filled up a sandbag sack?" He asked Nora in a hard whisper.

Nora shook her head.

"What sand?" He demanded of the staff members.

One of them sauntered from around the counter, yawning. He led them back out through the swing doors and pointed to a huge yellow mound.

"Fill them up with that." He said, beginning to enjoy himself.

"Do you have shovels?" Nora asked politely.

"And maybe some sandcastle moulds?" Roger added sarcastically.

They walked over to the mound after Nora had collected five long hessian sacks.

"I don't like this. No. This is ridiculous, completely impossible." His foot went into the puddle Nora had encountered and he swore loudly.

"We'll have to use our hands." Nora suggested.

"Sand stains." Roger was disgruntled.

"Well, we can treat ourselves to manicures. Oh look, the men are coming over." She had opened a sack and was attempting to add a heap but it collapsed.

"We decided we'll do it for you."

"As a favour." The other pointed out.

"Thank you. It's starting to spit with rain again and our bookshop was flooded." Nora said sadly and smiled at Roger who was glaring at the men.

"We would have gone back like…sand people." He said, stepping back and watching the two men easily fill up the bags with two trowels, muttering together and snorting with laughter.

"Like in Star Wars? Oh, it would be fun to enter the town on Banthas." Nora agreed wistfully.

"The rain's got into your brain." Roger decided.

They stood watching and chatting for a while until the last bag was filled and the man dragged them to the side of the van which Roger unlocked.

"Thank you. If you ever want a free book come to the Secondhand Bookworm and see me." Nora said.

One of the men looked at her as if she was potty, the other brushed off his hands.

"Do you sell Calvin and Hobbs?"

"Sometimes."

"I might come in and get one."

"Our pleasure." Nora said and choked back a laugh as they walked away, leaving Roger to hoist in the sandbags, shaking his head. "That was nice of them." She decided.

"How can they sell sandbags and sand separately?" Roger scoffed. "It's like us selling blank books and a pile of little words saying, 'here you go, add the words yourself'."

Nora howled with laughter, closing the van door.

"Come on, before it rains again." She said, sliding into the passenger seat.

Roger drove them back to the town and parked outside the shop where they unloaded the sandbags amidst much interest from the few passer-by's that were still lingering in the quiet town.

"Did you get flooded?" Spencer Brown asked, crossing the road to see them.

"Like nothing ever seen before." Nora sighed, wiping off her hands.

He cursed under his breath as he surveyed the floor through the window.

"Any books ruined?"

"No. It didn't go above a few centimetres. Just soaked the carpet. We're prepared now."

"I'll go and park the van." Roger said.

Spencer pondered the piles of maps and paperbacks.

"Well, I ran down for some computer ink in between showers. There's more rain coming. I'm working on my book and want to interview the singer Robbie Williams about his interest in UFOs so I'm sending him a letter."

Nora didn't get a chance to say anything because it started to rain again.

"I'm going back home before it tips it down. Good luck with that!" Spencer said and hurried off, white hair fluttering behind him.

Nora positioned the sandbags before the door, making sure there were no gaps and then opened up, climbed over them and picked her way across the slippery floor, using her foot to gather up the maps into small piles until there were seven mounds of drenched paperbacks and free maps. She stood catching her breath as Roger came in.

"I'll put the kettle on." He decided, stepping tentatively through the valley of books. "Would you like a cake? We deserve a bit of a breather."

"Well…."

"My treat."

The phone started to ring. Nora leaned across the desk.

"The Secondhand Bookworm."

"Oh hi, Nora. It's Georgina. How's it going?"

"We're back. Armed with five sandbags. We're about to clear up here but we'll need some form of heating. The carpet's soaked and we only have that little oil heater in the kitchen."

"I've asked Humphrey to bring a dehumidifier from his boat back with him. He'll set it up and it'll dry it out gradually. He wanted to head over there to help you straight away but he's stuck up in London sorting out some things with his business so he'll probably get there long after you've closed up. As long as we've got sandbags sorted out we should be fine. Do you want to contact your friend at Southern Water? He might be able to sort out the road because we certainly don't want to be flooded all the time there. I just hope it doesn't smell. That would be awful."

"If we dry it out thoroughly it should be okay." Nora nodded, noticing Sam stride across the square with a dead lamb over his shoulder.

"I've got a customer, I'd better go. Keep me informed." Georgina sounded bemused and rang off cheerfully.

There was a knocking on the door. Nora walked carefully across the slippery carpet to where a man was pointing to his left.

"Hello." Nora opened up.

"You've got a book in your window…holy macaroni!" He saw the paper mounds and wet carpet behind her. "Have you been flooded?"

Nora pointed to the pile of sandbags at his feet and he looked surprised.

"The book on Winston Churchill in the window. How much is it?" He asked while studying the barrier of bags.

"Seven pounds fifty." Nora remembered.

"Do you know the prices of all your books?" The man was impressed.

"Most of them."

"Okay, I'll let my brother know. He might be interested in it. Good luck with the clean-up. It's raining again." He pointed out the obvious and hurried away.

"Nora!" Billy was walking past from the delicatessen with a coffee, stomach preceding him as usual.

"Hello, Billy."

"Were you flooded? Bad luck. The deli got some in their kitchen and the antique centre was just pumped out by the fire brigade. They've just left." He shared.

"Poor things." Nora sympathised but felt a bit better that the rain hadn't just singled out the bookshop.

"I'll bring those books in I want to sell at some point." He called as he hurried off out of the rain.

Nora was sad she had missed the drama of the fire brigade pumping out the antique centre. As she stood staring up the road with the feel of rainy air whipping her hair and freshening her face her phone started ringing.

She dug it out the pocket of her jeans and smiled to see Humphrey's name on the screen.

"Hi." Nora greeted, leaning against the wet door frame.

The rain on the wood immediately seeped through the fabric of her sleeve so she grimaced and straightened up again.

"Hey. Is everything okay? Are you okay?" Humphrey asked.

"I'm fine." Nora assured, rubbing her wet arm. "How are you?"

"Georgina said the town was flooding and the front of the bookshop is soaked." He said, too consumed with her predicament to answer her enquiry about his wellbeing.

"Yes, it is rather." Nora nodded, glancing back into the shop. "I've had to use free maps and paperbacks to absorb most of the water but the carpet will need drying out."

"You're okay, though?"

Nora smiled to hear the concern in his voice.

"Yes. Apart from sandy hands and wet socks, I'm fine."

"Good. Glad to hear it." He cleared his throat. "I'll set up the dehumidifier when I've finished up here and turn it on so it will start absorbing the water overnight. That way the books won't get damp and you'll have a relatively warm shop to work in tomorrow."

"Thank you, that's really nice of you."

"My pleasure. Darn it, the lawyers and my ex-partners are all glaring at me. I'd better get back into my meeting."

"You left your meeting to call me?"

"Yes, I kept thinking about you and wanted to make sure you were alright."

"Humphrey." Nora said in a warning voice, although she smiled, touched.

"I know now so I can relax." He smiled too. "Speak to you soon."

"Bye, Humphrey." Nora said and rang off.

She returned inside The Secondhand Bookworm as it began to pour with rain again.

"Ah, it's nice to think that the water can't come in and destroy any more of the bookshop now." She said as Roger handed her a cup of tea.

He studied the rising puddle before the kerb and glowered at the traffic speeding down the hill.

"I feel like standing out there and shaking my fist at the drivers." He said, shaking his head as a wave hit the door.

No water came in; the sandbags were the perfect defence. Nora sipped her tea and then went off to the kitchen to hunt out a roll of black sacks.

Nora and Roger spent the rest of the afternoon bagging up the wet books and walking them around to the rubbish bins between the showers. They used the squeezy mop and bucket from the outside loo to dry out the flagstones and then wheeled through the oil heater from the kitchen, putting it on full so that they were soon so hot they had to open the door.

Roger's clothes had dried nicely so he changed back into them. Nora took down the *'Due to flooding we are CLOSED'* sign and they decided to open for the remaining half an hour, although the town was empty and they didn't have any customers.

While Roger wiped off the black cheap paperback boxes with paper towels, Nora contacted the man she had dealt with when the drains had been blocked before in the yard. He was alarmed to hear the drains in the high street were now blocked and said he would send Cole Highways out to investigate the roads.

Nora also finished off her Chagall sale which had been interrupted by the flooding and reserved it under the counter for the lady's sister to collect. Then she and Roger refilled the black boxes with fresh cheap paperbacks that were kept in crates under the stairs, topped up the free map box with the last remaining maps and Nora ran up the first flight of stairs to flick off the light switch behind the travel books.

"Home for a hot bath I think." Roger decided as they stood cashing up. He put a pile of twenty pence pieces into a little clear bank bag.

"Me too. Takings weren't too bad considering we were closed all afternoon."

"Are you on calls tomorrow?" Roger asked.

"No, on Thursday."

"I'm off tomorrow. I've got an event at the school my brother teaches in."

"Oh, that's right. I remember you booking it off when we did the roster. Are you giving a talk?"

"About the Elizabethans." He nodded.

"Are you dressing up?"

"Not this time, I do have a Tudor Day in the summer." He admitted, counting five pound notes and adding the float to the cash tin.

"That sounds really good. You'd make a good Henry the Eighth."

Roger looked offended.

"I'll drive the van to Georgina's and pick up my car from the garage now. Do you need a lift home?"

"I have my car. It's down along the castle moat today." Nora said.

They finished counting, locked the kitchen, turned off the downstairs light and set the alarm. The rain had eased off and they stepped over the sandbags, locking up.

"Excuse me."

A couple stopped behind them and the woman stared at the sandbags.

"Do you get flooded here?" She asked.

"Sometimes." Roger replied shortly.

"Is there a Halfords in town?" The man inquired.

"No. I'm afraid not."

"Is there a supermarket?" He next asked, looking disappointed.

"The nearest to a supermarket here is the shop over the bridge." Nora said and directed them down the road.

Nora and Roger walked down to the castle ruins where they parted ways and Roger headed for the car park to collect the van. While Nora dawdled down along the elm-tree lined road where other shop keepers and visitors to the town were collecting their cars she received a text message.

Smiling, she saw Humphrey's name.

'Everything still okay? I heard on the radio it rained down there again and there are weather warnings in place overnight for Cole. More rain. On my way back now, just stuck in a traffic jam on the M25.'

'Everything's fine here, thanks. The sandbags are working a treat so the shop will be flood free overnight. Sadly most of the free maps definitely perished today though.' Nora sent back.

A moment later:

'You must be devastated.'

Nora chuckled.

'Immensely.'

'Glad you're okay though.'

'I'm fine. A little wet. Home for a bath I think.'

After a moment.

'I would have thought you'd have had enough of water for one day. But that sounds very nice.'

'It should be. Followed by chocolate brownies and a good book.'

'Sounds delicious. Speak soon.'

Nora smiled

'See you, Humphrey.' She sent back and put her phone away, continuing along the moat.

The old moat ran all the way alongside the immense castle ruins. The moat was swollen with water and large puddles stretched across the path and the road. Several ducks swam alongside Nora looking for food and a huge Whooper swan was standing blocking the path ominously further ahead so Nora crossed over and walked through the puddles to her little Citroen parked by a children's play area.

Her thoughts filled with sand, crashing waves, Calvin and Hobbs and Humphrey, Nora left Castletown as it began to rain once more, secure in the knowledge of a great sandbag barrier protecting The Secondhand Bookworm.

5 WHITE-LIGHTNING JOE AND SHOUTING STANLEY

"I don't think it's too pongy in here," Nora told Georgina over the telephone the next morning as she stood on the damp carpet. "It's lovely and warm and the carpet just feels a wee bit damp."

"Does the dehumidifier need emptying again? Humphrey popped in on his way back up to London at five o'clock this morning and said the bucket was up to the top with water. Careful of the pipe, it's easy to knock out."

"What was Humphrey doing here at five?! Heading up for some more early meetings?" Nora was surprised and had the sudden thought he was returning back to his high powered job in the capital city.

"No. He was picking up our mother from the airport." She explained.

"Ah."

"She's back from visiting our older sister in Norway and I'm sure she'll be in a big grump because of the cold weather over there. That's why I sent Humphrey. She doesn't moan so much around him."

"Well, the dehumidifier's about half way full. I'll do regular emptying of it throughout the day," Nora promised, thinking about Humphrey.

"Cara and I are doing office work today, so Jane will be in the shop here."

Jane's distant voice called 'hello' and Nora smiled.

"Okay. Say hi back to Jane for me. Is her son better?"

"Yes, all fine now. She's sorry she missed the flood."

"It would have been fun with Jane here," Nora knew.

"Close for lunch for half an hour if you need to, Nora. It will probably be quiet over there all day but if you get hungry and need to eat without interruptions then close up for a break. And can you type out a calls sheet for tomorrow? We've got an interesting day looking at books throughout the County of Cole; hopefully we'll find some yummy things. I'll pick you up from your parents' house at nine in the morning and don't forget the money and calls file tonight when you leave."

"Okay." Nora scribbled a reminder on the message pad for the end of the day.

"I have a customer, I'd better go. Have a good day."

"Bye, Georgina." Nora said and hung up.

Once the boxes of freshly stocked cheap paperbacks, the postcard spinner, the crate of discounted pavement books and the few remaining free maps in their little wooden box were neatly outside in the sunshine, and the sandbags piled up out of the way to the side of the door to dry, Nora pulled out the diary and examined the following day's plan for calls.

"Do you have the latest Harry Potter?" A man in a top hat asked.

Nora wondered what it was with the top hats that week and resisted asking him if he was a wizard so directed him to the children's room on the next floor.

She opened up the calls sheet template on the computer and spread the diary open on the desk top, biting into an almond croissant she had bought from the delicatessen before she had opened up, as customers began to wander in and out of the bookshop.

It was busy again for a weekday in September.

Nora wondered if Castletown was finally becoming a year-round tourist attraction in the county of Cole. She *Googled* the town to see if it was in the news and saw there was an increase of interest due to rumours about the Duke of Cole planning to rebuild the castle. Nora found herself gazing at a photo of the Duke accompanying one disgruntled blogger's post. She hoped he would indeed rebuild his castle ruins and maybe move into his new citadel. Even though he was referred to as a bore Nora thought him very handsome and intelligent looking.

After a while the shop was teeming with people and Nora was interrupted endlessly as she worked on the calls sheet. Two men were browsing in the front room while discussing an episode of Stranger Things that had aired on Netflix the night before. A man with a bright spotty bowtie was browsing through the antiquarian section, his large behind nudging Nora's elbow every so often, so that in the end she abandoned finishing the calls sheet and typing an email to a woman looking to sell her collection of books about pumpkin carving and edged away, picking up a duster to dust the till instead.

"Do you do dry cleaning?" An old woman asked, standing on the doorstep and staring inside.

Nora looked up.

"Excuse me please." A woman pushed past the inquirer, holding a postcard.

"No, this is a bookshop." Nora replied.

"Do you know where there's a place that does do dry cleaning in this town?"

"I think the trophy engraver has a dry cleaning side line." Nora recalled. "He's in a shop along the road opposite. Go past the butcher shop and cross over the road there."

"Cheers." She turned and nearly collided with two more postcard purchasers who were speaking loudly in German.

"Do you sell stamps, dear?" The first lady asked at the counter.

"No, we don't, sorry." Nora said.

"The last of the big spenders I'm afraid." She smiled sweetly, handing Nora a five pound note.

Nora pretended it wasn't the one-millionth-time she had heard the comment, gave the lady her change and offered her a paper bag.

"No thank you, dear. Save the planet and all that." The woman scuttled off past the Germans.

"And one stamp!" A man with a large white moustache demanded.

"We don't sell stamps." Nora advised him.

"Hey, Nora." Spencer Brown glided into the shop.

"Hello." Nora greeted him, counting postcards from another German tourist.

"You sell stamps?" She asked with a heavy accent.

"Sorry, no."

"How's the carpet. Ah, it seems alright. It's warm in here." Spencer looked around with interest.

"Stamps?!" Another woman asked, passing a handful of cards to Nora.

"No, sorry." She repeated, scowling at another twenty pound note that would deplete the change in the till.

"I'll just go and look upstairs and see if anything new has come in. I'm looking for books about the Marquis de Sade."

Nora arched an eyebrow, watching him glide off to the back and begin creaking up the stairs.

"Do you need a bag?" Nora asked her customer.

"Yes!" She demanded.

"Do you sell stamps?" Another German tourist asked.

Nora thought about getting a t-shirt that said 'We don't sell stamps' printed in a dozen languages on the front.

When they had all left, Nora slumped down into the chair. The man browsing the antiquarian books behind her smirked.

"The last of the big spenders." A man chortled, coming inside with a postcard.

Nora looked past him, smiling blandly, distracted by one of The Secondhand Bookworm's regulars named Charles who had just pulled up outside on a bike. Charles got off, studied the window display and then folded up his bike, stepping inside with it as Nora took the exact money for the postcard and the man left.

"Hello." Charles beamed, tall and neat in his pinstripe suit, bicycle clips and trimmed curly blond hair.

"Hello." Nora returned with a smile, closing the till.

"Castletown has been invaded." He said quietly so that only she could hear. He stood to carefully take a book from the window display.

The browser near him walked off into the back and the man from behind her moved to before the counter with his selection of books.

"It's trade," he said, casting a business card in front of her.

Charles looked up and stared at the back of the man's shrunken head, meeting Nora's eyes briefly with a knowing look.

"Okay." Nora acknowledged the business card.

"How's Georgina?" The trade man asked pointedly, intending to convince Nora that he was a long-term friend of the family and was justified in expecting a discount.

"Very well." Nora studied the card and handed it back to him.

"Keep it." He shrugged, taking out his cheque book.

Nora placed it aside and began to run the prices of the books he had chosen through the till; a two volume set of Fairbairn's Crests, three A&C Black topography books, a vellum-bound poetry book and the one he had been lingering over, which was an early edition of 'Wuthering Heights' bound in calf's leather.

"Three hundred and Twelve Pounds and thirty five pence with ten percent off for trade." Nora concluded.

"What's the date?" He was bent over with round glasses on, writing his cheque.

Nora told him and started to bag up his books. Charles glanced at the man with interest and then continued studying the Virginia Woolf book he had picked out of the window.

The phone rang so Nora answered it as she waited for the cheque.

"Yeah, do you have a copy of Jonathan Livingston seagull? It's by er…Richard Bach." A voice asked.

"Could you hold on one moment please?" Nora asked her caller and took the finished cheque. "Do you need a receipt?"

"No, thank you." He took the two bags. "Goodbye."

Nora returned to the phone, smiling at Charles who glanced at her as the trade man left.

"Hello. Sorry to keep you. No, we don't have a copy at the moment; I sold the only one from the window last week."

"Oh." The caller was put out. "I lent my copy to someone and now I want to read it again."

"You could try our Seatown branch." Nora suggested.

"Oh yeah. The number's here. Thanks." They rang off and Charles indicated to the book he held.

"I'm very tempted. I have a first edition already but the dust wrapper isn't in as good condition as this. Oh, it's very tempting. Dare I spend forty pounds just for a wrapper?"

"It *is* very nice." Nora agreed.

She glanced at the door as more people sauntered in.

"Ask the lady." A man suggested, so the woman with him approached the counter bearing a frown.

"Hello, dear. I'm looking for a copy of 'Heartbeat' by Danielle Steel. It's her twenty-seventh novel and I've read all the ones before it." She said.

"All twenty six." The man with her rolled his eyes and gestured his head at the woman teasingly, winking at Nora.

"It was published in nineteen ninety one."

"Do you have any Barbara Cartland novels?" The man then asked.

"Well, all our fiction is upstairs…"

"Oh I can't do stairs!" The woman's smile vanished and she turned away.

"I can go up and look for you." The man with her was noticeably disappointed.

"No, come on, our coach is going soon. Goodbye." The woman walked out with the man following grumpily, only to be replaced by a little girl whose head barely reached the counter. Her mother stood behind her and prodded her shoulder.

"Do you…do you have Thomas?" She asked in a tiny voice.

"Thomas the Tank Engine." Her mother elaborated.

"We might have." Nora grinned at the little girl. "We have a whole room of children's books upstairs."

"Ooooh, shall we go and have a look Astrid?" The mother suggested and they followed Nora's direction through the walkway to the staircase.

Charles put the Virginia Woolf book back in the window, smiled and said goodbye, glancing at the book he had been browsing through longingly as he unfolded his bike outside and then peddled away.

Nora watched him go, glad when the rest of her customers scuttled off and The Secondhand Bookworm was left quiet and empty at last, as it should be on a Wednesday in mid-September.

Nora reached for her water bottle under the counter as a Skype message arrived from Seatown.

'Pls looks for any art books about Frida Kahlo. Customer here x'

'Checking' Nora sent back, stood up and scanned the art shelves before her.

'We only seem to have 'Pocket Frida Kahlo Wisdom' here which is a small green book mainly containing her quotes.' Nora sent back.

'Customer says no thank you! Back off up to the office now x'

'Have fun x' Nora sent with a small smile.

Her smile then faded when she saw a familiar form approaching the shop. White-Lightning Joe was about to enter The Secondhand Bookworm.

White-Lightning Joe was a little plump man with greasy black hair and eccentric mannerisms who lived just outside the town centre and worked in the old hotel as a bell hop. He collected every form of book and pamphlet about the history of Castletown even though he often complained of being short of money, and he slandered most of the townspeople. He was so named because he was almost always seen with a bottle of White-Lightning cider in his hand or in a plastic bag and sometimes singing in the square while dancing around a bottle on the cobbles. Once he had asked Cara out on a date and she had refused loudly, calling him a goblin.

"He-lo Nora." White-Lightning Joe greeted drearily, stepping down into the shop.

He was carrying his usual plastic bag which had his bottle of White-Lightning cider inside with a couple of squashed books. He looked red cheeked and his eyes were watering.

"Hello, Joe. How are you?"

He dropped his bag to the floor with a bang and stood before her with drooping shoulders.

"I've been made redundant!" He said, his bottom lip quivering.

Nora stared at him.

"What? Really!?"

White-Lightning Joe nodded forlornly.

"Yeah. That bloody hotel. After all the years I've worked there. They gave me a grand and made me and Roy the pot boy redundant." He sniffed, staring at her. "I'm heart-broken. And jobless."

"Oh. I'm really sorry to hear that." Nora said awkwardly.

His eyes filled up.

"And my girlfriend told me to bog off." He added, tears rolling down his cheeks.

Nora dived for the box of tissues under the counter, holding it out to him.

He grabbed some and used them and his sleeve.

"Can you lend me a couple of quid?" He then asked.

"Er…" Nora withdrew the box. "I probably can't actually."

"Oh. Right." He sniffed, picking up his bag. "Well…eeeeep." He withdrew a book with one of his unique sound effects and a flourish. "This any good to you? I've got loads of them at home."

Nora took the Blue Peter Annual. It was a little scuffed.

"It's a bit tatty, yeah I know but…eeeeep." He shrugged and pulled out a paper back. "This is a novel."

"Well…they're in quite bad condition."

"Can't you do a few quid on them?" He asked.

Nora felt sorry for him.

"They're not worth…"

"Just a quid?" He tried to persuade her.

"Okay, but they're not really worth it."

"I know, ah thanks Nora." He waited for the pound and rolled his tongue happily when she passed it to him.

"Well, I hope everything works out." She sympathised.

His eyes filled up again and he bolted for the door.

"Bye." He said in a high pitched voice and hurried out, squeezing between two people who were eating ice-creams and studying the paperbacks either side of the door.

Nora watched him bump into a man outside who frequented the town. The man was very skinny, had tattoos on his cheeks and sometimes stalked into the shop asking for books about machine guns.

"'Ere, Joe. Lots of people are mad at you 'coz you owe 'em money." Nora heard him say.

She tried to listen to their conversation in between serving a customer who bought some travel books followed by the little girl with her book about Thomas the Tank Engine.

"You shouldn't say that, Joe. It's two faced. HEY, LAURA!" Machine-Gun Man bellowed across the square to the lady who ran the Black Hart opposite.

White-Lightning Joe began to scurry away, laughing nervously.

"HE JUST CALLED YOU A WITCH." Machine-Gun Man shouted.

"No I didn't." Joe giggled, hurrying up the hill.

"YEAH HE DID. HE WENT 'THERE'S LAURA…THAT *WITCH'*." He shouted and tutted, shaking his head self-righteously.

Nora stared, passing the bag with the Thomas book inside to the girl.

"Oh dear." The mother shook her head as she listened to the shouting outside.

"Sorry about the drama," Nora apologised, walking around to watch the scene through the window as her customers left. She saw White-Lightning Joe walk up the road and then Machine-Gun Man decide to follow him. He followed Joe up and then across the road and down again, shouting threateningly while Joe giggled nervously and finally broke into a run where he disappeared past the butcher shop.

Then Nora saw Sam stalk out of the butcher shop, intercept Machine-Gun Man and stand in front of him. She ignored the phone ringing as she watched, until Machine-Gun Man shrugged, hung his head slightly and turned around, beginning up the hill. Sam watched him go, shaking his head before going back to the butcher shop, joined by Matthew from the trophy shop as well as Mr Sykes who had a room of stuffed animals in one of the antique centres. Nora left the window to answer the phone when it rang again just as Spencer came downstairs holding an armful of books.

"The Secondhand Bookworm." She greeted the caller.

"Is Georgina there?" A distant voice asked. "It's Devon the accountant."

"Oh, hello. She's in the office in Seatown." Nora explained.

"Okay, I'll try there." He said and rang off.

"Hello Nora, I found all these." Spencer put the pile of books on top of the cash book. "But I need to check if

I've got this one already, and this one and this one. Can you write them down for me?"

"No problem." Nora picked up a pen and a yellow Post-It.

"I'll definitely have this one, this one and, oooh la-la, this one."

Nora spotted the 'Letters from prison' by the Marquis de Sade in the pile.

"Anything about Aleister Crowley?"

"No." Nora turned her nose up

Spencer flicked through a thick book about aliens while she wrote down the titles and handed him the bright yellow Post-It.

"Thanks, I'll check these and get back to you. I didn't intend to come in again before the UFO convention but I've been working on my speech and going through my books. I lose track of the titles I already have in my library but I'm going through them to relocate the special ones in the top room of my tower."

"For special use?" Nora asked, curious.

"Yes."

"As another library?"

"Not really." He replied vaguely. "I should be able to read them easily once they've all been sorted."

"I had someone in last week who collects Collins Little Gem books."

"Those short, fat pocket-sized books about trees, insects, birds, etcetera?"

"Yes, those. He had a notepad with seven hundred and eleven titles in it, all the different editions of them, and he referred to it to check which ones he already had." Nora reminisced helpfully.

Spencer laughed.

"I don't fancy sitting down and listing all my titles but perhaps I should catalogue them one day." He watched Nora start to ring up his sales.

"I'm sure you've heard we have a new owner for the Indian restaurant?" Nora supposed.

"Oh, nobody here tells me anything." Spencer replied. "They're too scared of me. Although I was told a rumour once that someone thought I was a vampire and that I turned into a bat and followed people along the streets at night."

Nora felt her cheeks flush, hoping Spencer would never find out that was her.

"Oh. How silly."

"Is it though?" He asked mysteriously and grinned, showing his pointed teeth.

Nora yelped and edged back.

Spencer laughed.

"Relax. These are my real teeth. I just have sharp canines."

"That's nice." Nora said and hastily finished his sale, shaking her head.

Spencer paid by credit card, telling Nora all about a trip to Roswell he was going to try and persuade his wife to go on. Then he left, closing the door behind him.

As Nora was writing down his sale in the cash book she heard the sound of determined high heels advancing up the road. She waited to see what outfits the estate agents were modelling that day for their 'Main Street Catwalk' as Cara liked to call it. She smiled to see fur coats and red stilettos with loud laughter and loud voices clip-clop past with a client to view a house in the town.

Smiling, Nora decided to tidy the shelves in the Cole section that had been rummaged through and then plan a possible window display change while she pushed all thoughts of Spencer and his evening bat adventures firmly out of her mind!

Later that morning, Nora was bringing back the freshly emptied bucket to return to the dehumidifier when Mr Sykes entered the shop. She slowed down, silently surprised. He very rarely called into The Secondhand Bookworm.

"Billy tells me that the lovely lady in here has a book about taxidermy on display." He said, stopping before Nora.

He was dressed in green corduroy trousers, a checked shirt and fishing waistcoat. He smelt strongly of pipe tobacco.

"Oh." Nora put the bucket down. She placed the hose over the edge, glancing around. "Oh, yes. Billy was looking at it last week. It's behind here now."

Mr Sykes watched Nora retrieve a book from the rare and antiquarian book section, stroking his beard thoughtfully.

She passed it to him and he moved to a corner to study it.

"Did you see that the bakery has gone?" He asked without looking up.

Nora paused from picking up a pile of history books a customer had rummaged through, haggled about and then decided to leave.

"What bakery?"

He gestured his head to the window, turning the page.

"Next door to Lady Lane's." He shared solemnly. "Graham's bakery."

"What?!" Nora *hadn't* noticed.

She walked across to the window and stared past a gathering of school children on the cobbles.

"Closed up at four o'clock yesterday, swept out the windows and shelves and left for good. I'm surprised you didn't notice. Madam said it was to do with the rent from the landlord." He relayed, referring to his girlfriend who ran Lady Lane's on the street across the cobbles. "I doubt he'll be back."

Nora was stunned.

"Graham did the best carrot cake." She mused, more to herself.

"I'm glad we won't have all those cake wrappers littering the pavements anymore." He closed the book. "I used to have this one. You're charging fifty pounds I see. Since I don't have the museum anymore I don't really need it."

Nora looked at him.

"What museum?"

"The curiosity museum."

"Curiosity museum? Wait a moment. Was that *you*?" Nora stared at Mr Sykes with fresh eyes. "We often get asked about the old curiosity museum of Castletown. All the stuffed animals were dressed up and sitting around having tea parties or something."

"That was mine." Mr Sykes smiled proudly. "They were in various scenes and dioramas. There were mice wearing bowties and cats and dogs at a banquet. There was also the funeral of cock robin and a double headed sheep."

Nora chuckled.

"It would do well here with the tourists if was still open." She considered.

"Not tasteful today, apparently."

"What happened to all the stuffed creatures? Do you have them in your antique centre and at home?"

"I have a few in my shop." He handed her back the book. "I also stuff my own."

Nora's eyes popped.

"Fresh ones?"

"Lovely specimens I come across. Or trap."

Nora edged back and he smiled.

"Good luck with the book." Mr Sykes said and left, taking out his pipe.

Nora looked at the cover of the book and cringed, returning it to the shelf.

There was a message on Skype Chat so Nora sat down to read it.

'I'm sending Jane over to cover your lunch and finish the day with you, Nora. I'm having a meeting with Devon later and have had enough of paperwork in the office so I'll work downstairs with Cara. No need for three of us here and you all on your lonesome.'

Nora was pleased.

'Great. Look forward to it. By the way, I just had 'Bill Sykes' in. He used to have the Curiosity Museum in the town – the one people often ask about. With two-headed sheep and dead creatures.'

Keith from the occult shop threw open the door and walked into The Secondhand Bookworm.

"Hi Nora." He grabbed a book about spiders from the window and began to look through it, the scent of *Nag Champa* drifting towards her across the room.

"Hi, Keith. How are things at the occult shop? Busy?" She asked warily.

"No. But I had Spencer in. He's always good for a chat."

"Has he ever invited you up to his tower?"

Keith lifted his eyes to meet with Nora's.

"What? No, why?" He looked intrigued.

"Oh. I just wondered if you knew what he got up to in there."

Keith smirked.

"Probably best we never find out." He said, turning pages in the book before he returned it to the shelf. "If you ever get any detailed books about spider breeds can you let me know? I had one delivered to my house last night and I don't know what it is."

Nora stared at him. He grinned, beginning to leave the shop.

"What?"

"I rescue them. People drop them around my house who don't want them as pets anymore and I re-home them. I've got about eight tanks at the moment. Some monsters." He explained.

"That's hideous. Go away!" Nora shuddered.

A customer came out of the back room as Keith walked off chuckling. A new message flashed up on the computer monitor.

'Was 'Bill Sykes' part of the display? – Cara'

Nora saw the Skype message and bit back a smile, taking a biography about Hitler offered to her by a strange little man with a thin, pencil moustache.

"Can you do anything on the price?" The man asked.

Nora opened the book and saw the marking.

"I'm so sorry but I'm unable to change the price because it isn't my shop. It's seven pounds fifty."

"Where's the owner?" His tone was flat.

"She's with her accountant."

The man studied Nora.

"Can you phone her?"

"No. Sorry, I'm not able to change prices."

He stormed out without another word so Nora sighed, putting the book on the counter and sitting down.

She glanced at the clock, thinking about making an eleven o'clock cup of tea when Don strolled in.

"Any new Regimental Histories?" He asked again.

Nora arched an eyebrow.

"Not since yesterday, Don."

"I'll go out the back and have a look, just in case."

"Okay, knock yourself out." Nora sighed, bemused, and watched him as he strode past humming. She then followed him out with her empty mug to pop into the back kitchen and make a quick cup of tea.

Don stopped and stared blankly at the wall of military books.

"It's a little bit muddled." She noticed. "I'll try to have a good sort out of some sections this afternoon. We had a busy weekend."

"Yeah, it is all over the place." He agreed and stood in front of the military section with his hands in his pockets.

The kitchen door was already unlocked. Usually Nora kept it locked up because once she had found a man making himself a cup of tea and another time a man washing his socks in the sink. This morning she had left it unlocked because it was quiet and she thought she'd be able to keep an eye on who was in the back room.

When she opened the door however she yelped.

A man was sitting perched on the old wooden stool eating yoghurt while reading a book.

"Oh! Don't mind me." He said, turning a page.

Nora blinked.

"I'm sorry but this room is private. It's for staff use only." Nora exclaimed, wondering how he had managed to slip in.

The man frowned.

"Well, no one's been in here for the past hour." He defended, lifting his little spoon to his mouth. "I'll be done in ten minutes. I've almost finished this chapter."

"Is that one of our books?"

"It's from the royalty section out there. Keep your hair on!"

"Those books are for sale. This isn't a library or a cafeteria."

"Keep your hair on! Keep your hair on!"

"I'm going to have to ask you to leave now." Nora said firmly.

"Can't I just finish eating first? I'm not being a nuisance."

"You are, because I need to make myself a cup of tea and you're in the way."

The man sighed like a theatre thespian.

"Very well. I'll finish my yogurt in the reading room."

"We don't have a reading room!" Nora was beginning to feel exasperated.

"Keep your hair on! Keep your hair on!" He said, standing up from the stool. "I meant just out there."

"I can't allow you to consume food on the premises around our books. And that book is for sale. Are you going to buy it?"

A man's voice started calling from the front room. Nora hadn't meant to be long. She looked over her shoulder and saw Don filming her with his iPhone, grinning. Nora glared at him.

"I don't think I *will* buy it." The man with the yoghurt snarled.

"Then I think this conversation is over." Nora glowered, crowding him so he squeezed past her.

Nora dumped her mug on the worktop, filled up the kettle with fresh water, switched it on to boil, closed the door behind her and followed the man, making sure he had put the book he was reading back on the shelf and seeing him off with his yoghurt.

In the front a man stood in the middle of the room looking blank.

"Can I help?" Nora asked as the yoghurt man scurried away muttering.

The phone rang as the new customer began to speak and his voice rose loudly.

"I'm looking for a book about the history of Castletown. My family began here in the year thirteen sixty five. Now I have pension-itus and have my free pension bus ticket, I thought I'd come back to my roots." He almost shouted.

Nora kept a straight face, grabbing the phone.

"Bear with me a minute." She told him and answered the call. "The Secondhand Bookworm. Could you hold on one moment please?"

She walked around the counter to show the customer the local section and left him staring at it glumly, sucking his false teeth and clearing his throat loudly.

"Hello, sorry to keep you." Nora finally spoke into the receiver.

"Do you sell sheet music?" A well-spoken voice asked at the end of the line.

"We do keep a small section of sheet music in stock, yes."

"Hardback music." The lady clarified.

"Erm…we may have a few. What are you looking for? Piano?"

"I am selling it!" The lady declared. "I have some bound volumes and some miniature scores."

"Okay. We'd have to take a look at the condition."

"They are in mint condition." The lady was indignant. "I look after my music."

"Would you like to bring them in for us to look at?" Nora asked.

"I don't want to carry them in if you don't want them!"

"Perhaps you should speak to the owner. She's in our Seatown shop today." Nora suggested warily.

"And what is your name?" She demanded.

"My name is Nora. If you ask for Georgina Pickering she is the owner of our bookshops." Nora smirked.

"I have the number here, thank you. Goodbye." She hung up as the customer who had asked for Castletown books moved to stand in front of Nora.

"Any books by BB?" He asked.

"Well, no fishing books but we have 'The Wind in the Wood' by BB. It's a fairy tale." Nora replied.

"No thank you. I'm a pensioner now but my brain hasn't reverted to childhood yet." He huffed and puffed to the observer books and then checked his watch. "I'd better catch my free bus ride back to Seatown."

"We have a shop in Seatown as well." Nora said.

"Yes, I've spent my life savings in there." He nodded dryly and stepped out. "Farewell."

Quickly Nora grabbed the shop keys and hurried back to the kitchen where the kettle had boiled. She threw a small mint teabag into her mug, deeming it quicker than fiddling about with milk and sugar, poured a large splash of scalding water on top of it, locked the kitchen up behind her, glanced at Don who was typing on his phone and returned to the front of the shop, still stewing about the man with the yoghurt.

Nora was about to Skype an account of the event over to the Seatown shop when her gaze moved to the window and she gasped to see a familiar man marching across the cobbles on a mission toward the shop. She squinted, trying to make out his condition and winced to see him stagger slightly.

"Drunk-boy." She groaned, using the name she and Cara had given him after years of his antics.

Moments later he threw open the door and grinned broadly.

"Yeah…hi…hello." Drunk-boy said blearily, blinking and almost falling into the room.

"Hello." Nora replied flatly, pretending to type on the computer.

"Hello again." He grinned and sniffed, taking a great gulp from a can of coke and then belching loudly.

"That is really rude!" Nora rebuked.

He laughed and covered his mouth.

"Sorry…yeah, sorry." He laughed, slurring his words.

Nora stood up and faced him. He was handsome with a lovely smile, but his wide blue eyes were bloodshot and bleak, he was unshaven and wore dirty jeans, a scruffy t-shirt and filthy jacket with a pile of papers and magazines crammed under one arm.

"Do you need anything specific because you can't really hang out in here today?"

He looked really hurt.

"You're boring!" He sipped his coke and looked around, pointing with his can. "Yeah, yeah, I saw some Dali; his paintings are insane. What art do you like?" He smiled and staggered to the counter leaving his magazines there.

"Nothing." Nora glowered.

He looked hurt again.

"Come on, come on. Don't be boring, what art do you like?" He persisted and grinned.

"I won't have conversations with you when you're drunk." Nora reminded him with a sigh.

He stared at her.

"I ain't drunk!" He was offended. "Na, na I had a wild night man; I haven't been to sleep for seventy…seventy …seventy two hours. Phew it was wild; a whole night on magic mushrooms." He laughed, wobbling a bit and sipping his coke loudly.

Nora walked around the counter and he straightened up.

"Come on, don't be boring, Nora." He grinned. He dug into his pocket and pulled out a wad of fifty pound notes. "I want to buy a book."

"You don't want to keep spending all your money on books when you're high." Nora assured him.

He looked shocked and blinked at her.

"What? Let me buy an art book. Turner. Yep…Turner." He staggered towards them and his coke spilt a bit. "Whoops. Sorry. Sorry. Turner. Yep."

Nora stared at him, trying not to laugh.

"I'll have to get the owner, he's upstairs." She pretended.

Drunk-boy turned and looked at her, this time *really* offended. He frowned, his blue eyes tragic.

"This used to be a nice town." He slurred. "Now it's a Mickey Mouse state."

"Did you used to live here?" She asked.

His expression changed.

"I *do* live here." He was defensive.

"Where?"

"Up the road." He glowered.

"Where up the road?"

He stared at her steadily.

"Up the road of irritation." He slurred and Nora hid her smile behind her hand. "Ya boring." He decided to leave.

Nora picked up the magazines and her eyes widened when she saw what *kind* of magazines they were. He grabbed them off her.

"They sell this stuff and I buy it." He defended himself.

Nora watched him stagger out of The Secondhand Bookworm and then she moved to the window for a clearer view. He walked down the road, dropping his coke and magazines several times so that the coke spilt everywhere and the magazines scattered and then he stood talking to a woman who looked aghast at him.

Nora shook her head, turning around to consider the clock on the wall and thinking of Humphrey when the door flew open.

"HELLO!"

Nora flinched violently. She turned back to see Shouting Stanley, a customer who visited The Secondhand Bookworm several times a year, entering the shop.

"Hello." Nora replied, wincing to prepare herself for more shouting.

Stanley cupped his hand to his ear.

"I'M DEAF! YOUR SEATOWN SHOP SAID YOU HAD TEN WALTER SCOTT NOVELS. I HAD ONE PUT BY FOR ME ALREADY!"

"Oh, yes." Nora remembered and walked around the counter. She pulled out the novel that had been put by for him the previous week when he had telephoned. It had been a very interesting conversation that had left her ear ringing for a whole hour afterwards.

"AH." Stanley smacked his lips and picked up the book with the lone finger and thumb on his left hand. His fingerless gloves had been sewn up over the useless finger-holes where, he had once loudly explained, he had lost most of his digits through frost-bite. Nora tried not to focus too much on it. "YES! I'LL HAVE THAT. WHERE ARE YOUR OTHERS?"

"Well, we checked the ones on your list and didn't have the…"

"PARDON? I'M DEAF!" Stanley yelled.

"Attic room." Nora said and indicated upwards.

"I'LL FIND IT. I'LL MAKE MY WAY UP. I'M SLOW!"

Nora heard him stamping right up to the top.

She sat and sipped her mint tea, longing for Jane to arrive.

"Come along Jane. I'm lonely." She sighed into her mug, wincing as the mint steam stung her eyes in response.

Her watery gaze levelled on the view through the window into the cobbled square where she watched a man pushing a huge trolley of parcels along the street, a delivery of fresh bread arrive for the delicatessen, Alice sweeping something up from outside the deli door and an old lady telling off a workman up a ladder because she had to walk into the road to avoid it.

Shouting Stanley began back down the stairs, stomping so loudly that Nora flinched with each foot step. He sounded like a Stormtrooper.

"Hi!" A very tall man with bright yellow hair stooped into the shop.

Nora stared.

"Oh, hello," she greeted him.

"Any books about wine making?"

"Yes, on the next floor."

"Thank you." He said, making his way into the back.

"I'M SLOW!" Shouting-Stanley bellowed, letting him past.

Shouting-Stanley came into the front and roared with laughter.

"I WAS TOLD THERE WERE TEN NOVELS BY WALTER SCOTT YESTERDAY." He smacked his lips, laughing. "YOU MUST HAVE SOLD SOME OF THEM. YOU DON'T HAVE THE ONES THAT I WANTED."

He came to the counter and opened his bag.

"BUT I FOUND THESE. TWO OF THEM SHOULD BE A GOOD READ." He placed them onto the counter.

"I SAW THAT YOU HAVE MARY SHELLEY. HER FRANKENSTEIN WAS RIGHT ON THE BALL WITH WHAT'S HAPPENING THESE DAYS. SHOCKING, SHOCKING WHAT THEY'RE DOING TODAY. IT MAKES YOU LOSE FAITH, NOT IN RELIGION BUT IN LIFE. SOMETIMES YOU WANT TO COMMIT SELF-HARM OR SUICIDE BUT THAT'S FOOLHARDY. SO…" He smacked his lips and took out a wallet. "I MAKE IT NINE POUNDS."

"Yes, nine pounds exactly. Thank you." Nora agreed.

He passed her a ten pound note, she gave him a pound change and he placed the books into his bag.

"I SHALL BE BACK SOON. I LOOK FORWARD TO SEEING YOU. GOODBYE."

Nora watched him leave and head off down the street shouting.

Literally a moment later Jane bounded in, beaming amiably and carrying a yellow plastic box.

"I'm here! Hurrah. Hi, Nora! How are you?" She was a flurry of happiness and bounced in to place the box on the stool to the side of the counter.

Jane was one of Georgina's old high school friends and had recently started proceedings for her divorce. She was planning on opening a dance school in Piertown in the future but for now needed part-time work, so was doing the occasional day at the bookshop. She was very motherly and always happy and cheerful, which was amazing considering her husband was a serial cheater. She told everyone she was glad to be rid of him.

"Hello! At last! I've been lonely, endlessly interrupted and harassed." Nora welcomed her, grinning, as she stood to look at the box.

"I'm here now so hurrah!" Jane hugged her tight. "I must run to the loo. Do you have the key? Have a look through the transfer box; Georgina put a couple of Louis Wain books in there that someone sold her this morning, drawn before 'he went psycho' apparently." She laughed, taking the bunch of keys from Nora. "They're pricey so they need wrapping in a clear bag each. She already spoke to the Cat-Man about them but he said he would resist at the moment."

"Lovely. I'll take a look." Nora started to rummage through the box with interest.

"I ate a sandwich on the way over so when I'm back you can go and have your lunch if you like." Her voice sailed back as she hurried up the stairs to the bathroom.

Nora sat down to flick through the first Louis Wain book, finishing off her mint tea.

"'To Nursery Land with Louis Wain'. One Hundred and Fifty Pounds." She read aloud and studied the picture of three cats in a cradle with a cat in spectacles beside them on the front. "'Somebody's Pussies', by Louis Wain." She read the next title and her eyebrows shot up at the three hundred pound marking inside. She smirked at the bulging green eyes of the cats on the front before she rummaged around for the clear bags to put them safely inside. She popped them behind the counter on the antiquarian shelves.

"Ah, that's better." Jane was back looking relieved. She hung up the keys and turned to Nora. "Right." She flopped into the swivel seat and prodded Nora amiably. "Go and have a lunch break, sweetie. You've probably had a delightful morning here on your own and must be desperate to stretch your legs." She smiled knowingly.

Nora shrugged into her jacket and swung her bag over her shoulder.

"Thanks, I need it. Then we can get putting away and sorting some sections when I'm back." Nora hoped.

"I'm raring to go." Jane nodded, reaching for the phone when it began to ring.

Nora waved goodbye and stepped out into the sunshine, the light wind whipping her medium length brown hair as she turned left and started down the street.

The barber shop door was open emitting the sound of Jazz music playing inside while Johnny cut the hair of an old man who was tapping his foot. Next door, the estate agents looked empty of customers. The ladies inside were having a loud chat and screaming with laughter, one of them leaving to grab some lunch herself.

"Afternoon, Nora." Jeanette greeted, stepping out onto the street.

She was a thin woman in her mid-forties with fluffy black hair, bright pink lips, huge false eyelashes and an elegant, figure-hugging trouser suit.

"Hi, Jeanette."

"We're all interested in Georgina's brother, Humphrey. Word is you two are getting pretty cosy."

Nora glanced at her.

"What on earth? Why is my *friendship* with Humphrey Pickering the talk of Castletown this week?" Nora was exasperated.

"I suppose it's because nothing else happens around here and you and Humphrey are among the only few people under forty." Jeanette smiled, walking with Nora across the road. "So tell me all about it!"

Nora pressed a finger to her mouth.

"My lips are sealed." She decided to play into the gossip.

Jeanette linked an arm through Nora's.

"Oh how delicious. But I'll find out eventually!"

Nora shook her head, bemused.

Jeanette left Nora when they reached the newsagents, heading inside for a packet of cigarettes and a cheap salad.

Nora decided to buy a baguette and a slice of cake from the river café which was buzzing with people. She stood listening to various conversations as they made the baguette up for her, she chose a thick chunk of pecan pie and a steaming hot cup of chocolate and headed to the ruined abbey on the riverside with her lunch.

The various benches scattered about the little gardens and among the abbey walls were empty. Castletown was quiet at last. There weren't any coaches in the car park and only residents and locals were walking over the large stone bridge across the river. This was the September Nora was used to.

The castle ruins towered grandly in the distance behind her, imposing, ancient, with an interesting history and begging to be restored to their former glory. Nora thought about the Duke of Cole again, hoping the rumours were true and he would come to Castletown and build one of his new and impressive castles. And, of course, move in.

She sat down under an arch on a single bench beside a rose bush, hidden from view, entertained by a robin and a castle rook who were eyeing her baguette eagerly. In the peace and quiet Nora read a little of the novel on her Kindle as she ate and then threw some crumbs for the birds. After a while she gathered her things, stopping to walk around a small art exhibition in the scouts hut before she headed back to The Secondhand Bookworm, prepared to face the afternoon.

Back at the shop Jane was bagging up some books for an old man with a monocle. She gave Nora one of her looks as she listened to his diatribe about 'Country Gentlemen's Catalogues'. When he had gone, Nora popped her bag and coat under the stairs.

"Nice lunch?" Jane asked, writing down the sale.

"Lovely. I certainly needed it." She nodded.

"So now we're both energised! Shall I take those paperbacks up to the attic and put them all away?" Jane asked.

"How about you do an armful and then I'll do an armful." Nora suggested. "We can get them all on the shelves, have a hoover about, I think the carpet is dry enough now, empty the dehumidifier, sweep the stairs and then the shop's all tidy again. If we've time we can tidy up the travel section at the top of the stairs and the military section in the back room."

"Georgina also wants us to do a Wordsworth check so we can order more new ones in." Jane added, taking up the first armful of books to put away. "They're doing so well; it's nice that we do all those classics in new editions! I've printed out the list. We can take it in turns to do that too."

"I like our plan." Nora decided. "I love working with you Jane. We get so much done!"

"Aw, thanks Nora. I love working with you too!" Jane beamed and headed off whistling.

6 FAHRENHEIT 451

The bookshop was quiet in the late afternoon. After completing practically everything on their list, Jane and Nora served smatterings of customers while taking it in turns to put the rest of the books neatly away on their appropriate shelves in their sections throughout the shop.

The collection of new Wordsworth editions had been stock checked, the list scanned and emailed to Georgina for Cara to order that afternoon. Nora had sorted out the military section and the dehumidifier had been emptied twice. The carpet was slowly drying out so that no one would know there had been a flood the day before and all the bits trodden in by messy customers had been hoovered up.

The only drama that afternoon had been when a wasp had flown in through the open door and terrorized Jane, seemingly thinking she was a delectable flower. Nora had eventually managed to coax it back towards the doorway and wacked it out with a History of Cole book. She now stood at the desk adding up the sales taken so far while Jane was in the back room, humming as she placed the last few war and history books on the shelves

The front door swung open and a slim woman with long hair thrust up into a messy bun stepped down.

"You bought some books from me and I need one back." She said with an apologetic grin.

Nora looked up from her calculator.

"Oh, okay. When did you sell them to us?" Nora asked.

"About…ah, ten days ago. You came out to my car; a Golf?" She explained.

Nora stared at the woman but couldn't place her face. "Was it me?"

"I think so." The woman stared back at Nora hard. "You paid twenty pounds for about two hundred paperbacks. I need one back."

Nora bit her bottom lip, thinking.

"It may have been Georgina, the owner of our shops, because I can't recall it. We've had so many books in over the past week, the whole shop was piled high everywhere on Friday. We managed to get them away at the weekend and we've almost finished putting away today so the book you want is probably on the shelves."

The woman cringed.

"Isn't it typical? I shouldn't have been so ruthless in my sort out. Well, I'll go and have a look and see if you still have it."

"What kind of book was it?"

"A big fat novel."

"It would be in the attic room. It's in alphabetical order of author." Nora directed and the woman went up with her fingers crossed.

As she left, the door opened again.

A man in a bowler hat stepped down and closed the door behind him. He walked up to Nora, looking at the books on the shelves surrounding them, his blue eyes as round as marbles.

"Do you have The Hunting of the Snark by Lewis Carroll?" He asked.

"Yes, it's possible that we do."

"Possible? Can't you check your computer to find out for sure?"

"We don't keep a list of our titles on our computer."

"Oh! How bizarre!"

Nora smiled tightly.

"We do get copies of The Hunting of the Snark come in though." She assured him. "It would be in our humour section."

"Not hunting?" He was surprised.

"It isn't about a real hunt."

"Ah, so the Snark isn't a real animal then!"

"No, it's an animal which could be a highly dangerous Boojum."

The man looked blank.

"A what?"

"A Boojum. A fictional animal species."

"Do you have a fictional animal species section?" He asked.

"We have a section for beasts and mythology but The Hunting of the Snark is a nonsense poem."

"Oh! Would it be in poetry then?"

"No, I really think we keep it in our humour section." Nora insisted.

"Right, ho. So I'll look in the humour section then. Where would that be?"

"If you go through that walkway there, follow the staircase up and round and it will be on the landing opposite the Wordsworth books."

"Thank you." He set off towards the back of the shop.

The previous lady who was searching for the book she had sold came down clutching a big thick, glossy paperback.

"Found it." She breathed in relief, making for the door. "So I'll take it back then. Thanks."

Nora stood up.

"I'm so sorry but we bought it from you." She reminded her hastily. "And I don't actually remember it myself so I can't let you walk out with that book."

The woman skidded to a stop on the mat.

"Well, as I said you paid twenty quid for about two hundred paperbacks." She clutched the book possessively.

"I'm sorry but if everyone who sold books from us decided they wanted certain ones back and came in to help themselves there'd be some sort of book riot."

The woman thought about that.

"So, you want me to buy my own book?" She headed back to the counter, dropped it on top and took out her purse.

"The owner of our shop bought it from you." Nora hinted.

"But she only paid ten pounds for two hundred paperbacks! That's like, five pence each isn't it?"

"We don't pay for books equally. Sometimes we'll pay a pound or two for a paperback or yes, a couple of pence." Nora explained, hoping she didn't sound like a money-grabbing scrooge.

"Well, how much would you have paid for this one?" The woman glared, waving it in front of Nora's face.

"I would have offered you fifty pence." She replied warily, leaning back.

The woman sighed.

"Fine. Then I'll give you fifty pence."

Nora felt awkward but knew Georgina wouldn't be impressed if the woman simply walked off with it. Who was to say she wouldn't be back to help herself to more? And who was to say that book was actually one she sold in the first place? It was one of Nora's bookworm conundrums. She hated those.

"Thank you." Nora opened the book and saw three pound fifty written in pencil on the title page.

The woman snatched it back quickly. She dug out two twenty pence pieces and two five pence pieces and handed them over to Nora. Then she took up the book and walked off with her nose in the air.

"Oi! You there! Got any books about bowling balls?" A voice from the doorway shouted.

Nora straightened up and saw a large man with a shaved head shove the door against the wall. He remained on the step, looking like a bowling ball himself.

"Bowling balls?"

"Yeah, that's what I said!"

"I've never seen a book specifically about bowling balls."

"Call yourself a bookshop!" He shrieked and left, leaving the door open.

Jane came in from the back room studying a heavy black book.

"Where would you put this?" She asked.

Nora was still staring after the bowling ball man with wide eyes, so blinked and looked at Jane's book.

"Is it one of those books that don't seem to belong anywhere so we always put them on display?" She grinned.

"I think so." Jane agreed, holding it up for Nora to see closely. "Would you like a sausage roll? Honestly, it's all I can think about as I'm putting these books away out the back; a sausage roll and a mug of tea. My treat."

"I'd love a sausage roll." Nora accepted..

"Here you are." Jane handed the book to Nora. "You can deal with that and I'll get the sausage rolls. They do lovely crispy hot ones in the delicatessen."

Jane squeezed down the small corridor that led under the stairs behind them for her.

"That's lucky because the bakery across the road has gone." Nora said.

Jane straightened up, horrified.

"My goodness! Well, I'm glad I'm craving a sausage roll and not cakes at the moment. How thoughtless of them."

"Memoirs." Nora decided, holding up the book. She dropped it on the small pile that was left for upstairs.

"Good." Jane grinned. She squeezed Nora's shoulder and hurried off eagerly. A man replaced her, closing the door with a silent click.

"Hello, I…wow!" The man stood on the flagstones, staring around the room. "Well here's a fire hazard if ever I saw one. You'd go up like a bomb. Fahrenheit four hundred and fifty one!"

"Do we have it?" Nora asked.

The man looked at her.

"Eh?"

"Fahrenheit 451. The novel by Ray Bradbury." Nora prompted.

"Oh. I wouldn't know. I was just pointing out that the ignition temperature of paper is four hundred and fifty one degrees Fahrenheit, or two hundred and thirty three degrees Celsius. So you'd melt like an ice-cream in the height of summer if this room caught fire."

Nora cleared her throat.

"That's good to know." She said politely.

The man pondered the books for a moment, shrugged and turned to face her.

"What I wanted to know was if you knew a good pub in town."

Nora stared at him blankly.

"A pub?"

"Yeah, I fancy a Guinness. Where would you recommend?"

"There's a pub across the road. The Black Hart. I'm sure they sell Guinness." Nora said, wondering if The Secondhand Bookworm should double as the tourist information centre.

"Grand, grand. Off I go. Don't burn your books now." He winked, turning about and heading back for the door.

"I'll try not to." Nora assured and grimaced to see two postcard waving old ladies replace him.

"The last of the big spenders." The first woman chuckled.

"Do you sell stamps?" Her friend asked.

"No we don't but there is a post office on the corner." Nora directed, standing up to use the till.

The women clicked their tongues, shaking their heads.

"Shame, shame. Shame about that. How inconvenient." The first woman tutted.

"Yes, very inconvenient, Helen." Her friend agreed.

They poured out their purse contents on the counter together so that all the coins became muddled. This resulted in a loud debate about whose money belonged to whom with Helen baring her teeth making small hissing sounds until her friend backed down.

They paid, finally leaving as Jane returned holding two white paper bags.

"I'll put the kettle on." Jane offered.

"Okay." Nora nodded with a glance at the sausage roll bags on the side as a man entered the shop.

"Excuse me, sire. Is this the bookshop?!"

He was short and fat with very thick round rimmed glasses. Nora wondered if she looked like a guy or if he was a little blind.

"This is the bookshop." She assured, also wondering if having a thousand books in the front room wasn't a big enough hint.

"Oh. It looks like one long shop from outside going up half the street. I wasn't sure which door to come in! Do you sell books?" He looked Nora slowly up and down, holding the rim of his glasses.

"Yes. They're all for sale." Nora assured.

"What are the prices?"

"They're all marked up individually."

"Can you check your computer and see if you have a copy of 'The Pickwick Papers' by Rudyard Kipling?"

Nora paused.

"Don't you mean by Charles Dickens?" She asked politely.

The man stared.

"No. Rudyard Kipling. He wrote the Jungle Books."

"Are you after 'The Jungle Book'?" Nora wondered.

"No! 'The Pickwick Papers' by Kipling." He insisted and slapped his palm on the counter firmly.

Nora edged back slightly.

"Well, 'The Pickwick Papers' was written by Charles Dickens." She said hesitantly.

The man sighed dramatically.

"I read it when I was young and the copy I read was by Rudyard Kipling. There must be two books with the same name, one by this Charles Dickens fellow and the one that I read by Rudyard Kipling. I'm after the one written by Rudyard Kipling."

Nora's lips tightened.

"Well, in that case we don't have it. We only have 'The Pickwick Papers' which was written by Charles Dickens. Would you like to give that one a go and see if it's the same?"

"No, I only like Rudyard Kipling. He wrote many books and I'm after his copy of 'The Pickwick Papers'. Why don't you check your computer?"

"We don't have our titles listed."

"Where would Kipling's books be?"

"Up in the attic room."

"Oh I can't do stairs; I've had a knee operation. Can you run up and have a look for me?"

"I'm on my own and I can't leave the till." Nora fibbed, irritated.

"I'll watch it for you."

"I can't leave it with customers. I'm not allowed."

"How can I know if you have 'The Pickwick Papers' if I can't get up there and you won't go?!"

"I assure you that we do *not* have a copy of 'The Pickwick Papers' by Rudyard Kipling. But we most probably have it by Charles Dickens…"

"I don't want his one I want Kipling's! Oh, it's hopeless! Nobody ever has the one by Rudyard Kipling they only have this Charles Dickens fool! Forget it." He threw up his arms and stomped out.

Jane ran into the front room in hysterical laughter.

"Oh, oh dear, oh, I had my mouth covered around the corner with both hands as I listened, oh…" She was gasping between her laughter while Nora sat back in the chair, shaking her head with bewilderment. "I'm sorry I didn't come and back you up but that was so funny. I heard the silly man and…oh dear!"

"I was not going to run upstairs and look for a book that doesn't exist." Nora assured her.

"Oh dear, now I really need a cup of tea. The kettle's boiled!" Jane ran off to the kitchen still laughing leaving Nora writing a Skype message to Georgina asking if Rudyard Kipling wrote 'The Pickwick Papers'.

Five minutes later, Jane and Nora were sitting down discussing the different ways to swing a woman around a dance floor when a customer walked in from the back room. Jane was sitting in the swivel chair behind the counter so she put her tea down and wiped some pastry crumbs from her jumper as the man dropped a book before her.

"Would you do these for ten pounds? They come to twelve pounds fifty."

"Oh. I can't change prices I'm afraid." Jane said cheerfully.

"This one has a damp mark." He glared at Jane.

Nora arched an eyebrow.

"Well, it's priced at four pounds probably because of that." Jane said logically and picked up the book.

"It's not very saleable."

"Well, you want to buy it." She pointed out and Nora coughed into her mug to cover up her laugh.

"Yes, but not for four pounds!" The man insisted.

"They actually come to fourteen pounds together. I can't give you this one for free." Jane said with a polite smile.

"You should accept offers! You really won't? Bah. I get discounts in all the other bookshops." He rapped the books with his fingers angrily.

"We have to buy our books in."

"I doubt you paid four pounds for that one."

"No, but we need to make a little bit of profit."

The man shot a look at Nora who was pretending to read a book called 'The Evolution of the Wooden Ship' she had found on the pile of the last of their books to put away.

"I'll leave them then." He breathed severely. "You should be open to giving money off, especially on tatty damp stained books."

"It's not my shop." Jane smiled.

"Where's the owner? He always gives me a discount."

"Oh. Why?"

"He knows I'm a good customer."

"The owner is a she." Jane pointed out calmly.

The man flustered a little.

"Well, *she* knows me!" He stammered and then with a final glare he left, slamming the door behind him.

"Oh dear." Nora winced.

"All that fuss over a few pounds. We weren't forcing him to buy the books." Jane laughed.

"It happens all the time." Nora sighed.

The phone rang so Nora answered it while Jane sipped her tea.

"What do you mean did Rudyard Kipling write 'The Pickwick Papers'?" Georgina's voice at the other end was incredulous.

"According to one of our customers he did." Nora smiled.

"Oh dear! Typical Castletown. Is it busy there?"

"It's *been* busy. We're having a tea break and then we're going to sort a few more sections to keep us trim and fit." Nora explained.

"Oh good. Now about tomorrow. Remember to bring the calls file with you and I'll pick you up from your parents' house at quarter to nine. And don't forget the money, too. Sorry to go on about it but the last thing we want is to have to drive over to Castletown to pick them all up."

"I'll make sure I remember it all." Nora promised.

"Make certain we have a nice amount of cash; some fivers and pound coins and fifty pence pieces. I'm feeling mean. Have you done the calls sheet?"

"Yes, it's all done." Nora nodded, watching the door open and two men enter.

"Good. We've a full day all over the place with a whole variety of books and people including an actor off daytime television. The one your sister Heather has a crush on."

Nora laughed.

"Oh yes, *him*. That should be fun. Can I take some selfies with him?"

"Certainly not!"

"How dull."

"Now I don't want any complaining from you tomorrow."

"That sounds ominous. What do you have planned?"

"Just the usual, but I know you, and you start complaining."

"I'll try not to." Nora promised, watching the two men close the door after entering The Secondhand Bookworm.

"Hmm. Humphrey offered to go in my place. He seemed keen on driving you around in the van. Is there something going on between you I should be aware of?" Georgina asked with a tease in her voice.

"No!" Nora said emphatically.

Georgina laughed.

"If you say so." She chuckled. "See you tomorrow then. I've got a customer, I'd better go."

"Bye." Nora smiled and replaced the receiver.

The men who entered together looked like father and son. The older man wore a long, cream rain coat and had a large, long, thin nose, little blue eyes and a very soft, dreamy expression. The younger man looked friendly with a riot of greying black hair, a shirt, pullover and cords. Jane greeted them cheerfully.

"Good afternoon." The elder man replied slowly. He looked around. "I used to own a bookshop here in the town."

The younger man smiled, proceeding to scan the shelves behind him.

"Really?" Nora was interested. "Where was it?"

"Well it was over there." He indicated as if it was obvious. He sighed slowly. "Yes, I remember the previous owners here in this shop. Mr and Mrs Lodbrok."

"Yes, they retired." Nora explained.

"As did I, my dear." He studied her solemnly and Jane smiled, tidying some books on the counter next to Nora.

"What books did you sell in your shop, sir?" Jane inquired cheerfully.

He turned to regard Jane slowly.

"Antiquarian and rare books. In two rooms above what is now a shop for middle aged ladies clothing." He had noticed.

"Was it a good business?" Jane asked.

"I did very well." He assured. "There were four bookshops at one time in the sixties here, but Mr Stock committed suicide and Mrs McKnock had a dreadful fire and she lost all her stock." He shook his head forlornly.

"A fire? I expect that was a blaze." Nora mused, thinking of her earlier customer's comment about book-burning temperatures.

"Oh, yes, it was indeed. I wonder if it was done on purpose sometimes. Perhaps the council wished to reduce the amount of bookshops here since reading was thought to be a source of all the misery and corrupting ideas in the youth of Castletown. *'Give the people contests they win by remembering the words to more popular songs....Don't give them slippery stuff like philosophy or sociology to tie things up with. That way lies melancholy.'* That was the thought at the time." He said, quoting Fire Captain Beatty from Ray Bradbury's novel Fahrenheit 451.

"Oh dear." Nora frowned, hoping it wasn't an omen. She glanced around the room warily.

"Excuse me." Jane put down a book she held. "Did you say Lodbrok, Stock and McKnock all had bookshops here?"

Nora stared while the younger man chuckled into an open book called 'The Regency Road'. The elder man looked blank.

"Yes."

"Do you mind me asking your name, sir?" Jane asked, delighted with the thought that it, too, would rhyme.

"I am Mr Frederick A Speight." He replied slowly and sombrely.

Jane glanced at Nora.

"And are you revisiting the town here to reminisce?" Jane asked him, curiously.

He smacked his lips, thoughtfully.

"I am down from Kent with my son John and we have had tea in a lovely café called The Flowery Teacup and are now seeking crime and thriller novels." He indicated to the man behind him who gave a warm incline of his head, continuing to browse through the book he held.

"Ah, crime and thriller novels." Jane returned John's smile as Mr Speight rubbed his hands slowly and thoughtfully.

"In particular I am after two titles but I do not want Book Club editions. I would like hard back editions with original dust wrappers. I would like 'Killers must eat' and 'The men in her death'."

"They sound delightful, dad." John chuckled without looking up.

"Do you know the authors?" Jane asked Mr Speight.

"Of course." He sounded offended at the question.

"Would you like me to look for you or…?"

"I would like to look myself thank you." He assured.

"Come on dad, let's go and seek out the crime thrillers." John said, replacing 'The Regency Road'.

"They're upstairs at the top of the shop on the landing. You can't miss them." Jane indicated and Mr Speight bowed gratefully, John leading the way.

Jane stood before Nora, her eyes shining and a large smile on her face.

"Do you think it's true about Lodbrok, Stock and McKnock?" She asked. "Oh, I hope it is!"

Nora laughed.

"I know that Mr and Mrs Lodbrok used to own this shop before Georgina bought it because we still get post addressed to them. They're retired and living in a houseboat on the Thames now," she explained.

"Maybe they're with Mrs McKnock." Jane proposed and they stood laughing until the door opened once more to admit another two men. Nora sat down and Jane moved around to behind the counter.

The first man was old and wizened but stood tall, had a large gap where he was missing his two front teeth and was carrying a stick. He looked forbidding as he marched up to the desk, pulling out a slip of paper from his suit jacket. The man behind closed the door and smiled mildly.

"Do you sell fiction?" He asked.

His tone was almost confrontational and he stared piercingly at Nora.

"Erm...yes." She replied.

"Do you sell *hardback* fiction?" He asked, edging a little closer.

Nora edged back.

"Yes."

"And where is your fiction kept, missy?" He demanded.

"Upstairs."

"Upstairs?! Upstairs?! What about all the customers like me who can't do stairs?" His tone was soft but firm and Nora couldn't tell if he was joking.

"Would you like me to look for you, sir?" Jane offered, standing up.

"We can go up, Peter." The smiling man behind him suggested.

"Upstairs?! Upstairs?!" The man named Peter rapped his stick.

"Who is it that you're after?" Nora asked.

His blue eyes swung to meet with hers.

"I'm not after anyone, missy." He said. "I'm looking for a particular book. It's called," he unfolded his piece of paper, 'Dagger before me'."

"Do you know the author?" Nora asked.

"If I knew the author I wouldn't need to ask you, missy!" He said severely.

There was the sound of pattering feet and in a moment Mr Speight rushed in from where he and his son had been side-tracked by the motoring books. His faded blue eyes were wide.

"I do apologise but I overheard your question and I believe that I can help. I used to own a bookshop here and I believe that the book you are after is by Peter Cheney." He said, breathlessly.

John followed his father, smiling with interest.

The man before Nora drew in his breath and suddenly seemed taller.

"Peter Cheney?! Peter Cheney?! It most certainly is NOT." He was affronted and Mr Speight stuttered and rang his hands.

"Oh please forgive me, please forgive me, I made a faux pas, a terrible faux pas." He shook his head tragically. "I mistakenly thought that Peter Cheney wrote 'Dagger before me' but of course no, it was a faux pas, no it was Manning O'Brine, Manning O'Brine who wrote 'Dagger before me', of course!"

"Are you *sure*?! Because if I climb up some stairs and it turns out that you have made a faux pas and I look for the wrong book I shall be very put out!" The tall man was severe.

Mr Speight rang his hands and his son grinned, enjoying the scene. Nora cleared her throat.

"I'll have a look on the internet and see if I can check the book author." She suggested hurriedly.

Peter turned his gaze back on her.

"Do you mean to tell me that you could have looked on your computer all along?" He breathed.

"No." Nora cringed, typing quickly. Her cheeks felt as though they had risen to four hundred and fifty one degrees Fahrenheit. "We don't have our books listed."

"Well, why not?" He spoke as if she was a child and Nora felt like running away.

"Oh, look, there it is." Jane interrupted quickly and loudly, pointing at the monitor. "You were right Mr Speight. It *is* a crime thriller by Manning O'Brine."

"A crime thriller?! A crime thriller?! I assure you I do not read crime." The man with the stick declared in affront.

The man who had entered with him burst out laughing.

"That's not true, Peter. You like a good crime novel. Shall we go up and have a look?" He suggested.

"We're heading up there too. I do apologise for my faux pas." Mr Speight repeated tragically.

Peter beheld him aloofly and deigned to follow the party.

John grinned as his father led the way.

"I thought there was going to be a fist fight then." He said quietly to Jane and Nora and followed them amidst apologies about the faux pas and complaints about the stairs.

Jane sat down again and she and Nora looked at one another.

"He's like Steptoe from that programme 'Steptoe and Son' on UK Gold." Nora said and Jane covered her mouth with laughter.

"It's true. Oh dear, he was very scary! I hope we have a copy of 'Dagger before me'." She said, shaking her head.

"I hope not. He may get ideas." Nora smirked.

A woman then arrived, large, manly and with a unibrow frowning angrily over her dark eyes. She stepped down into the shop, leaving the door wide open so that five crisp packet wrappers sailed in and landed on the mat.

"Do you have a copy of 'Burning Bright' by Tracey Chevalier? She also wrote 'The Girl with a Pearl Earring'." The Unibrow asked.

Nora looked around warily.

"If we did it would be in our attic room." Jane replied enthusiastically.

The Unibrow's face fell.

"Oh. I don't do stairs!" She turned away.

"I would be happy to look for you." Jane offered cheerfully.

"No, I won't ask you to. What if there was a fire and the building became a towering inferno? You would be trapped and burned alive and it would all be my fault. No, sirree Bob. Don't worry; I'll check the charity shop." The Unibrow said and left quickly.

Jane and Nora looked at one another.

"Burning Bright is part three in Fahrenheit 451." Nora grimaced.

"The novel by Ray Bradbury?"

"Yes. It seems to have been a worrying theme this afternoon. I hope it's not an omen."

Jane smiled and shook her head.

"No, of course not." She assured and gave Nora a hug. "Shall I make us some more tea? I think we need it." Jane suggested, standing up.

"We certainly do." Nora agreed and Jane headed off to boil the kettle leaving Nora pondering the books around her uneasily.

7 THE REMAINS OF THE DAY

While Jane made tea Nora dug her iPhone out of her jeans pocket having heard a text message arrive. She smiled to see Humphrey's name on the screen.

'Hi. How's your day going?' He had written.

Nora typed her reply.

'It's been the usual kind of bookshop day here. Crazy customers and fearing for my life as usual.' Nora joked. *'How's your day going?'*

'Busy. Georgina now has me sanding down her back door. Maybe you need twenty-four hour protection there?'

Nora chuckled.

'I've often thought about getting a bodyguard.' She teased.

'I'd be more than happy to apply for the position.' Humphrey joked.

'Thanks. Good to know!' She sent back.

Nora sat thinking about Humphrey for a moment, picturing his nice suits, easy manner and his grin. The shop door opened, interrupting her musing, and some leaves dropped down onto the mat with a rustle. A woman entered The Secondhand Bookworm, closed the door firmly behind her and straightened out her hair. Nora placed her phone back into the pocket of her jeans.

"Hello." She greeted.

The woman pushed her glasses back from her nose slightly, approaching the desk.

"Hello. I have some books for sale."

"Oh yes?" Nora smiled, picking up some paperclips she had just sent scattering with her elbow.

"I don't have them with me but I have a list of the titles. They're all novels by Charles Dickens." She placed her bag on the desk and sniffed, opening the clasp.

"Are they a complete set or individual editions?"

"They were *part* of a complete set. The mice ate one box full which had half of the set in." She admitted dryly.

"Oh dear." Nora looked at the list. "It's very difficult to sell incomplete sets of Dickens."

"I thought it might be." She nodded, withdrawing the list and folding it into her bag. "What should I do with the remaining ones?"

"Erm…."

"Give them to the mice?"

Nora smiled.

"You could do."

The lady sighed and picked up her bag.

"Okay, well, it was worth a try. I decided to bin them if you didn't want them."

As she was turning to go the door opened and Billy's large stomach preceded his entrance accompanied by his loud guffaws.

"Goodbye." The lady said while Nora stared at Billy who stepped down into the shop, speaking into his mobile.

"I'm in the bookworm emporium. Call you back in a moment." He said and hung up. "Nora! I have these books." He announced loudly, letting the lady past who gave him an unimpressed look. "The books I mentioned that I wanted to sell."

"Oh. Yes." Nora nodded grimly.

Billy dropped a plastic bag onto the counter, opening it up, pausing for a mighty coughing fit and then wiping his eyes before drawing out the book on top.

"Oh dear, blasted dust." He coughed and handed Nora a tatty old tome. "There are seven and all the boards are detached. Looks like they had bookworm at some point. See the burrowing. They were part of a house clearance last week. Any good to you?"

Nora looked at the offered volume.

"No!" She assured him.

"Well *I* won't be able to shift them. I thought *you* might, with your bookworm fetish."

"We don't have a fetish for bookworms! We're called The Secondhand Bookworm in honour of people who like to read secondhand books." Nora explained for the umpteenth time.

"Eh?" Billy looked baffled.

"People who devour books are fondly referred to as bookworms."

Billy frowned, coughed and then cursed as his mobile phone rang.

Nora turned her nose up at him as he turned his back on her and shouted into his phone, laughing loudly. She returned the munched up book to the bag, prodded his back and handed it to him.

"Hold on a sec." He told his caller. "You can't give me a tenner for them, Nora?"

"No!"

"Not even a fiver? Think of your bookworms."

"No!"

He shrugged, smiled and headed off with the bag while still bellowing into his mobile.

"Was that 'Billy Bunter'?" Jane asked, finally returning from the kitchen carrying two mugs of fresh steaming tea.

"How could you tell?" Nora replied flatly.

"He never has anything decent to sell. He just tries to palm off the ones that are falling apart and is obsessed with half eaten books." Jane knew.

The front door opened and a man marched in.

Jane sipped her tea while Nora greeted him politely.

"I have some ghastly old books I want to get rid of. They're tatty, monstrous things. Would you be interested in buying them from me?" He asked.

Nora stared at him.

"Not if they really are as horrific as you say they are." She replied.

"Well, I don't want to dump them. They belong on a tip but if I can get some money from them it would be good. Shall I bring them in? They're in loads of black sacks in the boot of my car. All subjects, like Arthur Mees encyclopaedias, Haynes car manuals, Reader's Digest condensed novels; some of them have dog sick on them."

"Are you having a joke?" Nora asked.

The man frowned at her.

"What?"

"Why would we want to sell, or even more to the point how *could* we sell 'ghastly old books with dog sick' on them?" Nora was completely insulted that he could even offer them to The Secondhand Bookworm.

"Well, you're a bookshop, you sell books." He defended.

"But we can't sell them covered in dog sick to begin with, and those subjects and titles we find very difficult to sell anyway."

"Well, I'll donate them to you, save me going down the tip. They're all in black sacks." He decided.

"No thank you!" Nora was adamant.

"You don't even want them for free?!"

Nora put down her mug of tea, getting irritated.

"If you look around you won't see a section that says 'Books with Dog Sick On Them'." Nora stressed and heard Jane snort with laughter into her mug.

The man glared at Nora.

"Fine! I'll dump them then." He snapped and swung around, stomping out of the shop.

Before Jane or Nora could react, another man replaced him, almost falling into the room.

"Whoops. Mind the step!" He told himself.

Nora stared expectantly as he approached the counter.

"Do you have anything about the Olympics?" He asked, peering around at the shelves of books lining the room.

Nora tried to recall if she had seen any Olympic books.

"If we did they would be upstairs in the sports section." She explained.

"And what colours are they?" The man asked, taking out a handkerchief to wipe his glasses.

"Pardon?" Nora watched him rub a lens.

"The books." He said.

"What colours?" Nora repeated blankly.

"Yes."

"Er..." She was aware of Jane shaking with laughter into her tea behind her. "I don't know."

"It has to be a blue book about the Olympics." The man explained, rubbing the second lens before placing his glasses back on.

"May I ask why?" Nora questioned.

"Well, blue is her favourite colour and she loves the Olympics. It's for my missus. It's our one year anniversary." He explained.

"Well, that's very thoughtful, but it's probably hit-and-miss that any books about the Olympics will be blue."

He screwed up his nose.

"Oh dear. Can you order me one?" He asked.

Nora arched an eyebrow.

"What?"

"A blue book on the Olympics." He said.

"We don't order books I'm afraid." Nora explained, beginning to feel exasperated.

"Oh, that's a pity. I'll go and have a look and see if you have one anyway." He decided and headed off towards the stairs.

Nora turned and looked at Jane.

"I will be in servitude to the madness of bookworms until the end of my days. I feel it in my bones." She growled.

Jane was wiping her eyes from laughter tears but couldn't say anything because the group of four men from the crime thriller section were finally returning, talking loudly, accompanied by the banging of Peter's stick and Mr Speight's apologies about his earlier faux pas.

"You see, I used to own a book shop here but I forget, I forget lots of titles and authors." He was saying. "So I do oftentimes make a faux pas."

"I think we get that now, dad." John's weary but smiling voice said and they came into the front room.

"You didn't have the 'Dagger before Me'!" Peter said, in his slow intimidating tone.

"Oh dear. Sorry about that." Nora apologised uneasily.

"Hmmm." He looked at her pointedly, leaning on his stick.

"Thank you very much, we had best bid you goodbye." John grinned. "Come on dad, let's get going and leave these good ladies in peace."

"Nice to meet you, Mr Speight." Jane said.

"Thank you, thank you." He nodded solemnly and they headed towards the door.

"We'd best be going too, Peter." His friend said.

"Do you order books, missy?" Peter asked with a rap of his stick on the carpet.

"No, we don't." Nora said determinedly.

He tutted against the gum of his missing front teeth.

"Oh dear. Very disappointing."

"Come on, Peter." His friend smiled, following Mr Speight out.

"Goodbye." Peter smiled, showing the gap in his teeth.

Jane and Nora politely bade him farewell and the door rattled against the wind slightly once it had closed.

"This afternoon is becoming a typical Bookworm afternoon." Jane laughed and Nora flopped into the swivel chair.

"I'm glad I'm on calls tomorrow." She decided.

The man who had inquired about the Olympics book came down the stairs and into the front room, flicking through the pages of a book.

"This one is really good, but the cover is yellow. Do you have a blue cover?" The man asked.

Jane looked at the book he held.

"But that's the dust wrapper. That's how it came." She pointed out.

"Hmm." He turned it over and over. "I could take the wrapper off, no, it's orange underneath."

Nora could see that Jane was about to burst out laughing.

"You could use blue wrapping paper." Nora suggested.

"No, it will still be yellow on her book shelf and she only has blue books." He explained seriously.

"Really?" Nora blinked.

"Yes, it's her favourite colour. I'll have to leave it I'm afraid. Do you know where else I can get a blue book about the Olympics?"

"No."

He shrugged and headed off.

Jane picked up the phone.

"I must tell Georgina about our afternoon." She laughed and Nora sat down, shaking her head.

It was quiet in the shop as Jane spoke to Georgina so Nora added up their sales so far. Jane wrote down some titles to look for that Georgina gave her from customer requests in Seatown.

"I'll look for the novels." Nora offered, picking up the list.

"Okay, and then I'll look for the sailing books." Jane agreed.

Nora headed off out of the front room, through the narrow walkway and soon began climbing the creaking stairs.

It was peaceful in the depths of The Secondhand Bookworm. Nora realized she hadn't had much of a chance to take a quiet walk throughout the shop for a while. Usually when she worked on her own she only made a quick trip up to the toilet which was located at the back of the next floor in the children's room. Today she had hurried throughout the shop putting books on the shelves without taking a moment to enjoy her literary environment.

Working in The Secondhand Bookworm meant she didn't have much of a chance to browse so she climbed the stairs slowly, perusing the shelves and checking on the vast array of stock.

The stairwell circled up through all the floors culminating in the attic room which was full of fiction organised in alphabetical order of author on a hundred shelves. On her way up Nora picked a chocolate bar wrapper from the first flight of stairs and a clump of mud probably from the bottom of someone's hiking boot.

She straightened some philosophy books and removed a children's book that was lying across a row of Garfield books in the humour section, almost tripping over some Giles annuals someone had rummaged through on the second floor landing and left in a pile on the floor.

"Excuse me. Do you work here?" A woman asked as Nora stopped to put the children's book on its correct shelf.

The woman stood in front of the cookery section.

"Yes." Nora smiled.

"Do you have any Delia Smith books? Or any Mrs Beaton books or books by Mary Berry? I've looked all through here but I can't see any?" She said, brow furrowed.

"This is where they would be." Nora knew. "They are all popular cooks so we could be out of them."

"Oh well. I live locally so I can just pop in from time to time." The lady decided cheerfully. "Do you have any books about herbal remedies?"

"If we did they'd be on the next floor in health and self-help."

"Okay. Up I go."

Nora followed her, picking up a biography that was left idly on a stair before she finally reached the attic room after directing the lady to the correct section. The attic room was bright and pleasant with two big windows and a skylight, a brown carpet and green walls. There were many corners, endless books and three piles of paperbacks on the floor waiting to be sorted and put away.

The attic room had once been a store room. Georgina had transformed it into an extra room for books a year after she had purchased the shop which meant that it was the only room in The Secondhand Bookworm that had a more modern feel to it.

"Let's start with 'A portrait of a lady'." Nora said aloud, consulting her list and following the cases of fiction around to the section where the authors' surnames began with 'J'. Nora crouched down, pushing some paperbacks into a neat, level line with her finger until she reached Henry James. There were a couple of other titles of his but no copy of 'A portrait of a lady'.

"'Moby Dick' by Herman Melville next." She shuffled along on her knees, scanning the shelves, faintly aware of someone entering the attic room.

"Got any Stephen King?" A man asked.

Nora looked up to meet two heavy lidded eyes.

"We should have." She gestured further around the room. "Horror is separated out into its own section there."

"Yeah, horror." He nodded. He moved over to the section where he stopped, staring silently.

Nora looked at him before she continued scanning. She saw a copy of 'Moby Dick' so pulled it out, noting the price inside. She had two more to check.

As Nora neared the partly open window looking for Edward Rutherford's 'The Forest', which she couldn't find, she was aware of music drifting out from the flats above the Indian restaurant. She stood to scan the area, seeing a tall hookah pipe positioned on the windowsill of one of the rooms. Ladders and paint pots, dustsheets and the sound of hammering accompanied Max's voice.

"Hey, Nora!" Max came to one of the open windows and waved at her.

"Hello, Max." Nora called back.

"Fancy that tour yet?" He asked.

"I can't at the moment. I'm working." She held up the book she was holding.

"Just let me know any time." He winked.

Nora smiled politely, watching him turn back to a workman holding a saw.

"Got any Dean Koontz?" The man in the room then asked Nora.

Nora glanced at him where he stood still staring at the shelves.

"They'd be in the same place." She replied.

"Got any G.M. Hague?" Was his next question.

"Erm…" Nora decided to look for him, deducing he wasn't having much luck. "There are all the Stephen King's."

"I got all them." He told her.

"There are three Dean Koontz."

"Oh yeah. No I got all them."

"I can't see any G.M…"

"Hague. He's an Australian horror writer. Quite hard to find." He said.

"I can't see any."

"Didn't think you would." He sighed drearily.

Nora glanced at him. He sniffed loudly.

"Got any Dragon Lance?"

"Who wrote them?"

"Different authors." He shrugged. "You won't have any."

"Are they horror?"

"Fantasy."

"Look over there." Nora indicated and returned to hunt for her last book on the request list.

"'The Flirt' by Kathleen Tessaro."

"What?"

"Just speaking to myself." Nora said, scanning the shelf. "Why is there a 'Doctor Who' novel here?!" She pulled it out and then gave up looking for the last title, leaving the room with her copy of 'Moby Dick', followed by the customer who sneezed loudly behind her. Nora displayed the 'Doctor Who' book on a shelf near the stairs before she began to walk down.

"Got any books about Shamanism?"

Nora stopped, looking back.

"The room behind you. On the right." She indicated.

He turned and stomped off so Nora hurried down the stairs, pausing to let a man past.

"Sorry! Thank you." He smiled, stopping at the humour section.

Nora reached the bottom of the staircase with a sigh. She walked through to the front room where Jane was speaking with a small group.

"No, no, they're certainly not politically correct these days but we do see them." Jane was saying.

"I have a good collection but I'm still after this title." A lady was explaining proudly.

Jane noticed Nora and turned to her.

"Do we get 'The Gollywogs go Fox-Hunting'?" She asked.

Nora placed 'Moby Dick' on the counter by the computer monitor.

"No. It's quite hard to come by and would be about three hundred pounds if in a reasonable condition." Nora knew.

"Yes, that's what we thought. Well, we ask every time we go into a secondhand bookshop don't we Vera."

"Yes we do Doris." The lady beside her nodded.

"Well, thank you ladies. Shall we go and get some afternoon tea, Vera?" Doris suggested.

"Yes, Doris. Where would you recommend is a good place for a cup of tea?" Vera asked.

Jane looked at the wall clock.

"Well, it's four o'clock."

"Oh yes, they might all be closed now." Doris said.

"You could try down by the river." Jane suggested and the women headed off, thanking Jane and discussing their tea plans.

"I found one." Nora said.

"Wonderful!" Jane wrote down her previous sale. She checked the sailing list. "I'll see if we have these. It won't take me a moment."

While Jane was in the back room, Nora sat down in front of the computer to let Seatown know about the novel she had located. Cara Skyped through the name and number of the lady who had asked for it with instructions to bag it up and put it by to be sent over to the Seatown shop, so Nora put it in the transfer box.

The transfer box was a tatty cardboard box kept on the shelf under the till. When Georgina drove home from Seatown to Piertown she dropped into The Secondhand Bookworm in Castletown to collect any books that needed transferring and dropping off any books from the Seatown branch. It was a system that worked quite well.

"No luck with the sailing requests." Jane's cheerful voice announced.

"Oh well. We found one on their list so that's good." Nora said, standing up.

A new customer arrived.

"Good afternoon." He greeted, stepping down and closing the door.

Jane was now sitting at the computer, Skyping her message with one finger.

"Hello." Nora smiled.

The man had a white trimmed beard and moustache, round spectacles and a long raincoat with a tweed suit underneath.

"Might you have a copy of a book called 'The Passenger Tramways of Pontypridd'?" He asked. "Or, a section about trams where it might be?"

"We do have a section of books about trams and buses." Nora led the way through the walkway into the back.

"Oh, splendid. I'll have a look through. It's this particular book I am searching for but I would be delighted to look through your sections."

"Well, here are the books about trams and buses. There are some railway books above it too." Nora indicated.

"Okay, thank you." He began to browse.

Nora returned to the front room where Jane was now bent over humming as she dug out the dusting spray and a duster.

"I thought I'd clean the PDQ machine and the till." Her muffled voice explained. "It's so dusty again."

"Good idea." Nora approved. "It gets dusty in just one day." She then gave a small gasp.

Jane looked up as the door opened and the Goat-Lady walked in.

The Goat-Lady was one of Nora's regulars; a short, thin woman always with a patterned scarf wrapped tightly around her head. She had several teeth missing and a crinkly face. She bred rare breeds of sheep and goats with her husband Bill and often grazed them in a field outside the town, popping into The Secondhand Bookworm whenever she was in the area with her unique perfume of pungent goats that stank out the whole shop.

The Goat-Lady was from a very well-to-do family but she now spent her days in a tiny caravan about the

Cole countryside with Bill. She was nice and friendly, if a little aromatic.

"Hello, Nora!" The Goat-Lady greeted loudly.

"Hello." Nora was immediately engulfed by the strong smell of sheep, goats and manure. Jane quickly sprayed a large dose of dusting spray which soaked the till and PDQ machine.

"How are you?" The Goat-Lady asked, stopping before the section of books about the County of Cole opposite the front door.

"Very well. You?"

"Well!" She exhaled a dramatic sigh. "The caravan heating packed up so Bill and I have been freezing; mother had a fall, the car's failed its MOT and I have a hideous splinter. But apart from that we had a wonderful day in Wall Town with the markets and the sheep fair on Saturday, and, seeing as I'm related to the Witch Master's General, as you well know, I sniffed out all those with the evil eye at the goat fair we put on in Little Sea on Sunday, drove their curses from us and we were able to sell eight boxes of goat's cheese."

"That's good news." Nora said, covering her nose with the sleeve of her jumper.

"Yes, yes. I'm currently trying a new concoction for our next market in Large Town. Goat's cheese and gooseberries. There's a bush of gooseberries where we've parked our caravan. I managed to pick a basketful before the sheep ate them all. I'll try to remember to bring some in for you to try. It smells glorious."

"Thanks." Nora winced, attempting not to breathe.

Nora and Jane listened to the Goat-Lady's update about her life amidst sheep, goats, farmer's markets and manure while she browsed through the books about fields and towns in Cole until a horn sounded.

"Oh. That'd be Bill in mother's car. Come and say hello to him, Nora."

Nora saw Bill leaning out of his car window as he held up traffic in the road before the bookshop, leering at Nora with a crooked smile half hidden behind his scraggly black beard.

"Oh, no, I'm okay, thanks." Nora refused.

"Until next time! Goodbye, ladies!" The Goat-Lady bid and hurried away, climbing into her mother's car while deflecting imagined curses from impatient car drivers.

She left the entire shop smelling like a cowshed.

Nora ran around to re-open the door.

"What a smelly woman." Jane grimaced.

"She's still not as smelly as 'The Smelliest Man in the Universe'." Nora insisted, waving her arms about to disperse the scent of goats.

"I can't believe that." Jane said with her nose covered.

"One day you'll encounter him and see. 'The Smelliest Man in the Universe' will never be beaten. He is truly appalling. Cara and I used an entire can of air freshener the last time he was here." Nora shuddered.

Jane laughed.

"Oh dear."

The man who had asked for the 'Passenger Tramways of Pontypridd' returned from the back and politely didn't mention the smell, apologising for not buying anything but saying he would call back in the future.

Nora and Jane sat down behind the counter in the welcome late afternoon silence at last.

When it was almost five o'clock Nora and Jane started to close up The Secondhand Bookworm for the day.

Jane was picking up the box of free maps and Nora struggled in with the large revolving postcard holder as the phone began to ring. Nora dived for it breathlessly.

"The Secondhand Bookworm."

"Yes. Hello? Hello?"

"Hello?"

"The line is very faint. I'll phone you back." The voice said and rang off.

Nora waited patiently, watching Jane hoist in a box of paperbacks from the boxes either side of the door.

"Who is it?"

"Someone who couldn't hear me."

Jane pulled a face.

The phone rang again so Nora answered it once more.

"The Secondhand Bookworm." She repeated politely.

"Yes. Hello? It's a very bad line!" The lady shouted at the other end.

"Yes it can be a bad connection here, we're in the hills." Nora agreed.

"Pardon?"

"How can I help?" Nora asked.

"DO YOU BUY BOOKS?" The woman shrieked.

"YES." Nora shouted back.

"I have a lot of fishing books. My husband died and he was a hoarder." She said.

"Okay." Nora glanced at Jane as she placed the last box onto the flagstones.

"Well!? Do you want them?!" The lady on the phone demanded.

"It depends what they are."

"Pardon? It's a bad connection."

"I said, it depends what they ARE."

"I just told you they were fishing books."

"If they are very *general* books about fishing or books about fishing in *bad condition* then we couldn't sell them on."

"They are a variety. A variety of specific fishing types; fishes, rods, flies, ponds, rivers and all in a variety of conditions. About a thousand books."

"They sound interesting." Nora decided. "Would you like to phone our Seatown branch and speak with the owner there? She may like to call around to you to see them."

"Pardon?"

Nora repeated herself loudly and gave her the number, hanging up when the lady was finally satisfied.

"Was she deaf?" Jane asked, smirking.

"No, but I think I might be now." Nora laughed.

"Excuse me. Are you just closing?" A voice spoke into the shop.

A man stood on the doorstep, his wife behind him licking a large green ice-cream.

"In a few moments." Jane replied.

"Do you restore books?" He asked.

"I'm afraid that we don't." Jane shook her head.

The man sighed sadly.

"Do you know anyone who does?"

"No, we don't have anyone to recommend at the moment. We don't have books restored."

"Oh. I thought you might be more helpful. I'll have to go somewhere else then."

Jane arched an eyebrow.

"Sorry about that."

"The nearest one in the Yellow Pages is in Long Town." He said, shaking his head. "They don't know, Mavis." He shouted into his wife's face. "I thought they'd be helpful."

"Sorry." Jane apologised again.

Jane closed the door behind him and turned the sign around to 'CLOSED'.

"Jane. Be more helpful!" Nora exclaimed.

Jane laughed.

While Nora began to cash up for the end of the day, Jane checked there were no more customers lurking upstairs, switched off the lights and locked up the kitchen. Once the money was counted, bagged up and the float placed in the little safe for use the next day, Nora popped the organised takings for the calls in a couple of bank bags and the purse, shrugged into her jacket and popped the monies for pay outs into the prepared calls file. She placed it in her bag.

"It's been surprisingly busy this week. Usually September is quiet in Castletown." Nora said as Jane opened the door.

"Yes. Good news for book trading."

"An increase in bookworms." Nora agreed, making sure the desk was left tidy for Cara. "Do you think it's to do with the Duke of Cole?"

"Oh, I heard the rumour that he's thinking about rebuilding his ruins into one of his magnificent palaces."

"A palace?!"

"Alright, a castle." Jane laughed. "I hope so."

Nora agreed with a smile.

"It looks like it's a nice evening." Jane pointed out as Nora turned off the front lights, punched in the alarm code and ran around the counter, stepping out onto the pavement with Jane. "I might go for a walk along the beach with my son. The fresh air will do him good after his stomach bug."

"That sounds nice." Nora nodded, locking the door to The Secondhand Bookworm.

They dragged the sandbags in front of the door just in case it rained heavily overnight and there was more flooding in the street. Once the bags were nicely positioned, Jane and Nora stood brushing the sand from their hands.

"I can see this is going to be a lovely new daily routine." Jane grimaced.

"Hmm." Nora sighed grimly.

She turned to begin walking up the hill with Jane towards their cars but suddenly found herself facing a wall of expensive tailored suit instead. Humphrey was blocking their way.

"Hello!" Jane greeted enthusiastically.

Nora stepped back, surprised.

"Hi." Humphrey took off his sunglasses, his blue gaze levelled upon Nora.

"Humphrey. What are you doing here?" She asked.

"Offering you my protection." He replied.

Jane nudged Nora's arm.

"She won't say no to that, will you Nora. I'll leave you to it then. Bye, Nora. Bye Humphrey."

Nora watched mutely as Jane hurried up the hill, looking back over her shoulder while winking enthusiastically at her.

Humphrey chuckled.

"Sorry, I didn't mean to surprise you."

Nora smiled.

"You didn't. Not really."

"HUMPHREY!!" Imogene's loud yell made them both jump.

Nora looked past Humphrey who turned around, alarmed. Imogene was sprinting across the cobbles towards them.

"Hi, Imogene." Nora greeted.

Humphrey was frowning at Imogene as she crossed the road and stepped onto the pavement between them, turning her back on Nora so that Nora stepped back.

"Hello again!" Imogene purred, gazing up at Humphrey. "Oh, have you been working back up in London at your high-powered business job? How handsome you look."

"No." He levelled a cool gaze upon her.

Imogene giggled.

"Then why are you dressed so smartly. You look like just like Harvey Specter."

"Who?"

"Harvey Specter. From the TV show Suits?" She prompted, fluttering her eyelashes.

Nora saw Humphrey move around Imogene and felt his hand on her elbow.

"I've come to take Nora out to dinner. Nice to see you again...Irene wasn't it?"

Imogene's smile faded.

"Imogene. We met in the bookshop the other day, remember?" She looked at Humphrey's arm as it snaked around Nora's waist.

"No, sorry." He shrugged.

"I was given the impression our meeting could lead to more."

"Not by me you weren't." Humphrey assured.

Imogene stared as he led Nora away.

"The Italian restaurant tonight wasn't it?" He asked Nora loudly.

Nora nodded.

"Yes, that's right. Bye, Imogene."

"Bye, Nora." Imogene said through gritted teeth.

Nora was led carefully across the road and onto the cobbles towards the Italian restaurant opposite The Secondhand Bookworm.

"I thought you'd come to rescue *me*." She laughed.

"Now I owe you one." He looked relieved to see Imogene heading away down the street, casting them jealous looks over her shoulder.

"Okay." Nora chuckled.

"How about dinner then? As a thank you." He suggested, stopping outside the green painted windows of the restaurant.

Nora pondered.

"I'm not sure."

"As friends?" Humphrey suggested.

He let go of her waist, smiling as she thought about it.

"Hmm. Seeing as how I did just save you from Imogene." Nora finally agreed.

Humphrey nodded, pleased.

"Great. I've already booked a table for us."

"How presumptuous of you."

"Well, I know you can't resist a good calzone," he said, referencing their night out in Piertown when they had devoured pizzas on the pier.

Nora chuckled, watching him open the door for her.

"You're right. I can't." She smiled, stepped inside the restaurant and decided it would be a very interesting evening.

8 THE POLISH COUNT AND THE SOAP OPERA STAR

Little Cove was a small village on the seaside about ten minutes' drive from Castletown. There was a scattering of farmhouses along twisting and turning lanes leading to a row of cottages, some of which backed onto little cliff walks or down into the main cove where there was a network of smugglers' caves. Further along, a housing estate stood amidst groves of ancient chestnut trees. Various streets wound off between houses, blocks of flats, cottages and a row of village shops.

Georgina drove her bookshop van towards a neat terrace. Nora was already waiting at the kerbside outside her parents' house where she was currently staying with her younger sister Heather, two younger brothers, Seymour and Milton, and their mum. Her father often worked abroad and he was currently away. Nora's older brother Wilbur had his own house but was regularly over for free home-cooked meals.

It was noisy, crowded and messy and although Nora loved her siblings and her mum she had spent a whole hour browsing local flats for sale on the internet after her dinner with Humphrey the evening before. Cara was right. She needed a place of her own. Hopefully the right flat would come along for her soon.

As the little bookshop van pulled up outside the house, Nora waved, finishing putting on her lip balm. Several dogs bounded about on the grass while Heather sat tugging on Wellington boots to take them for a walk along the beach.

Heather was almost twenty and sometimes worked for Georgina with Nora in The Secondhand Bookworm on Saturdays. She was due to work that weekend and enjoyed encountering the many different customers and locals.

Heather waved to Georgina, calling goodbye to Nora who closed the gate and pulled open the van door.

"Good morning." Georgina greeted, turning off the radio.

"Morning. How was the gym?" Nora asked, climbing inside with the calls file which had the money inside it too.

"I ran for twenty minutes, swam for half an hour and then I had a huge bowl of porridge." Georgina said, suppressing a yawn.

"Impressive." Nora nodded. "I don't know how you can be bothered. I lay in for as long as I could."

Georgina laughed, watching Nora sit down, pull on her seat belt and focus on the satnav.

"I've already put the first call in." Georgina said.

"Okay." Nora studied the list again. "Three in Littlesea, oh, the daytime soap actor is third."

Georgina scoffed with a wry smile.

"That should be fun."

The bookshop van made its way out of Little Cove to join the main road. Nora and Georgina talked about the expectation of certain collections they were viewing that day while Nora secretly hoped Georgina wouldn't mention Humphrey.

"Mr Caramac has a library of Punch annuals." Georgina explained.

"Caramac? Isn't that a chocolate bar?"

Georgina laughed.

"Oh yes, it is. What a funny name to have. I think the lady in Walltown has a super shooting collection. I have several trade customers lined up for it if it's as good as she says it is. We'll drop into Seatown to have a lunch break. Roger is there with Jane. Cara's in Castletown isn't she?"

Nora nodded.

"Yes. I've left her a few warnings about customers due in to pick up various books."

"She'll be fine on her own today. I've given her a large file of paperwork to do if it goes quiet."

"She's good at that." Nora nodded, sipping her water.

The van drove through the coastal towns until they pulled up outside their first house.

"Is this right?" Georgina frowned at the large but tatty garden. The building looked condemned.

"Erm…yes, number thirty."

"It looks empty and abandoned. Okay, off we go." Georgina stepped out, Nora grabbed the calls file and they took in the sight of rows of over flowing bins, over-turned car, two broken lawnmowers, a broken pram and three Tesco shopping trollies that were scattered about the Cul-de-sac.

The house they were calling at looked in great need of repair. The garden was wildly overgrown and a cat darted across the path, making Nora yelp.

Georgina finally located the doorbell behind thick, leafy ivy and pressed the button. When there was no reply Nora rapped on the window until they finally heard immense coughing coming from inside. A shadow loomed up to the door and a woman in a dressing gown tugged it open.

"Mrs Baker? We're from the bookshop." Georgina greeted, coughing as she received a face full of cigarette smoke.

"Yeah? Come in." Mrs Baker returned huskily. "Out the way Daisy! They're my mum's dog and cat."

A fat Labrador welcomed them excitedly, almost bowling Georgina over.

Georgina followed Mrs Baker inside and Nora left the door ajar a little, waving the calls file in front of her to disperse the trail of smoke from the cigarette between Mrs Baker's teeth.

"I got the welfare officer coming round so I ain't dressed yet."

"Hello puss-puss." Georgina greeted a tabby cat on the back of the sofa and stroked it. She then span around, looking at Nora with a repulsed expression.

Mrs Baker sat on the arm of the single chair and flicked ash into an ash tray on the side of the coffee table.

"It's my mum's house but she passed to the other side. Daisy! Stop it!" She coughed as Daisy ran at Nora and placed her snout between Nora's legs.

Nora arched an eyebrow at Georgina questioningly while trying to move Daisy's head away.

"Mrs Baker. Where are your books?!" Georgina demanded loudly, glancing about, unable to locate any.

"Oh, yeah. They're upstairs." Mrs Baker said and heaved herself up, dragging her feet as she led the way toward a stairwell in the hall. She had a mass of black and silver curls and a heavily lined face with black teeth. Nora was reminded of a character from a Charles Dickens novel.

They followed Mrs Baker and Georgina walked behind her, wiping her hands on the sofa and curtains as she did so much to Nora's baffled amusement. They climbed the stairs and came to the first room.

"There's some in the bottom of that chest and some on them shelves." Mrs Baker pointed out.

The doorbell rang and she coughed violently.

"I'll leave you to look while I deal with the welfare woman." She said and tore down the stairs, almost tripping over Daisy who was on her way up.

Once alone Georgina shook her head, beginning to skim the shelves with a narrowed gaze.

"Ugh. She told me on the telephone that she had a great collection of books on various subjects. We do *not* want any of these." She said, disgruntled.

"Shall I dive into the chest?" Nora smirked.

Georgina's mobile phone began to ring so Nora passed her the calls file where it was hidden. While Georgina dug out the phone Nora started to move a pile of blankets and an old telephone off the chest and opened it up. She lifted out some pictures and bags of knitting and came to some mouldy Agatha Christie novels with some crushed children's books.

"We're in a mad house at the moment." Georgina was telling Roger who had phoned. "Yes, yes, just pay him ten pounds for them. We'll be with you at lunchtime. Goodbye." She hung up as Mrs Baker came coughing back up the stairs, preceded by Daisy who almost bowled Nora into the chest.

"DAISY! Get out." Mrs Baker shouted, leaning against the doorframe. "Find anything?"

"I'm afraid not." Georgina replied as Nora heaped the objects back into the chest while stroking Daisy. "Sorry."

"Ah, I didn't think you would. My mum died in here."

Nora and Georgina stared at her.

"Oh, sorry to hear that." Georgina said, quickly making to go.

"She was ancient." Mrs Baker shrugged. "Thanks for your time." She led the way down and Georgina and Nora followed, covering their noses in the smoke trail.

The welfare officer was perched on the sofa, wiping her hand with a repulsed expression and watched Mrs Baker see out her visitors. The cat ran out ahead of them as Georgina and Nora made for the van.

"Oh dear." Nora smirked.

"That cat had the most hideous sores on its back!" Georgina said, flopping into the driver's chair, reaching for the wet-wipes which they always kept a supply of in the van door.

"EEEEEWWWWW!" Nora was aghast.

"I gave it a big stroke and ugh! Yuk. What a complete waste of time. And she knew it. Let's hope that doesn't set the trend for the day!" Georgina muttered, frantically wiping her hands. "I expect Mr Kowalski is covered in sores. We're going to him next."

"Lovely." Nora laughed. She opened the calls file, writing 'zero spent' next to Mrs Baker's name before putting the next address into the satnav.

Mr Kowalski was in a large nursing home. Georgina warned Nora about him wryly as they turned into the long driveway, passing some staring gardeners.

"He's a Polish Count and he made a big hoo-ha in the shop in Seatown at the weekend. I think he's slightly mad but he has some books he wants to sell and I felt sorry for him so said we would call in." She explained as they approached the big sprawling building.

"A Polish Count?"

"Apparently he escaped his country decades ago. That's possibly true, but now he's quite mad."

They parked, looking at the building.

"This is weird." Georgina frowned, stepping out of the van. "He said to go into reception at the front but part of it is boarded up."

The place looked desolate. There were chairs piled up before the doors. Nora and Georgina stopped before what looked like the main entrance.

Georgina pressed a button and a buzzer sounded weakly before petering out.

"This looks very strange." She frowned.

"You don't think he's lured us here and has some sinister designs on us?"

"Nora!" Georgina checked the calls file. "I'll phone him."

Nora peered through the murky windows before stepping back to wander around, looking in the other parts of the building through dusty, grimy glass. She turned a corner and almost jumped out of her skin.

"Are you lost?" A man in overalls was standing there.

"Erm…"

"This is the old building. The nursing home moved to the new building over there." He indicated.

Nora smiled.

"Oh. Thanks."

She turned and hurried back to Georgina who was speaking to Mr Kowalski loudly.

Nora pointed behind them, laughing.

"Goodbye." Georgina hung up. "He says he's in his apartment and he's not dressed yet but can we go up anyway."

"Well, we're at the wrong building; the nursing home is over there somewhere. This is the old location." Nora explained.

Georgina sighed.

"Come on then."

They set off, passing the gardeners who stood watching them with amusement.

"This is much better." Nora said as they walked on little neat pathways and under lattice archways that were sprawling with pretty flowers to the main door.

"Hmm." Georgina opened the door and two women approached them.

"Hello ladies, who are you here to see?" The first one greeted confidently.

"We have an appointment with Mr Kowalski." Georgina explained.

The woman blinked and glanced at her companion. "Do you?"

"Yes. He was in my bookshop and he has some books for sale."

"Oh." She blinked again. "Okay." She picked up a register. "He's in room sixty one A. I'll take you." She started to lead the way.

Nora looked about. A piano was being given a pounding a few rooms along and a woman was walking towards her in a nightdress with her arms outstretched.

"Not now, Janet. This way, dear." A carer called.

Georgina and Nora followed the manager through endless corridors.

"Mr Kowalski is a very important man." The manager said. "He was a Count in Poland but his whole family was deported during the Second World War."

Georgina gave Nora a told-you-so look. Nora didn't look convinced.

There was a certain pungent smell throughout the whole home. They passed a room where a hairdressing shop had been set up, and avoided elderly people sitting in chairs or walking around with Zimmer frames.

"Here we are." The manager smiled and rapped on an open door. "Visitors, Mr Kowalski."

Nora peered past Georgina to see an old man sitting on the edge of his bed in leather slip-on slippers, blue boxer shorts and an open dressing grown. The room was so hot that the heat met them in the doorway, but several fans were blowing and the endless sheets of paper and clutter on many units and desks fluttered about in the wind.

"Yess. Yess. Hello." He greeted with his strong accent, his tongue protruding outwards after each word.

"Hello Mr Kowalski. We're from the bookshop."

"Hello. Hello. Yesssss. Forgiff me. I am not drezzed yet."

He stood up as Georgina walked in, looking around the tiny room.

A carer stopped behind Nora.

"I'll come back and dress him when you've finished." She chuckled and went off humming.

"Yes, yes. You aff come to see my boogz." He said grandly and pattered to the desk next to the door.

"Yes. What do you have for sale, Mr Kowalski?" Georgina asked loudly.

"I aff zis, zis, zis and you like zis one?" He prodded several books on the desk.

Georgina side-glanced Nora and picked them up.

"Yes. I can use this one and this one." She said.

"Zis, zis is a conspiracy book. All I knew before I read zis was liez, liez, but zis tell the truth. I used to believe but zis tell me all is liez." He said.

"Do you have any more books?" Georgina asked loudly.

"Yess, yess, more here." He pattered across to another desk.

The walls were surrounded with newspaper cuttings of conspiracies accompanied by numerous photographs. Nora studied them with interest while Mr Kowalski prodded a selection of books.

"Zis told me that all the Egyptians lied. Yess, yess, and I study more and zis is all conspiracy." He pointed out the books to Georgina who pulled out a few.

After a while the heat became overwhelming. The carers kept looking in, anxious to dress him, so Georgina made a little pile on the first desk by the door. Nora remained out of the way.

"Well, these are the ones I can use, Mr Kowalski. They would be worth fifteen pounds to me."

"Ah, ah, I see. Hmm, fifteen, yess, yess, this vood be acceptable, yess." He agreed.

Nora opened the calls file and took out the purse.

"Okay, Mr Kowalski. Thank you." Georgina picked up the pile of books. "Are you keeping well?"

They chatted while Nora handed him the money.

"Goodbye." Nora bade as they left.

They started to walk down the corridors, passing a carer heading to the room eagerly.

"How do we get out of here?" Georgina muttered, leading the way quickly. "Argh, I always get lost in these places."

They ended up encountering several people with Zimmer frames like an army filing slowly down a corridor and had to double back where they almost collided with someone singing dreamily while facing a wall, hastily avoided a carer pushing a wheelchair determinedly towards them and kept meeting a man pointing and laughing demonically in several of the endless hallways before they finally fled for the exit doors and took in gulps of fresh air out in the rockery.

"Argh, okay. Let's go." Georgina said, leading the way hastily towards the van in the distance by the old block.

The winding road to Littlesea was busy. The bookshop van passed a line of cars turning into the owl sanctuary, slowing down a little to join a queue of traffic by the little harbour where the tide often came in to cut off the road into the village. It was a lovely bright sunny day. Georgina drove quickly toward their next call.

"Opposite the road mirror, sharp left." Nora read the note that Georgina had told her to type on the calls sheet.

"Yes. It's a difficult location; I'd better slow down as we're nearing it." She nodded, her brow furrowed in concentration.

Someone beeped their van behind before revving loudly past them with a glare. Georgina ignored them, looking for the house.

"It's called 'Streamside'. Keep an eye out for it." She told Nora.

Nora leaned forward.

"There's a house coming up. Oh, look, and a road mirror is opposite it. It must be…yes! It's Streamside." Nora pointed at the open brown gate, large gravel drive and sprawling big house set back in the hedges.

Georgina slammed on the brakes, indicated and turned left amidst another car horn and an angry screech of tyres.

"Patience is a virtue," she smiled, pulling up between a sports car and a land rover.

"Wayne Baxter, daytime soap star extraordinaire," Nora grinned, considering the house as Georgina turned off the engine.

"Hmmm. Watch out because he is a bit of a *ladies man*. My sister read his biography. He's on his fifth wife. He'd better have some good books." Georgina frowned.

"Heather watched him in that daytime soap he's in when she broke her ankle and was off college for six weeks." Nora grinned. "Are you sure I can't get her his autograph?"

"Don't you dare ask for it!" Georgina warned and they climbed out of the van.

The house was large with many wind chimes, stone Buddhas of various sizes, lots of 'beware of the dog' signs, gnomes, pots of plants and three pairs of green Wellington boots on the front entrance step. Georgina rang the bell and Wayne Baxter glided into the porch with a grand smile. He pulled open the door.

"Hello." He greeted smoothly and winked.

"Hello. We're from the bookshop." Georgina returned politely.

"Yes, yes. Do come in." He gestured them inside, continuing to smile.

Nora stared at him before looking down at a big black dog he caught by the collar.

"Do you mind dogs? Buster won't hurt." Wayne Baxter said grandly.

"We don't mind dogs." Georgina assured, stepping into the house and looking around.

Wayne Baxter closed the door. Buster ran off.

"Did you find the house alright?" He asked confidently, indicating the way. "The books are through here. They're probably bloody awful and no good whatsoever for you but it's good of you to come and see them."

"We were in the area so it's no problem." Georgina smiled.

They passed through a many-angled brick, wood and wind-chimed foyer into a vast open plan kitchen-diner. A large Buddha sat on a brick plinth and Nora spotted Buster through the windows, chasing the gardener, who was on a motorised tractor, around the large gardens.

"Well. Here are the books. Sorry I couldn't make it earlier but I had to do some autograph signing and I'm driving up to film this afternoon." He said smoothly with a wave of his arm towards the table of books where they were all arranged in neat piles across the polished top.

"It was no problem." Georgina assured, stopping before the table.

"Hello." A woman with red hair and a kind face strolled in carrying some washing.

"Ah, this is my wife." Wayne Baxter introduced.

"Hello." Georgina smiled.

"Did you offer them tea, Wayne?" His wife asked.

"No. Sorry. Tea, ladies?"

"No thank you, we just had one." Georgina declined politely.

Nora noticed a waterfall surrounded by mist in the corner of the room as well as crystals hanging in the window catching the light. She stopped at the table of books, scanning them curiously.

"We've had a clear out. Most of them are mine; lots of gifts from fans." Wayne Baxter grinned.

His wife walked away and out of the room while Georgina smiled patiently.

"Well, what we'll do is go through them and pull out any that we can use and make you an offer." She explained.

"Ah. Right." Wayne Baxter nodded, picking up the kettle and walking to the sink to fill it anyway.

"Nora, why don't you start on those ones?" Georgina indicated.

Nora stopped studying the actor and grinned, making a start on the books. They pulled out about three or four boxfuls.

"Can I take a photo of him with my phone? I'll be discreet?" Nora whispered.

"No!" Georgina whispered back.

After a short while Georgina calculated how much she would pay and made Wayne Baxter an offer.

"Erm…well, I shall sheepishly go and ask my wife." He said and walked off, leaving Georgina and Nora in the room.

"What a lovely garden." Nora pointed out.

"Yes. A lovely house." Georgina agreed. "He thinks he's very important." She added in a whisper. Nora chuckled.

"I don't see why I can't secretly take a photo of him."

"If he saw you he might be furious. He's in his private home and if you put it on Facebook it would be a breach of his privacy!"

"Would I do that?" Nora asked.

"You took a photo of that male model in his boxer shorts we called around to the other month."

"Sorry about that but I thought Cara would be amused." Nora apologised. "And it got over three thousand likes on Instagram."

Georgina smirked.

Wayne Baxter came back with his wife.

"They've made an offer of eighty pounds, darling." He explained. "Shall we go for that?"

"I think so, darling." She nodded. "We don't want them any more do we?"

"No, no we don't darling." Wayne Baxter agreed. "Alright, eighty pounds it is."

"Would you like a cheque or cash?" Georgina asked.

"What do you think, darling?" Wayne Baxter asked his wife.

"A cheque would be preferable." She decided.

Georgina dug out the van keys.

"I'll just ask Nora to go and get some boxes from the van." She said passing the keys to Nora.

Nora wandered off, leaving Wayne Baxter telling Georgina about an awards ceremony he was due to attend that weekend. Once at the van she pulled out four collapsed boxes and dawdled back inside the house while looking about at the pictures, photographs and little Buddhas until she reached the dining room and opened up the boxes.

"What marvellous boxes. Very handy aren't they darling?" Wayne Baxter pointed out to his wife.

"Yes, they're very useful." Georgina said, beginning to load the books inside.

Once the books were all packed into three boxes, Nora laid the spare one across the top of her one and bent her knees, hoisting it up.

"Here. May I take one out for you?" Wayne Baxter offered cheerfully.

He took up a box and walked with Georgina and Nora to the van.

"Now, be careful on that road, it's lethal." He told them as they loaded the boxes into the van and then slid into the front seats. "Thank you for coming. Goodbye ladies. I'll bring some flyers and posters to the Seatown shop about the talk and play I'm in for you to advertise, Be sure to come along and see me in it! Cheerio."

"Goodbye." Nora waved.

Georgina started the van engine and Nora was silent so that Georgina could concentrate on leaving the drive. They were soon on their way back along the road. Nora opened the calls file to write down how much they had spent.

"Well I'm glad that wasn't too much hard work." Georgina sighed. "His wife had him under control."

Nora laughed.

"He was nice enough." She decided, focusing on putting the next address into the satnav.

"Two more calls in Seatown and then we'll go to the Seatown shop, unload and have some lunch before our final few." Georgina decided.

"Sounds good." Nora nodded, sitting back as the satnav calculated a new route.

The woman's voice announced the first phase of directions and Nora yawned, picking up her bottle of water and thinking about replying to Humphrey when the van phone began to ring. Humphrey's name came up on the display so Nora smiled.

Georgina pressed the button to answer it.

"Hello, Humphrey." She sang cheerfully.

"Hello, how's it going?" Humphrey's voice filled the cab.

"Well, Nora and I have been to visit a woman from a Dickens's novel, a Polish Count and a daytime soap opera actor so far." Georgina replied.

Humphrey roared with laughter.

"Did you get any books?" He asked.

"A few boxfuls of general shop stock. We have some good calls coming up though."

"That's good. Georgina, can I use your car? Mum wants me to take her to Tesco's and she moans about mine."

Georgina laughed.

"Yes, that's fine. She's certainly not a fan of sports cars. Keys are in the kitchen."

"Thanks. Someone's on the other line. It's probably mum. I'd better go." He said.

"Bye." Nora and Georgina said together.

"Bye, have a good afternoon. Bye Nora." He added warmly.

"Bye." Nora repeated, flushing red.

Georgina pressed the button to hang up and looked at Nora knowingly.

"Humphrey was back later than I expected last night. And he said he'd already eaten."

"Did he?" Nora asked, gazing out of the window next to her.

"Hmm. He didn't say where and who he was with, but I'm not daft. He has a smile when he talks about you." Georgina chuckled. "In fact, this is the happiest I've seen Humphrey in years."

Nora's cheeks flushed a bit more.

"We went out to dinner after work as friends and I've assured him that's all we are."

"Well, the biological clock is ticking." Georgina pointed out.

"Thanks for that." Nora shook her head, amused.

"Humphrey's a good boy." Georgina assured. "I know, he's a *man*, but he'll always be my little brother. He's often helped out with the bookshop business since I bought it off of mum and he's always looked after mum, even when he was in the midst of running that high flying firm of his in London for the past eight years. I told him he's too young to retire but I'm glad he did and is staying at my house at the moment. I was afraid he'd have a heart attack with all that stress and work and he's only twenty eight. Well, twenty nine next week "

"Oh! Happy birthday to Humphrey."

"I'm sure he'll invite you to the dinner I'm putting on for him at my house next weekend. I won't ask you first. I get the feeling he'll want to do that."

Nora grinned.

"Thanks. It sounds lovely. We're about five minutes away from the next call." She noticed.

"Hopefully Mr Foskett has some good books." Georgina sighed. "It's a lot of theology, African books and heaps of philosophy apparently. His father has gone into a nursing home."

"Would he know Count Kowalski?" Nora asked dryly.

Mr Foskett was waiting outside his father's house with the door behind him wide open. He was speaking into his phone.

"Hello." He greeted Georgina and Nora after ending his call. "Right on time. Come this way."

They walked up the path, Nora looking at the front of the large old house with a curious gaze.

"How is it going? How is your father?" Georgina asked conversationally.

"Oh. He's settling in. It's hard for him. We've had to sort out most of his things and he made me promise his books would go to a good home." Mr Foskett sighed, gesturing them inside.

"Oh yes. It's almost empty." Georgina noticed, looking around.

"Just the books and some haberdashery left." He nodded. "There are thousands of books! I'll show you where. And they all have to go."

"Well, I can help you with the ones that are saleable for me, but I won't be able to use them all." Georgina explained.

"What shall I do with the ones you can't use?" He asked, pointing to the first room.

"Either a charity shop or…"

"Dump them?"

"I'm afraid so." Georgina apologised.

"That's fine. It's his life's collection. He was a Professor at Cambridge and at Oxford. I hardly knew him; he had me when he was in his late fifties. When he and my mum split up I went with mum. I was five. But I promised him I'd do what I could with his books. Right. These cases here." He led them into the room opposite. "Those cases there." Out in the hall. "Those boxes there." Up the stairs. "In this room, all of these."

"There *are* thousands." Georgina arched an eyebrow at the walls and walls of books.

"That's not even half of them." Mr Foskett led them up another flight into the refurbished attic rooms. Three rooms and the landing were full of books, floor to ceiling.

"Okay." Georgina checked her watch. "It will probably take us about an hour or so to go through these. I'll be able to do it quickly because they are specific subjects and I'll know straight away the ones that are saleable."

"I'm meeting my wife for lunch at one thirty so you'll be finished by then?"

"Yes, should be."

"Okay, I'll go down and get on with the haberdashery and leave you to it."

"My goodness. There are *loads*." Nora said, looking around.

"Just go along each shelf and pull out any you think we can sell on. I'll check them afterwards. It shouldn't take too long." Georgina assured.

Nora pulled out a book.

"Oh! Er….this one has been munched!" Nora announced.

"Argh! Bookworm." Georgina exclaimed and grabbed it.

There were twisting and swivelling lines and holes in all of the pages and both end boards.

"This isn't good. We can't have bookworm."

"But we're called The Secondhand Bookworm." Nora teased and pulled out another book which had been equally munched. "These look like the kind of books Billy from the antique centre would think we would love. Oh dear."

"It looks old. It might have died but…okay, we'll pull out what we think and if it has had bookworm we'll have to leave it. I can't risk that in my shops."

"No way." Nora agreed and began on the shelves before her.

The entire first room was full of theology. Nora had a nice time making sure a large set of *Summa Theologica* was complete and flicking through various tomes about the Early Church Fathers, Latin Bibles, writings of Saints and metaphysical works. Most of them were free of bookworm but a whole run of the writings of Saint John of the Cross had been eagerly eaten. She sat crossed legged making various piles and checking for bookworm, pleased to discover an early collection of G.K. Chesterton books which were un-munched.

They made several piles and then moved onto a room of African books. Georgina decided they were too specialist and she would suggest a specific African bookshop dealer instead. After a while they had various piles everywhere. Mr Foskett interrupted them several times until they reached the ground level, pulling out books amidst his haberdashery.

"So we'll leave the ones with bookworm." Georgina explained, calculating what she would offer for the ones they had chosen.

Nora leaned against the bottom stair rail studying a case of poetry magazines.

"That was when they were in Africa. They were fumigated before being shipped over." He explained, picking up some pens from the stairs.

"Yes, but I'd have to convince all my customers of that and I can't risk it." Georgina said.

"Understandable." Mr Foskett nodded.

"Okay. For all the ones that I have shown you I would pay five hundred pounds." She offered.

Mr Foskett stood stroking his chin, looking indecisive.

"Five hundred pounds. For all of them?"

"For all of them." Georgina nodded.

"Hmm. Well…yeah, go for it. We need to get rid of them. Yes."

"Okay. Nora. Can you go to the van and bring in all the boxes and make room for all of these to go in when they're filled up. Would you like cash or cheque, Mr Foskett?"

"Cash please."

"Okay. Well, I'd have to go to the bank as I don't carry that much cash around with me."

"That's fine. I can pop into the bookshop in Seatown this afternoon?"

Georgina nodded.

"I'll sort it out for you."

She handed Nora the bunch of keys.

"All of the empty boxes." She indicated.

"Okay." Nora nodded and set off.

It took them another quarter of an hour to load up the boxes, carry them downstairs, down the path and organise them in the van before Mr Foskett thanked them and hurried to close up the house so as to leave and meet his wife. Nora was exhausted and started yawning.

"One more call and a well-deserved lunch break in Seatown." Georgina agreed, wiping her hands on the wet-wipes. "We acquired some good stock though."

She started the van while Nora opened the calls file.

"Mr Swan." Nora read.

"He told me he has coin books." Georgina recalled.

Nora was putting the address into the satnav when the van phone rang again and she jumped. She pressed the button to connect and Cara's voice filled the interior.

"Helloooooooooo." Cara sang cheerfully.

"Hi Cara!" Nora greeted. "How's Castletown?"

"Quiet." She sighed and there was the sound of the till beeping. "Sorry, I just leant on the till. A man wants to bring some books in and I have to give him a specific time that you're in Castletown."

"Er…." Georgina glanced at Nora shuffling the call's sheet.

"We've three more calls after lunch so we should be with you at about four?" Nora replied.

"What are the books?" Georgina asked.

"A big variety. Gardening, leather bound, music, railways and some sets." She began to crunch something.

"Tell him we'll be there at about four o'clock, Cara, and if that's no good I'll phone him for another appointment." Georgina said.

"Okay." Cara agreed. "By the way, you have loads of post. It looks like bills."

"Oh, goodie." Georgina said with light sarcasm.

"Bye." Cara sang.

Nora continued typing in the address to the GPS machine and it told them they were a few minutes from their destination.

Mr Swan's bungalow was set back in an overgrown garden. There was a fat ginger cat on the path which ran away with a hiss as they approached. The television sounded really loud even as Georgina and Nora entered the garden. Georgina had to rap several times before the dingy door opened. Mr Swan stood there.

"Hello. We're from the bookshop." Georgina greeted.

"Eh? Oh yeah. Come in." He was a little stooped man in a brown shirt with the waistband of his trousers almost under his arms.

Georgina gave Nora a look.

"This way." He took them through the dark hall into a dining room. "I've put them into piles for you."

Nora arched an eyebrow to see the whole room covered in little piles of books arranged on the bureaux, chair seats, table and the floor. They were each piled in stacks of three.

"Okay." Georgina's eyebrows lowered as she looked around.

"This is them. They're what were left over from a boot sale." He said with a sniff.

Georgina spun around and stared at him.

"A car boot sale?"

"*Yeyp*." He nodded, leaning back to look down the hall towards his television.

"Well, I doubt there'll be anything for me if they've already been in a car boot sale." Georgina was irritated. "Where are your coin books?"

"There." He prodded a finger towards the table before edging away. "I'll leave you to look through." He said, obviously missing something on television that he wanted to see.

"These are *magazines*." Georgina shot a glare at Nora who watched Mr Swan hurry away. "He told me he had coin *books* and he never told me he had done a car boot sale." Georgina seethed. "A waste of time…"

"Here's a book about fruit growing." Nora spotted, picking one up.

Georgina screwed up her nose and began scanning the books. She sighed.

"I suppose it's no good me being snotty about it." She grumbled and had soon made a small pile of about ten general books. "Do you want to call him back?"

Nora leaned out of the doorway.

"Helllooooo? Mr Swan?" She called.

"Oh…oh yes." His voice sailed back before he came along stoopingly.

"Three pounds on these ones, Mr Swan." Georgina offered.

"Thank you." He accepted.

"You never told me you had had a car boot sale." Georgina added as Nora took out the purse. "You should have called me first."

"We sold 'em." He said, holding out his hand for the coins.

Georgina stared at him.

"Hmm. And I thought you said coin books. They're magazines."

"Yes." He said blandly.

Nora paid him, biting the side of her lip.

Georgina began to leave.

"Thank you." She said, leading the way out of the house.

The cat was on the doorstep and Georgina almost stepped on it. It hissed again, bolting into the bushes. Nora laughed.

"Sorry, I just scared your cat." Georgina apologised.

"It'll be back." Mr Swan shrugged, said a hasty goodbye and closed the door, running back to his television.

"Oh, what a waste of time." Georgina sighed. "Now I'm grumpy because I'm hungry. Let's go to the Seatown shop."

"Good plan." Nora agreed.

They placed the books in a box in the van, climbed into the seats and sped away.

9 A ROOM WITH A TREE

"Good afternoon." Roger greeted when Nora and Georgina stepped into The Secondhand Bookworm, Seatown. He was seated behind the little front counter with a steaming mug of tea.

"Hello. How's it going?" Georgina asked, taking off her sunglasses to look around.

"We've had some nice sales today." Roger said and stood up.

Jane waved from the kitchen which was at the far end of the little bookshop and called out 'hello'.

"Oh good. That's what I like to hear. We have some goodies for you to mark up this afternoon," Georgina told them as Jane closed the kitchen door and bounded down to the front of the shop.

"Hello, hello, hello. How have calls been?" She grinned.

"Don't ask," Georgina warned, placing everything she was carrying on to the desk top.

The counter was very close to the front door with the little walkway between it and the wall being the only entrance and exit for people. A small queue comprising of an elderly lady, a business man and a tourist waving postcards soon formed. Georgina and Nora edged around to let them through and Nora grabbed the shop keys.

"Can I rush to the ladies room?" She asked, beginning to hurry away.

"The men's room." Roger corrected.

Nora rolled her eyes, heading off.

The Seatown bookshop was quite different to the Castletown bookshop. It was smaller and narrower with one less floor of books, but it did very well with its regulars and tourists. Because it was located in a more modern town it had a noticeably different vibe. The stock was slightly different since Seatown had more art galleries, museums, theatres and motor-racing festivals than Castletown.

There were four rooms of books on various subjects in total, with a large stock of book-themed greeting cards, postcards, book posters, wrapping paper, deckchairs with Penguin book jacket designs and pens for sale. Several people milled about browsing happily.

When Nora returned to the front of the shop, Georgina was speaking with a woman in a long white dress with a big white bow in her hair.

"Don't you find," the woman with the white bow in her hair whispered dreamily, "that everybody is eating these days."

Georgina stared at her and then met Nora's amused eyes.

"Jane has had her lunch and is just parking the van for me. Roger has gone off to have his and when Jane is back I'll grab a sandwich. Do you want to go off to have your lunch?" She asked Nora.

"My point exactly." The woman with the bow said softly before seeming to glide towards a section of books about art techniques.

Nora stifled a laugh.

182

"Yes, I'll go and grab some lunch thanks."

"Can you just hold the fort while I use the ladies room?" Georgina then decided, picking up the keys.

Nora sat down in the swivel chair, listening to the conversations taking place outside. The bar opposite The Secondhand Bookworm sent pounding music into the street; there were steady streams of shouting teenagers going past on lunch breaks from the nearby colleges and a delivery lorry was reversing in the road outside while announcing repetitively, 'Attention! This vehicle is reversing!' in an aggressive robotic voice.

"How's your granddaughter?" A lady turning the greeting card racks outside asked her companion.

"Oh, she's still ugly." Was the reply.

Nora gaped, leaning forward to see them until a large man blocked her view.

"*Hellope*." He greeted gruffly and hurried into the shop to the back room.

He was followed by a young woman covered in face piercings.

"Where's your self-help?" She demanded of Nora.

"Self-harm?" Nora asked, unnerved.

"What?" She looked dangerous and began to chew her gum fiercely.

"Er…oh! Self-help." Nora realized. "Upstairs in the front room."

A businessman followed the woman with the pierced face as she stalked off with a glare. He asked for some paperbacks and Nora directed him to the correct section.

"This please." A loud voice stated.

Nora turned to see a woman holding out an astrology book. She opened it to find the price.

"Five pounds please."

"I couldn't see the book I wanted but that's really good." The woman bellowed.

Nora hastily dealt with the sale while another man entered just as Georgina came back from using the loo.

"Do you have any Tarot cards?" He asked.

Nora looked at Georgina.

"Possibly. Up in the occult section." Georgina recalled.

"I'm not going upstairs." He decided and stood there in the way.

"I'll go up and look for you." Georgina offered patiently and headed for the staircase in the corner of the room.

Nora smiled faintly at the man waiting who examined a book on the counter before helping himself to some business cards and leaflets. She then sold a book to a customer who refused a bag.

"Save the planet and all that." He said as he left, squashing his book into his rucksack and squeezing past the man who was waiting for the Tarot cards.

"We have a pack here." Georgina revealed, returning from upstairs.

She passed it to the man who took them and examined them.

"What can you tell me about them?" He asked.

"Well. I don't know much about them." Georgina replied.

"What?" His head snapped up. "What do you mean you don't know much about them?"

Georgina's eyes narrowed.

"They're Tarot cards." She pointed out.

"But what is their history?"

"I don't know. I just bought them." Georgina stressed.

The man lifted the pack as if to hit Georgina on the head with it.

"You don't know their history or anything about them?" He repeated, changing his mind about the attack.

"I don't. And I don't want to really." Georgina said firmly. "If you don't want them I can put them back."

The man looked at the cards.

"How much are they?"

"Seven pounds." Nora pointed out, glaring at him.

He glanced at her.

"Fine. I'll take them. But it's a shame you don't know about their history."

"Probably some gypsy woman had them in her gypsy caravan?" Nora suggested.

He shot her a glare and paid for them.

When he had gone Nora looked at Georgina.

"He was going to bash you with that packet." She was indignant.

"I know." Georgina shook her head, wearily.

"I'd have boxed his ears with Roger's tea mugs if he had." Nora decided, standing up.

Georgina laughed.

"Go and have your lunch."

Nora grabbed her bag.

"See you in a bit." She smiled and left the shop.

Outside The Secondhand Bookworm in Seatown the streets were teeming with people. A group of teenagers were having a fight, a man was pretending to be a statue, at least fifty pushchairs containing screaming babies were causing. Nora was wondering where to eat when further down the street she spotted Roger coming out of a barber shop. He saw her and waved solemnly.

"I've booked to have my hair cut." He explained.

"Jolly good."

"Where are you going for your lunch?" He asked.

"I don't know yet." Nora replied, edging out of the way of a knot of tattooed women pushing prams.

"Do you fancy a pot of tea and cake in the cathedral tea rooms? We can sit outside in the garden," he suggested.

"I've never been there. Okay!" Nora agreed.

"I'll lead the way." He said, taking her towards the gatehouse squashed between an underwear shop and a bakery. "So, how were the calls this morning?"

Nora told Roger the morning's events as he led her through the old stone archway that was part of the ancient town walls and then down a street. They walked past a little row of cottages to some covered stone passageways leading to the cloisters of the large cathedral. Nora looked about in interest. She then smiled with pleasure as they slipped through an arched doorway into the tearooms.

The tearooms were bustling with people and smelt strongly of coffee and toasted sandwiches. They grabbed some trays and Nora picked a prawn sandwich, a pot of tea and a slice of chocolate cake. She joined Roger in the gardens at a circular table amongst the autumn flowers. When she sat down she gazed up at the cathedral spire close by.

"This is like being on holiday." Nora decided.

Roger snorted at that, pouring tea from his own teapot which was pink and spotty.

They discussed the bookshops, customers that had been in that morning to The Secondhand Bookworm, Seatown, and the history of the cathedral while they ate. The sun was warm, it was peaceful and cheery and the time flew by until Nora finally drained the last of her tea and Roger brushed crumbs off his trousers.

"Ah, lovely. I feel ready to do the afternoon calls now." Nora decided, standing up.

"Thank you for your delightful company." Roger said.

"It was more relaxing than the last time we had lunch." Nora pointed out and they both laughed, making their way back to the bookshop.

Jane and Georgina were chatting and laughing in the empty front room when Nora and Roger returned.

"We had a man determined to sell his scruffy paperbacks to us all at the same price he had paid for them new." Jane announced.

"Oh dear." Roger shook his head.

"We also had a cancellation of one of the calls." Georgina revealed, beginning to gather her things. "Mr Caramac. So we can get to Castletown earlier and do some things in the shop there."

"Oh good." Nora was pleased. "Did Mr Foskett drop in for his money?"

"Yes, all done."

"Great!"

They organised themselves and then Jane collected the van, soon pulling up in the road outside the shop.

"Quickly. Before the tyrannical wardens come along." She urged, handing Georgina the keys. "I used to be one so I'm familiar with that thirst for ticket writing!"

They hastily unloaded some boxes of books that they had bought that morning for Jane and Roger to go through and mark-up during the afternoon and then finally, Nora and Georgina climbed into the van, checked that they had everything and left.

The first stop was at a lovely cottage where a husband and wife both welcomed Nora and Georgina at the door.

"Do come in." Mrs Button greeted politely.

"Sorry we're a little late." Georgina apologised, stepping into the circular hall which only had a grandfather clock and a roll top desk in it. The wallpaper was very flowery and overwhelming.

"No problem." The couple assured in unison, leading the way through the house.

"This is where the books are." Mr Button pointed to a highly polished dining table.

There were a variety of large books so Georgina studied them, going carefully through each one.

"Well, sadly you're missing the dust wrappers off a lot of these."

"Yes. They were in my workshop. I'm a carpenter." Mr Button nodded.

"It does affect the value of selling them on though." Georgina explained. "But books are for reading and using so I'm glad they were well appreciated."

"They were." He nodded proudly.

"My husband made all the furniture in the house." Mrs Button said.

"Really!" Georgina was impressed.

"Did you see the grandfather clock in the hall? My husband made that? And the table you're leaning on he made." She explained.

Mr Button stood smiling proudly.

"Four of the chairs are reproductions which he made." She added.

"They're exceptional." Georgina agreed and Nora felt the wood of the table top, impressed.

"Every single item of furniture in the house he made." Mrs Button stressed and began to recount each one.

Georgina and Nora listened to the history of all the items and Mr Button demonstrated through many of his books the sections he had used to make them until Nora wanted to scream. Eventually, Georgina gathered the books into a pile that she could use and made an offer on them. Mr and Mrs Button conversed about accepting the offer or not and then decided to. Georgina paid them and she and Nora were able to carry the pile they had bought to the van without boxes.

"Thank you for coming. Goodbye." Mr and Mrs Button called in unison as they both stood on the doorstep waving and Georgina pulled away in the van.

"Hmm, quite difficult to sell on but they were nice books. To the right customer they'll be perfect." She convinced herself.

Nora smiled.

"We know where to go if we are ever in need of furniture." She decided, putting in the address of the next call.

The satnav took The Secondhand Bookworm van out of Seatown and further into the hills of Cole. It soon reached Walltown. Georgina drove up and down a particularly narrow, busy road looking desperately for a place to park since the house that they were calling at was on the corner. In the end, she pulled up onto the pavement, deciding they would have to cause an obstruction or they would never get out of the vehicle. Nora was conscious of glares from drivers having to wait to let the traffic on the other side of the road pass because of the van in their way. The road seemed very oppressive with its extremely high walls lining both sides amongst the houses and the constant drone of vehicles.

"Quickly, knock on the door." Georgina cried so Nora climbed some steps and pressed the button of a bell.

After a while they heard a lady's voice sounding faintly above the traffic.

"Oh, hello." Georgina greeted a woman who stood at the side of the house on some uneven cobbles.

"Please do come this way." She urged, beckoning with a small hand.

Georgina picked her way carefully over the cobbles in her high heels, Nora following.

Once they were walking down a narrow alleyway to a back gate away from the road, Georgina addressed the woman.

"Are you Mrs Drury?"

"I am Mrs Drury." Mrs Drury affirmed.

She led them through a gate and closed it behind them. They found themselves in a pretty, well kept, long garden that ended in a low flint wall overlooking a vast expanse of hills and fields.

"I don't use the front door." Mrs Drury explained.

"Oh. Well, I'm Georgina and this is my colleague Nora." Georgina introduced them.

"Hello." Mrs Drury indicated to the back door. "The books are down in the study room. They were my late partner's. All of his shooting books."

"Your shooting partner?" Nora asked curiously as she tried to imagine this wisp of a woman wielding a giant gun.

Mrs Drury stared at her and then looked a little flustered.

"No, no. My husband actually. My life partner." She corrected.

"Down here?" Georgina had noticed a small staircase leading down into basement rooms.

"Yes." Mrs Drury nodded, leading the way.

It was a small but beautiful study with low beamed ceilings, window seats, choice ornaments and beautiful bookcases. Nora had to bend slightly until she found a place between the beams to stand up comfortably. Georgina was shorter than her so found the room quite nice.

"Is that a…" Georgina stared and cleared her throat.

"It's a tree. I like it growing into the room." Mrs Drury assured stuffily and Nora gaped at a big trunk with branches and leaves growing through the plaster walls on one side of the study. "These are his books. Shooting and fishing. This case and this case. These are my books which I don't want to sell."

Georgina turned her attention to the books for sale.

"Ah, yes. A very nice collection." She noted.

"Shall I leave you to go through them?" Mrs Drury started to walk away.

"Thank you. We'll let you know when we're done." Georgina nodded and Mrs Drury climbed the stairs, leaving them alone.

Georgina and Nora gave one another a look. Nora sat down on a tall wooden seat, trying to ignore the tree but found that she couldn't. She wondered if tree creatures emerged at night and crept through the house.

"I'll go through these because there are some unusual ones here." Georgina said so Nora watched her carefully pull out the good ones and look pleased, pile them all on a table and then call Mrs Drury back.

"It's a bit strange to have a tree growing in your house, isn't it?" Nora whispered as they waited for Mrs Drury.

"Very." Georgina assured. "But each to their own."

Nora bit back a small grin.

Mrs Drury came down and accepted the offer that Georgina made, saying that she wasn't interested in shooting so had no need for the collection anyway.

Once Georgina had paid for the books it was an ordeal to bring the empty boxes in from the van across the uneven cobbles and down the alleyway, down into the basement and then all the full boxes in the reverse. After ten separate trips they made room in the van for the last few boxes, arranging them amidst the constant roar of the traffic until Georgina wanted to cry and slammed the van door once the last box was inside.

"Come on. Let's go to Castletown before I go mad!" She announced through gritted teeth.

Chuckling, Nora climbed into the van.

Georgina manoeuvred the van away from the pavement, clearing the roadblock and, amidst beeps and a box of books crashing over in the back of the van, they left Walltown, heading for Castletown, glad it was the last of their calls.

Georgina pulled up outside the butcher shop where, incredibly, there was a space. She climbed out of the driver's side and looked in the butcher shop window to consider the rows of various offerings of meat before turning to unload the van and carry the boxes across to the bookshop. Tim was staring at Nora and smiled at Georgina.

"They do such lovely meat here." Georgina pondered as they carried a box each, pausing on the kerb to let a bus pass by. "Lovely chipolatas."

"Chops for tea?" Nora asked.

"Perhaps." Georgina mused. They hurried over the narrow road, stepping into the bookshop. "Afternoon!"

Cara was seated behind the counter cutting out some signs for a display of mountaineering books that she had put in the window. She blinked and smiled.

"Hello! How was it?" She asked.

She put down her scissors and signs and stretched.

"Tiring." Nora decided as she put down her box.

"Can you help Nora unload?" Georgina asked Cara. "It's quiet here isn't it? I'll run to the loo! I must have a bladder the size of a pea!"

"Here you are." Cara grinned, handing Georgina the keys and moving around the desk to go to the van with Nora.

"Has it been busy?" Nora asked.

They hurried across the road before a stream of cars coming along reached them.

"Yes actually. Lots of people in and lots of sales. I sold some mountaineering books which is why I ran up and grabbed a load for the window as its gone quieter now."

"They look good. It needed changing but I never got around to it." Nora confessed.

Cara grinned and they reached the van.

"I think we're taking it all in and marking it up this afternoon." Nora said.

Cara grimaced at all the boxes.

"Fun!" She glanced at her watch. "Two hours. We might do it," she pondered doubtfully.

"If it goes quiet and we all madly price them up then we will." Nora was optimistic. She hoisted a box towards Cara. "This isn't too heavy."

"I'll manage it on my own." Cara assured her, grabbing it firmly and lifting it out of the van.

She headed back to the shop leaving Nora to climb into the van and arrange the boxes so that they could unload easily. Nora refilled the box that had crashed over, dragged the heavy ones to the back which would need two people to carry them and manoeuvred all the lighter ones to the side just as Cara came back.

Nora stepped out of the van and took up a box, passing it to Cara.

"Any new mountaineering ones? There's one more gap in the window." She asked.

Nora took up a box and they began back to the shop together.

"I don't think so."

"I'll find something else." She decided, contemplating the window as they approached it.

Georgina was back from the toilet and speaking on the phone, making an appointment for the following week with the man that Cara had called about.

It was a hectic and exhausting process as Nora and Cara continued to unload the van, soon joined by Georgina who helped with the heavier ones until it was totally emptied. She handed Nora the van key to go and park it in the short term car park around the corner. When Nora returned from doing so, Cara was sitting on the floor surrounded by books. There was a mug of tea on the counter for Nora. Georgina was sipping hers, looking through the sales written in the cash book.

"Catch." Cara said and a pencil sailed towards Nora.

She caught it, passed Georgina the van key and sat on a box, sipping her tea with a satisfied sigh.

"I thought this could go in the window." Cara smirked, holding up a book with a pen and ink drawing of an ugly woman on the cover.

"What's that?" Nora asked, screwing up her nose.

"Aubrey Beardsley. People like his drawings." Georgina defended.

Nora and Cara smiled at one another and Cara cast it onto her marked up pile.

"Where are all the customers? We've scared them away." Nora said, peering out of the window into the square.

"You spoke too soon." Georgina indicated as the door opened.

Nora continued to sip her tea, watching a man in a red t-shirt with a big camera around his neck come into the shop. Georgina said hello and he smiled, looking around.

"You don't sell fridge magnets do you?" He asked.

Cara sniggered, leaning over her box of books.

"No. This is a bookshop." Georgina pointed out.

He smiled weakly and turned around.

"Thank you." He said and left.

"That's the third time I've been asked for fridge magnets." Cara chuckled.

"Well we're not selling those." Georgina insisted.

Nora pulled out a pile of books, pondering them as she finished her tea.

"We need a pile behind the counter of books to look up and check the prices of." Georgina reminded them, looking under the desktop for a book put aside.

"Okay." Cara nodded, placing some gun books in a small pile that looked as though they would mark up higher than the standard shop stock.

Georgina soon went off into the depths of The Secondhand Bookworm with a list of books to look for, requested by Seatown, leaving Cara and Nora to continue the mammoth task of pricing. Soon there were three empty boxes and several tottering piles of books about the carpet. Two customers, interested in the new stock, began rummaging through an unmarked box much to Cara and Nora's annoyance.

"Do you have any ladybird books?" A man with great horn-rimmed glasses asked Nora after twice knocking over her pile of freshly priced stock.

"Upstairs." Nora indicated, pointing towards the back.

She then gathered a leather-bound Dickens set and carried it to behind the counter, huffing and puffing.

"I'll have a look Edith. Are you coming up?" He asked his wife.

Edith was peering at an unmarked box, deciding whether or not to attempt to empty it before they were priced. Cara drew it towards herself and began to price it up with a small smile.

"No. I'll look at these art books." She refused, turning to scan the shelves.

Her husband set off so Nora sat back down on her box with a look at Cara.

Two more customers entered and left the door open.

"Would you like a bit of my nougat?" They heard a woman ask someone outside.

"No thanks, love." Was the reply.

Cara giggled.

"You've had a change around!" A man in a suit exclaimed.

"We took over this shop about five years ago when the previous owners retired, so we moved the counter." Nora explained.

"Shows how long it's been since we've come to Castletown." He clicked his tongue. "Have you moved the stock around, too? You used to have children's books down here."

"They're upstairs now." Nora indicated.

"Oh dear. Dear, dear, dear." He looked disappointed and sighed, deeply. "Well, we'll have to find our way around again." He accepted, leaving for the back room, shaking his head.

A young woman entered next. She closed the door behind her and smiled faintly at Nora and Cara.

"Where's your medical section?" She asked.

She wore a black lace dress with black arm-length gloves, chunky black boots, black lipstick and heavily made-up eyes.

"On the top floor." Cara indicated.

"Thanks."

The young woman drifted off; pausing to consider the leather bound books behind the counter.

"I hate it when the books are like that!" Edith grumbled from beside Cara. "Sideways. I get a neck ache reading the titles. Can't you put them differently?!"

Cara raised an eyebrow.

"Well, they'd be hard to get to if they were piled up on their sides." She pointed out.

Edith sighed, continuing to scan the titles, rubbing her neck and clicking her tongue.

Nora carried armfuls of books to behind the counter, past the woman looking at the leather books.

"Do you have any old medical books?" The girl in black asked.

Nora sat down in the swivel chair.

"I don't think we have actually." She admitted.

"Books about surgery with detailed illustrations and pictures of the insides of bodies and that?" The woman elaborated and her eyes shone eagerly. "I'm a photographer for a morgue and I collect old medical and surgical books."

Nora stared at her.

The girl in black grinned.

"Well, you could look upstairs just in case we have some up there." Nora suggested faintly. "But I don't think there are any special ones back here."

"Okay. I'll check upstairs."

She left and Nora glanced at Cara who shrugged, grimacing.

Georgina returned with a couple of books.

"Success with two but no luck on the others." She declared.

Nora pushed herself out of the chair to let Georgina sit down and Skype the results to Roger and Jane in Seatown.

Edith's husband returned and Edith stood by the door, flicking through a book about village pubs as she waited for him.

"Do you have the ladybird book on fossils?" He asked Georgina.

"Did you look upstairs?" She asked him.

"Yeah, it wasn't there with your ladybirds." He sighed. "I particularly want that one. I know the fellow whose fossils were used in the book. You've got the one on rocks and minerals but they weren't his rocks and minerals. They were his fossils though in the ladybird book of fossils."

"That would be the only place you'd find it if we had it." Georgina said. "Would you like me to check our Seatown branch and see if they have one there?"

"Oh, you have a shop in Seatown? We're going there tomorrow. We can pop in and have a look ourselves."

"Are all your books sideways on the shelves though?" Edith cut in, frowningly.

Georgina stared at her.

"I get such a neck ache." Edith complained.

"We'll pop in there tomorrow, dear." Her husband said and left optimistically. "Thank you. Goodbye."

Georgina gave Nora and Cara a blank look before picking up the phone that had begun to ring. She passed it to Nora who answered it cheerfully.

"Look at Skype." Roger's voice commanded after Nora's greeting.

"Eh? Okay." Nora moved around to the computer and saw a message flash up.

'She is annoying.'

Nora bit back a smile.

"Okay."

"Do you have anything about Tiny Town?" Roger asked flatly.

The Skype Chat flashed:

'Very annoying.'

"I'll have a look." Nora said and leaned around the wall by the till to see the Cole section and the shelf where any books about Tiny Town would be.

'Incredibly annoying.'

Nora scanned the shelves.

"No. Nothing here."

'Astronomically annoying.'

"Okay. I said I would ask. Thanks. Bye." He said dryly and hung up.

Nora laughed as she read his comments.

'She keeps looking in the wrong section. I keep showing her Cole and she keeps going to Somerset. Now she's blocking the door. Extremely annoying.'

"They're having as much fun as us then." Georgina said, pleased and started to write the titles of the books she had found for them, grinning to herself.

'It has to have pictures as she is short-sighted and can't read anymore.' Roger wrote.

Georgina chuckled, continuing to type.

A group of women entered The Secondhand Bookworm, speaking loudly and admiring the shop. Cara grabbed some books to take upstairs and put away as there wasn't any room for them all piled up in the front. Nora remained on her box, almost finished with her marking-up.

"Oh look, Hannah. Old children's books." One of the ladies exclaimed.

There was a loud babble of excitement and then the lady who had spoken stared down at Nora who was perched on her box with her pencil.

"Do you have any books about Amelia Anne Stiggins? I've been looking for them for you for ages, Hannah." She told her friend. "Every bookshop that I go into."

Hannah was touched.

"Oh, have you?" She stood before Nora too. "That's so kind of you, Jennifer." She looked down at Nora as well. "Yes, Amelia Anne Stiggins; she went to a tea party while all the little Stigginses were ill in bed so she filled up her umbrella with food to take back for them even though they told her it wasn't going to rain, but one of the cruel children put up Amelia's umbrella so all the food fell out and then told everyone that Amelia had been stealing, but when the landlord heard it was for the little ill Stigginses he sent them a hamper. I've been looking for it for ages. Do you have it?"

Nora was almost spellbound and looked across to Georgina.

"We have more children's books upstairs." Georgina said loudly as other customers came into the shop.

"Oh, have you?" The women said all at once and had a long, loud debate about whether or not to go upstairs. It was decided that only Jennifer and a lady called Claire would as their knees functioned better. The rest of the ladies would go for ice-creams and meet Jennifer and Claire at the ice-cream parlour.

The room emptied except for a newly arrived lady who took off her sunglasses.

"Have you seen my husband?" She asked Georgina.

"I don't know your husband." Georgina returned with a polite smile.

"He came in here." The woman assured.

"Yes, but I don't know him."

Nora picked up a book, listening.

"Well, do you have any people in here?" The lady next asked.

"There are several upstairs." Georgina was concentrating on her typing.

"Is one of them my husband?"

"If he came in here."

"Well, did he come in?" The woman persisted.

"But I don't know your husband." Georgina stressed, looking up.

"He's got white hair and he's tall and is wearing a green fleece."

"You could call him. The shop goes up and up." Nora suggested.

At that moment, the man described came in from the back room.

"There he is. I knew you would have seen him come in. This lady forgot that you came in." The woman said, almost smugly.

The man looked blank and followed his wife off who said she wanted to buy some chipolatas from the butchers.

"Chipolatas are popular here." Georgina said ironically and continued typing.

It was almost five o'clock when Nora reached the bottom of her final box of marking. Cara unclipped and carried in the cheap paperback boxes from either side of the door and the young woman who had inquired about medical books returned, delighted to have found a nice selection of gruesomely detailed volumes. She offered to send them some of her photographs, paid and left happily, leaving Nora rather pale.

Nora helped Cara bring the postcard rack inside, leaving the last few unmarked books in her box in a small stack on the counter to finish off pricing the next day.

Georgina left to fetch the van. A moment later she parked outside the shop to load in the empty boxes.

"Agnes will be with you tomorrow." She told Nora.

"The new girl." Cara elaborated.

"Okay." Nora nodded.

"She just wants to work on Saturdays but she was free tomorrow so I thought you could see how you get on with her." Georgina explained.

"That sounds good." Nora agreed.

Cara turned the sign around to say 'CLOSED' while Georgina made sure she had her mobile phone and handbag.

"We'll leave you to cash up and empty the dehumidifier for tonight, Cara." Georgina decided. "Don't forget to put the sandbags across the door, just in case it rains heavily overnight."

Nora waved goodbye, sliding into the passenger seat of the van.

"Okay." Cara agreed cheerfully and locked herself in the shop.

Georgina slid behind the wheel. She turned on the air conditioning even though it was getting dim and cold.

"Right then. I'll drop you home, Nora." She said.

"Thanks." Nora smiled and leaned back.

The van pulled away from outside the shop at what felt like one hundred miles an hour and weaved through the little roads as if it was a Formula One racing circuit, soon leaving Castletown behind. They reminisced over the day's calls as Georgina drove to Little Cove.

"Any exciting plans tonight?" Georgina asked as they neared Nora's parents' house.

"Flat hunting and then Heather, Milton and I will probably head over to Seymour's theatre. He's got us painting the lobby. He calls it free slave labour."

"Sounds fun." Georgina grinned. "I'm looking forward to it being finished and opening soon."

"Me too."

The van pulled up outside Nora's front gate. She climbed out and gathered her things.

"Have a nice day tomorrow!" Georgina smiled, waving goodbye.

After waving back, Nora made her way towards her house, knowing she would probably have a lot of book-wormy-dreams that night filled with Polish Counts, daytime soap opera actors, mad cats, little old telly addicts, hunters, fishermen, rooms full of trees and a library full of bookworms!

10 MR HILL

The following morning Nora was yawning loudly as she drove towards Castletown, having worked late in Seymour's theatre painting the foyer and trying on costumes. The town still seemed asleep and the sky was overcast as she drove across the bridge over the river. The old town mayor was crossing the road at the mini roundabout and paused a moment to clutch his chest as though having a heart attack. He did that a lot so Nora wasn't worried. Sure enough, he sneezed loudly and then continued along happily.

Nora parked her car at the top of the hill once more in the long road where parking was free all day. A slight breeze rustled the magnificent trees in the grounds of the castle ruins, their branches hanging over the tall surrounding walls in several places. There were many ancient walls and turrets left standing from the medieval castle and grounds; exciting areas to explore and climb, with tea-rooms, gardens and a gift shop down by the river entrance.

In the summer the ruins held festivals, tournaments or craft fairs. It was an exciting feature for the town and one that attracted a lot of tourists. Once a film had been made by the castle keep about medieval zombies, and in the 1980's an episode of Doctor Who was filmed up at the Duke's folly. You could still get a postcard from the town museum of a Cyberman walking past some local ducks.

Nora locked up her car and slung her bag over her shoulder, making her way past a row of large town houses. When she rounded a corner by the popular, rambling old restaurant 'The Duke's Pie', Nora saw White-Lightning Joe sitting on a bench against a brick wall, looking forlorn.

"Oh dear." Nora sighed and approached him warily. When she stopped before him he looked up in a daze.

"Oh. Hel-lo, Nora." He greeted glumly.

"How are you, Joe?" She asked.

"Yeah, yeah okay, you know." He made a little squeaking sound, shuffling with his shirt collar and tie. "I've got a meeting about my redundancy pay this morning so I'd better go down to that damned hotel. Any more local history books in?" He stood, the top of his greasy head only reaching Nora's shoulder, and picked up his bag.

"No, nothing new for a while."

"Oh, well. Eeeeep! I'd better go!" He scurried off determinedly, leaving the aroma of cider in his wake.

Nora followed slowly, waving at Albert from the Print Shop who was coming back to his shop after walking his spaniel.

"Hey, Nora."

"Morning, Albert."

Down on the cobbles Sam was carrying a whole pig carcass from the back of a large van to the butcher shop.

"Good morning." Nora smiled, trying not to look at the animal.

He winked at her, hoisted the pig so it was more comfortable and set off whistling.

Penny was filling up the flowerpots outside her knick-knack shop with windmills and chatted to Nora about the water pipes being dug up down the alley beside her and having to use the public toilets all day because of it.

"Let's hope something other than water pipes and rude tourists occurs today to make our trading lives more stimulating." She chuckled.

Nora laughed.

"Yes, lets." She agreed, bade her goodbye and took out her keys.

Once Nora was at The Secondhand Bookworm she moved the sandbags to the side of the door, stuck her key in the lock and opened up the bookshop. The phone was ringing so she glanced at the clock, flicking on the lights.

"I know that's you Mr Hill." She said aloud and just managed to lock the door behind her before hurrying to the counter and picking up the handset. "The Secondhand Bookworm."

"Hello. It's Mr Hill." The familiar voice greeted her. "Who's that?"

"It's Nora, Mr Hill."

"Nora. In your war section, back room, five shelves up, do you have a copy of 'Military Uniforms of Britain and the Empire', volume four? It's red cloth." He asked.

Nora turned on the computer and walked patiently into the back of the shop. A light was buzzing and flickering on and off. She grabbed the ladder and climbed up to push back a row of precarious looking volumes hanging dangerously over the edge of the top shelf before scanning the other shelves for Mr Hill's book.

"Yes. It's here."

"Oh, it's there is it? And how much is it?"

Nora stepped down, opening it up on the radiator.

"It's priced at seven pounds fifty."

"Seven pounds fifty. I'll take it. Could you put it by for me?"

"I can send it to Seatown for you?" Nora offered hopefully.

"No, I shall come over today by bus. What time do you close?"

"Five o'clock."

"Can you put it by for me and I'll be over at about mid-morning to purchase it? Thank you, b-bye."

He rang off and Nora sighed, walking back to the front with the book.

Moments later, as she was filling up the till with the float, he phoned again.

"Nora. It's Mr Hill. I shall be getting the quarter past ten bus from Longhill and coming to you. Can I pay for the book with a cheque because my funds will be cleared on Monday?"

"Yes." She agreed, dropping some coins and watching a five pence piece roll away across the counter top.

"I can? Oh good. I'll see you later. B-bye." He hung up again.

Literally a moment later he phoned back.

"Nora, is it seven pounds fifty on the book I've reserved?"

"Seven pounds fifty." She affirmed, climbing the stairs, flicking on the light switch behind a tatty Russian travel book that would illuminate the rest of the shop.

"Seven pounds fifty." He repeated carefully. "I shall be with you mid-morning to purchase it with a cheque."

He hung up without saying goodbye.

Nora ran back downstairs to empty the dehumidifier and make a cup of tea. There were some emails and the

Skype Chat alert was flashing a message so Nora sat down to read the latter. The message was from Georgina who was with Cara in the Seatown shop that day. Georgina was letting Nora know that Agnes was due in to Castletown at eleven.

'She's really nice. As I said, I worked with her on Saturday. You'll get on fine.'

'I can introduce her to Mr Hill. He's due in.' Nora typed back.

She then sipped her tea and left her steaming mug aside so as to open up. When she reached the door she saw a man peering in through the window.

"Good morning." Nora greeted, opening up.

"Can you put up a poster? It's about a new Yoga class I'm running in the scout's hut." The man asked dreamily.

"I'm terribly sorry but we don't have any room for posters here. Almost all of our wall space is taken up by book shelves and cases and we like to keep the windows clear." She explained, hoisting the postcard rack onto the pavement and wheeling it round next to the door.

"Okay." He smiled and walked off.

"Excuse me." A miserable looking man smoking a pipe addressed her.

"Hello."

"Do you sell fridge magnets?"

"Only books I'm afraid." Nora couldn't help but grin. She thought of Georgina's determination never to sell fridge magnets and wondered if it would be worth persuading her she should. They were always being asked about them.

"Oh, bother! Where can I get one from?!" The man seemed angry.

"Try next door. Lizzy sells lots of gewgaws, doodads, whatnots and tchotchkes so fridge magnets are something she might stock." Nora gestured, using some odd words in the hope of lightening his mood. "She's closing down soon so could have some *fantabulous* bargains."

It didn't work; the man continued to look miserable.

"Fine." He grumbled and set off.

Nora heard Lizzy's talking mirror in the doorway of the shop next door call out, *'hello, handsome!',* and then wolf-whistle at him when he entered, much to his annoyance.

As Nora was arranging the cheap paperbacks in the boxes outside, a voice next to her ear made her jump.

"Any new Regimental Histories?" Don asked and laughed to see her flinch.

Nora dropped the last paperback into the box.

"You made me jump."

"Sorry, Nora! I wondered if you have any new Regimental Histories." He repeated, following her into The Secondhand Bookworm.

"No!" Nora assured, almost despairing at his persistence.

"I'll have a look anyway." He shrugged and stomped across the carpet towards the back room.

"Why not. Some could have magically appeared overnight without me knowing." Nora muttered sarcastically and frowned at his retreating form.

Once the box of free maps was positioned before the bay window outside, Nora closed the door to keep out the September chill. She scanned the shelves behind the counter for a book to place in the window, choosing a crime novel with an interesting dust jacket from the fifties.

"Cinderella goes to the morgue." She read the title aloud, popping it on the shelf, facing outwards.

A couple slowed down and read the title, laughing loudly. Nora turned to see Don saunter out of the back room.

"No, no. Nothing today. One day though," he said, hands in his pockets. "By the way, your video has had over five thousand views so far."

Nora stared at him.

"My *what*?"

"Your video. The one of you the other day telling that man eating his yoghurt in your kitchen out the back to get out. I put it up on YouTube and it went viral. Five thousand views already. You're a star."

"I really wish you hadn't done that!" Nora said, aghast.

Don chortled.

"Ah, relax, Nora. I didn't use any real names and you can't be recognized. It was funny though. Ha-ha-ha. Check it out. It's called '*Bookseller throws a barney at yogurt-eating intruder*'. Five thousand views and rising. If you like I'll mention The Secondhand Bookworm and put it on the map…"

"NO!" Nora exclaimed and then smiled politely. "No, best not. And please don't ever mention it to Georgina."

Don shrugged.

"Fair enough. I don't want you to sue me." He winked and left,

Nora sat down, cheeks burning.

She turned to the computer, brought up the web browser and quickly went to YouTube. After typing in Don's title she quickly discovered his video. It was jerky and wobbly and the sound was terrible and the image a little blurred but she could make out her loud voice telling off the man who had helped himself to the bookshop kitchen to eat his yoghurt and read a book.

Nora cringed.

Georgina would probably go mad if she found out about it. And that poor customer looked like he was being told off like a little naughty schoolboy.

With a groan, Nora closed the site and prayed no one from Castletown or The Secondhand Bookworm would ever discover the video!

Picking up her tea, she stared out the window opposite the counter. Through the glass she could see that the town was still empty and looked like a typical mid-September day, dreary and cloudy with a dim light.

The butler from the mansion on the edge of the town suddenly arrived, whistling cheerfully as he stepped down into the shop.

"Good morning, Nora." He gave a small bow, putting his bag down before the Folio Society books.

"Hello, Edward." Nora replied.

Edward straightened his tie, adjusting his soft crimson vee-neck sweater and pondered the shelves of leather books.

"Sam said he saw you and Humphrey Pickering out to dinner the other evening."

Nora inwardly groaned.

"Why is my personal life of sudden interest around here?"

Edward glanced at her.

"Because most of us are over eighty and you young people entertain us."

"You're only in your forties!"

"I *feel* eighty. Old Madam drains the life from me like she's a vampire. In fact, I feel like I'm a vampire's familiar."

Nora couldn't help but smile.

"To set the record straight, Humphrey Pickering and I are just friends."

"Ah, I see. That's dull. I'll pretend you're living an exciting love triangle. Old Madam will prefer that story when I get home with her camomile teabags and goats cheese pastries. Now, I'm looking for a small birthday present for her." His gaze honed in on a little leather bound poetry book with gold edged paper. "Ah-ha. This may be just the thing." He took it off the shelf to study it carefully.

The door opened and a woman leaned in, remaining on the step.

"Excuse me. Where can I get some playing cards?" She asked, peering around.

"The gift shop opposite sells playing cards." Edward suggested, not looking up from the book he was examining.

The woman and Nora glanced at him.

"Oh. Thanks." She nodded, left and closed the door.

"Yes. This will do nicely." Edward decided and approached the counter.

"Do you need a bag?" Nora asked.

"No thank you. I'm giving it to a bag." He replied and Nora smothered a laugh.

"You really shouldn't speak about Lady Augusta like that." She warned him as she entered the price into the till. "She's related to the Duke of Cole."

"She's his twelfth cousin, twice removed." Edward explained with a screwed up nose. "If the Duke ever does move back here and rebuild his castle I shall be heading over there to offer him my services at the first opportunity, I tell you. I doubt he'll drain me of all life."

Nora gave him a sympathetic look, he paid, gathered his things and left whistling, only to be replaced by an old lady.

"The last of the big spenders." She said, stepping down brandishing her postcard. "You'll be able to close up and go home, ha-ha-ha."

Nora took the card.

"Do you need a bag for it?"

"No, I'm going to write it. Now, where's my purse?" She hoisted a big handbag onto the counter and started to rummage through masses of tissues that seemed to fill it up to the brim. Nora waited patiently until the purse came out and the woman began to count her coppers. "Do you sell stamps?"

"No sorry we don't, but the post office is on the corner." Nora indicated.

"Thank you dear." She counted out the money, dropped the card amongst the tissues and left shuffling with her bag only to be replaced by a tall man with a buzz cut, dark sunglasses, a tight fitted black t-shirt and black trousers. He was very muscled and sweaty with a handsome, sharply angled face, square jaw and serious expression. Nora immediately thought of 'The Terminator'.

"Any Beano annuals?" He asked Nora, easing his shades back into his buzz cut while looking her up and down.

Nora sat down behind the counter self-consciously.

"Yes, probably upstairs."

"I want all of your Beano annuals and Dandy annuals. Can you get them all down, and all of the ones from your Seatown shop too?" He asked.

"I can look later when my colleague is here." Nora suggested.

He stood staring at her for a long moment before nodding.

"I'll be back." He said determinedly, his voice taking on a slightly European accent.

Nora stared.

"Okay. Can I take a name to put with them?"

"I'm Harry. I've just moved into Castletown, a flat above the greengrocer shop down Market Street. Do you live here too?"

"No. I just work here." Nora explained warily.

"Ah. Now I know you're here I'll come and visit you. I have to be somewhere in five minutes else I'd stay and chat you up. But…I'll be back." He said, slipped his sunshades down, turned and walked off.

He paused and came back.

"I'll give you my mobile number. You can let me know about the annuals and send me a text if you like." He winked.

"Erm. Okay, yes, I'll write down your mobile number and we can let you know about the annuals."

"And anything else." He winked again and then checked his watch. "Shame I have to be somewhere."

"Yes, shame." Nora agreed with as little sarcasm as she could.

He gave her his mobile number, watching her write it down next to his name.

"I'll be back." He said once more, turned and swaggered off.

Nora watched him leave and shook her head, adding a note beneath his name and number to remind her to gather all the Beano's and Dandy's for '*The Terminator*'. She chuckled, sipping her tea.

The window cleaner arrived and stuck his thumb up at Nora through the glass in the door. He was deaf and mute so communicated by 'thumbs up' or 'thumbs down' to the shop keepers about the town while he cleaned their windows. Georgina had inherited him from the previous owners; he had turned up one day and just cleaned the windows without even negotiating with Georgina, but because he did such a good job she just let him carry on.

Nora waved,

A woman came in, carrying a box of books which the window cleaner helped her with, holding open the door for her. He stuck up his thumb.

"Are you buying any books at the moment?" The woman asked, huffing and puffing with the box.

"I can take a look." Nora offered, propelling herself out of the chair and walking around to the front where the woman dropped the box onto the carpet.

"They were all my daughter's books." She explained.

Nora knelt before the box and began to pull out the Lemony Snickets, Lucy Daniels and Jacqueline Wilsons.

"We can use these." She said, leaving some books about sea creatures and pirates but pointing to the others. "They'd be worth five pounds to us."

"Lovely. That'll buy us a couple of ice-creams." The woman accepted, picking up the box. Nora carried the books to the desk, opening the till for the money.

Once she had been paid, the woman left and let two people in who began to browse by the Cole section. Two others entered with the window cleaner.

"Good morning." One of the two new men greeted her.

"Hello." Nora returned, handing the window cleaner his two pounds.

He stuck his thumb up and left.

"Oh, look Geoffrey, there's Alan's book!" The lady by the Cole section announced loudly.

"Oh yes. Alan, good lad. Let's see if *we're* in here. It's about our town." The man said, equally as loud.

"How old are the castle ruins?" One of the men who had entered with the window cleaner asked.

"Erm…well, all the bits have different ages actually." Nora replied.

"Hmm, hmm. Is it worth a visit round them? You have to pay to go in the grounds."

"It's very nice." Nora nodded. "And a lot of the rooms are still intact with big, high walls and some ceilings. The largest turret is also free to climb but the top is missing."

"Very well. I may have a wander around." He decided. "Where are your westerns?"

"Western novels?"

"Yes."

"In the attic room at the top of the shop; they'll have a label, at the end of the general fiction." Nora indicated. She watched him and his companion head off to look as the telephone began to ring again.

"Good morning, The Secondhand Bookworm." Nora greeted cheerfully.

The voice at the other end was faint.

"Yes." The man cleared his throat. "I am looking to sell some books. We're downsizing from a large house into a flat. Would you be interested in purchasing some of our goods, dear?"

"We can certainly have a look." Nora replied. "Do you want to bring them in or would you like a call out?"

"I can't carry them in my dear." He assured and coughed feebly. "I would much prefer someone to call out."

"If you would like to telephone our Seatown branch then the appointment diary is there and they can arrange a day for you?" Nora suggested.

"I have the number here." He said. "Thank you dear, I'll do that."

As he hung up two more people entered the shop. Nora thought of the Duke of Cole and fondly blamed him and his plans to rebuild his castle as being behind the reason why The Secondhand Bookworm was so popular that week. The newcomers appeared to be a couple and were laughing loudly; a woman with a pierced cheek, red shiny dress and Doc Martin boots and a man in shorts, a pink tie-dyed t-shirt, long curls and a huge beer-belly.

"Can I have a look at the book in the window darlin'?" The man asked loudly.

"He's not gonna read it." The woman laughed.

"I can't read. I've never read a book in my life." He assured, looking around. He then stood in the middle of the room. "Do you sell books?" He asked loudly and they both roared with laughter.

The couple by the Cole section pretended to ignore them. Nora stood up.

"What book is it from the window?"

"I can grab it. It's here in the front." The woman said and picked up a large tome about Egyptian travel.

"My brother killed himself, my nan just died and my mum's in hospital." The man said.

"Oh dear." Nora sat back down.

"Yeah, woe is me." He took the book from his friend. "She'll love this. I'll send it to her."

He slammed it on the table and began to rummage for some money.

"I'll pay for it!" The woman decided, swinging her bag off of her shoulder and almost sending some books flying.

"Shurrup!" The man bellowed and they laughed as he pulled out his wallet and began to rummage.

Nora opened the book to read the price. She punched it into the till.

"It's seventeen fifty." He said, taking out a twenty pound note. "We won't be able to feed mum for a week but at least she'll have something to read."

They both almost doubled up with laughter.

"Do you need a bag?" Nora asked loudly, glancing at the Cole customers who made a hasty exit with a repulsed glance back.

"Yeah…is it free?" He looked suspicious.

The woman nudged him hard.

"Shurrup!" She laughed.

"It's free." Nora nodded, unhooking one.

"Ah! So mum will get an egg for breakfast at least." He shouted and hit the desk with his fist, laughing.

Nora bagged up his book fast and handed him his change.

"What you doing tonight darlin'? I've only been here two minutes and I've pulled already." He told the woman.

Nora gave a hollow laugh while they screamed hysterically.

"Just ignore him. He's drunk!" She shouted, grabbed his arm and dragged him from the shop.

They left singing pub songs and Nora stared silently after them. A moment later the phone rang so she grabbed the receiver, determined to live up to her name and be jolly.

"It's Mr Hill." The voice at the other end said amidst heavy breathing.

Nora held the phone away from her ear slightly, screwing up her nose.

"Hello, Mr Hill."

"Nora. That book I've put aside. I've had a change of plans and won't be able to come over today after all. Would you be able to transfer the book to your Seatown branch for collection over there?"

Nora sat down.

"That's no problem." She tried to keep the sigh out of her tone.

"It's the 'Military Uniforms of Britain and the Empire', volume four. It's red cloth."

"Yes." Nora tried not to sound despairing.

"Could you put it to go to Seatown please?"

"Yes."

"And when will it get there?"

Nora paused.

"Erm, well, probably not until Monday."

"Oh dear. That is a nuisance. Oh dear." He breathed loudly for several seconds. "Oh dear. Well. Perhaps you could put it back into stock then please."

"I can keep it under here for you…"

His breathing grew heavier.

"No, no…I shan't be requiring the book after all. Thank you." He hung up and Nora almost threw the phone.

A man came in from the back room and dropped a book onto the counter.

"Is someone having a laugh?" He began slowly away, looking at the book as if it would explode.

"Pardon?"

"Is someone having a laugh?" He repeated, edging away while staring at it.

Nora saw a huge white sticker on the back of the book that was facing up which read *'£1.99 – bargain'*. It was a thick new biography. Nora turned it over and opened it.

"Our price is seven pounds fifty." She pointed out.

"Someone was having a laugh." He was almost at the door, still looking back at it. He smiled, embarrassed.

"Yes." Nora smiled dryly and pulled off the sticker.

He left the door open and Max from the Indian restaurant peered in.

"Hello. Do you have a car parked out the back?" He asked.

Nora shook her head.

"No way. It's not us." She assured.

"Someone's blocked the road and I've got a skip being delivered. Okay, see you." He smiled, looking a bit harassed, and walked away scanning the area about him.

The phone rang again.

"Hello, it's Mr Hill." The voice said followed by more heavy breathing.

"Hello." Nora greeted with forced cheerfulness. "Who's that?"

"It's Nora, Mr Hill!" Nora replied tightly.

"Yes, Nora. Do you have a book in your stock called…'Anthony and Cleopatra'?"

"I can have a look for you." Nora grimaced and headed toward the area by the start of the staircase.

"It would be in the Egyptian section, by the staircase, two shelves down. It has a yellow dust wrapper and it's called ANTHONY AND CLEOPATRA." He said and coughed, breathing even louder.

Nora held the phone at arm's length away from her ear. She spotted the book straightaway and pulled it out.

"I have it."

"Oh…oh." He sounded excited. "And what is the price?"

"Six pounds fifty."

"Six pounds fifty? Can you put it by for me? I won't be requiring 'Military Uniforms of Britain and the Empire', volume four, which is red cloth. But I would like to purchase Anthony and Cleopatra."

"Okay Mr Hill." Nora said patiently and placed the book on top of the military uniforms."

"I shall be in at some point to collect it but I shall have to make arrangements. B-bye." He hung up.

Nora tentatively returned the phone to its cradle, expecting it to ring again but after a few moments of silence she stood up and ran to make some more hot tea.

Just before eleven o'clock Nora was polishing some leather bound books in the peace and quiet when a young woman with a riot of bright red curls bounded into the shop carrying loads of bags.

"Hello! I'm Agnes! Are you Nora?" She greeted with a large grin.

Nora blinked.

"Hello. Yes, I'm Nora." She replied as Agnes hurried around the desk, huffing and puffing.

"Sorry about the bags. I feel like a bag lady. I've just raided the library. I'm surprised they let me take more books out after I just paid a twenty seven pound fine. My brother thinks I'm mad as I was coming to a bookshop but I don't want to keep books about economics and maths for the fun of it; I may as well hire them out."

Nora watched her shove the bags out of the way and then turn and shake out her hair.

"Oh my goodness. Sorry, I must seem like a mad woman."

Nora laughed.

"Well, if you are then you've come to the right place. It's been rather mad here all morning."

Agnes grinned, looking around.

"So I'm here until four today. What would you like me to do?" She offered, peering at the cash book with interest.

"We've had endless paperback sales this morning." Nora indicated.

"That polish smells nice."

"This one's lovely. That pot there smells of cow manure." Nora pointed.

Agnes laughed and picked it up.

"Is it a special cow cream?"

"Hmm, it's for leather sofas but I couldn't bear my house to smell of that. It does bring the books up nice though so Georgina makes us use it on all of our leather volumes. It makes them look lovely." Nora explained.

Agnes sniffed it and pulled a face.

"Yes…cow manure." She agreed and twisted the lid back on.

"Well. The paperback room needs a bit of a tidy and sort if you'd like to do that?" Nora suggested. "It'll get you familiar with all the titles up there because we get asked for a lot of fiction."

"Oh sure!" Agnes was keen. "I'll keep popping down to see if it's busy and if you need a break."

"Thanks." Nora appreciated. "It's been busier than usual for this time of the year."

At that moment a man stepped into the shop and Agnes stared at him with interest. Nora turned to watch him look around and then approach the counter.

"Yes, yes. Hallo. I am a trade buyer. I buy lots from your other shop. If I buy a hundred books, what discount can you give me?" He asked, peering around through squinting eyes.

Nora added some more red polish to the leather binding she held and buffed it up with the duster.

"We can only give ten percent off all of our books for trade." She explained.

"Oh, but your prices! They are always so high. I make a big pile and you do me a deal? I am from Greece." He said in a whining tone.

Nora rubbed the leather slowly, staring at him.

"I'm afraid I can't do more than ten percent off for trade. We have some good American trade customers especially in the summer and they spend hundreds of pounds, sometimes six or seven hundred pounds and we still only give a ten percent discount." She said.

Agnes tided up some of the leather books, trying not to look like she was eavesdropping.

"But I been before and I spend a lot on many books." He whinged.

"Yes, these trade customers do return and still we only give ten percent for trade; it's our policy."

He sighed and shook his head slowly with a big shrug of his shoulders.

"I start small pile. You write them down with prices for me as invoice please." He said.

"Of course." Nora put the lid on the polish and grabbed some wet wipes to clean her hands.

"My shipping company will collect them in five or ten days." He announced and headed off into the back room.

Agnes grinned.

"That's exciting."

"Perhaps the paperback room should wait until we've done these." Nora decided and Agnes agreed.

They cleared a space on the side of the counter, squashing the computer monitor aside and bringing the invoice template up onto the screen. In the midst of sorting themselves out they sold a handful of postcards and Agnes had to give directions to the castle ruins. Then the Greek trade man brought his first large pile through.

"This is all the old sailing stuff we've had for ages on the shelves." Nora whispered, pleased.

"Excellent!" Agnes nodded.

"If you read out the titles and prices I'll type them out." Nora suggested so Agnes took up the first book.

Soon there was a large pile which they managed to work through quite quickly as it was quiet. Agnes used the calculator to add them up when the trade man had finished. They took off his ten percent and he handed over his card, whining about not having a bigger discount as he was spending two hundred and fifty pounds.

"My shippers will come and collect. You box up and put a copy of invoice inside?"

"Yes, that's fine." Nora assured, handing him back his card.

He gave them a business card and left them to box up the books.

"We can use this big box here that contained the toilet rolls we ordered last week." Nora said from under the stairs, dragging out an empty cardboard box that looked like it would hold the collection.

Agnes laughed, taking out the blue display tissue paper that was stored inside. She started to wrap the books in piles of three or four.

"Perhaps we should wrap them in toilet paper." Agnes suggested and they chuckled.

The books fitted perfectly. Once they had placed the invoice inside they taped it up with parcel tape and then pushed it under the stairs out of the way.

"They can take one to three weeks to come and collect it." Nora knew from experience.

"That was fun." Agnes said.

"It took ages." Nora noticed. "I think I might take my lunch break after all of that!"

"Okay." Agnes flopped into the seat behind the till.

"Are you alright using the till and PDQ machine?" Nora asked her.

"Yes, I worked at a clothes shop over Christmas and Georgina ran through these machines with me at the weekend. *And* the subjects are listed at the bottom of the stairs if anyone asks for something so I'll be fine." She assured.

"Okay. Well, I've got my lunch with me today so I'll go and eat in the kitchen." Nora decided.

"Enjoy." Agnes smiled, turning to greet an old lady with uncontrollable flatulence who stepped down into the shop clasping a handful of postcards.

Nora shook her head, leaving Agnes's shoulders shaking with silent laughter. She headed to the back of the shop and into the kitchen, closing the door behind her and turning on the light.

The room was small and cosy but perpetually cold because it had a plastic roof. It was an extension so not as old as the rest of the shop but still a little bit tatty. Nora dragged a tall stool towards her, sitting down. With a sigh she washed her hands, took out her sandwiches and her Kindle and settled down to read.

11 THE TWITS

When Nora returned to the front of the shop Agnes had finished the polishing, tidied the books up on the floor and had taken over one hundred pounds in sales.

"It's been quite mad." She grinned. "And a Mr Hill phoned several times to say he will be here at five past three to collect an 'Anthony and Cleopatra' book."

"Lovely." Nora sighed. She spotted her earlier note about the Beano's and Dandy's for 'The Terminator' as she dropped her bag safely behind the counter. "Do you want to go and have something to eat?"

"I'm okay at the moment." Agnes assured.

"Well, just say when you want to go. I'll run up and look for these annuals."

"I can do that if you like?" Agnes offered, standing up. "I love the children's room."

"Okay." Nora agreed. "The customer said he wants all our Beano and Dandy annuals."

Agnes quirked an eyebrow and, smiling, headed off. When she had creaked upstairs the telephone started to ring.

Nora picked up the receiver, pausing as three boys sat down outside against the front of the bay window and there was a small bang as an elbow hit the glass. Nora walked around the counter, watching the boys begin to wrestle and laugh. Familiar heavy breathing sounded down the phone line.

"One moment, Mr Hill." Nora said distractedly.

She put the phone onto the counter as another elbow smacked the glass. Nora stalked towards the door, pulled it open and stepped up.

"Please come away from the window!" Nora said to the boys with clenched teeth.

They all stood up as if the windowsill was on fire and stared at her.

"The glass is thin and it will crack."

"Sorri!" A blond haired boy with a northern accent stuttered and they ran off.

Nora smiled, pleased that she was obviously scary and returned to the shop.

A man was waiting at the counter with a paperback.

"Oh hello. Sorry, I interrupted a telephone call. Bear with me a moment." She grabbed the receiver and the customer shrugged, picking up a book on the counter called 'In praise of flowers'.

"Sorry, Mr Hill."

"Is that Nora?" Mr Hill asked.

"Yes." Nora tried to sound polite.

"Nora. It's Mr Hill."

"Hello, Mr Hill." Nora said tightly.

"Nora. I've had to change my plans today. The book about 'Anthony and Cleopatra' that I've put by." He paused for some heavy breathing. "I'd like to pick it up on Monday please. Is that alright?"

"Yes!" Nora replied. "That's fine."

"Thank you. I have some business with the bank to reimburse some funds. So on Monday Nora, I shall catch the train over to Castletown and purchase the book from your premises. B-bye." He hung up before Nora could reply and she pressed the end call button several times with her thumb, shaking her head in despair.

The man in front of her arched an eyebrow, putting down 'In praise of flowers'.

"Just that one for you?" Nora smiled pleasantly, returning the receiver to its cradle.

She picked up the paperback and opened the cover.

"It's two pounds." The man pointed out as Nora read the pricing.

"Two pounds fifty." Nora said.

"What? They're two noughts." His finger jabbed the pencil mark and the cover closed.

"That's my number five for fifty pence." Nora said. "Sometimes it looks like a nought. If it was just two pounds I would have just pencilled a number two. But it's not important. Two pounds please." Nora said and rang it through the till.

"No, no, no. If you wanted two pounds fifty then I'll give you two pounds fifty, love." The man insisted.

Nora added fifty to the till.

"Thanks. It is a nice copy."

"It's for my mum." He said, handing her three pounds.

"I'm sure she'll enjoy it." Nora assured. "Fifty pence change. Would you like a bag?"

"No thanks; save the planet and all that." The man replied, stuffing the book and the change in his pocket. "Goodbye."

A woman walked into the front of the shop.

"I want to buy that set of Robert Stevenson novels." She said, pointing to a green cloth set that was between two globe bookends on a shelf by the doorway. "I was looking at them earlier. It says twelve volumes for twenty five pounds. Would you take two hundred and fifty for them?"

Nora stared at her.

"What?!"

"Two hundred and fifty pounds for the set?" The woman repeated, indicating with her head towards them.

"It's twenty five pounds for the twelve volumes as a set." Nora explained.

"OH!" The woman was shocked.

"You can pay two hundred and fifty if you like." Nora grinned.

The woman laughed.

"I really thought it was twenty-five pounds per volume. I left my brain at home today." She slapped her forehead but looked really pleased.

Nora walked around the counter to the books.

"They are a lovely set but they're not exceptionally rare." Nora assured.

"Oh I'll have them! They're a fantastic price!" The woman enthused and helped Nora to stack them up on the counter.

As Nora was taking payment by credit card, Agnes came down with an armful of annuals. She put them on the floor and helped Nora box up the books in a cardboard box that had had a delivery of carrier bags in it. The woman left cheerfully, carrying the box and almost colliding with a man in the doorway. Nora smiled to see Humphrey. He took a half-eaten long apple pastry from between his teeth and gestured the lady with the box through, standing aside.

Today he was dressed more casually, wearing a dark grey sweater with a small silver zip at the throat, black jeans and boots. Nora hadn't ever seen him in anything other than his suits and was surprised at how ordinary he now looked.

"Thank you." The woman called back, leaving the shop with her books.

"Bye." Nora called, smiling at Humphrey.

Agnes stood next to Nora, watching Humphrey step down and give a small wave with the pastry he was holding, sending a chunk of apple onto some walking guides.

"Sorry." He said, stooped and picked it up.

Nora laughed.

"I've just been to McDonalds." He explained, swallowing his mouthful and gesturing with the pie.

"Is there a McDonalds here?" Agnes was startled.

"No, I've just come back from my flat in London. There's one between here and Walltown." Humphrey explained, passing Nora the little piece of apple from the carpet.

She placed it in some tissue paper and threw it in the bin.

Agnes stared at Humphrey as he took another bite and then offered it to Nora.

"No, thank you." Nora declined.

"And while I was in McDonalds, Georgina phoned me. Who are you by the way?" He looked at Agnes as he leaned against the front of the counter.

Agnes just stared at him.

"This is Agnes." Nora explained, nudging Agnes's arm. "She's started working here and is going to be doing Saturdays."

"Hello." She squeaked, locked in Humphrey's piercing blue gaze.

"Oh good. I hope you're mad. You have to be mad to work here. It seems that all of the customers are mad." He smirked. "The residents too."

"I am." Agnes nodded enthusiastically.

Nora bit back a grin and Humphrey smiled.

"She's already encountered Mr Hill." Nora assured.

Humphrey almost choked on his pastry.

"My favourite customer so far." He coughed. "I hope you found his book, put it back, found it again, put it back..."

Nora's laugh was pained but Agnes continued to stare, nonplussed.

Humphrey's attention returned to Nora.

"So, Georgina phoned and said that mum wants to go to the theatre." He continued.

Nora pressed the date and time button to secure the till after her last sale.

"Oh, yes."

"So I bought two tickets." Humphrey explained. "It's in Seatown at the Guild Theatre, box seats, very nice." He cleared his throat, watching Nora who smiled at him, curious.

"That sounds lovely. What are you going to see?"

"It's a Dickens play." Humphrey sounded really enthusiastic.

"Dickens?" Nora pondered him, suddenly suspicious. "You told me over dinner the other night that you've never read a Dickens novel; that they sound stuffy and long-winded and a real bore and to give you a crime thriller any day, but now you're excited about seeing one performed?"

He smirked.

"I love Dickens." Agnes joined in. "The play is 'Nicholas Nickleby' isn't it?"

Humphrey glanced at her and nodded, finishing off the last of his apple pastry.

"Nora's favourite." He revealed.

Nora arched an eyebrow.

"It is. Did I harp on about it?" She grinned.

"It's a beautiful sounding harp." Humphrey said. He then cleared his throat and the top of his cheeks flushed slightly.

Nora stared at him, studying his expression.

"So anyway, I was eating my cheeseburger on the drive back." He continued, picking up some more pastry flakes from the cash book. "And I thought; Nora would enjoy this 'Nicholas Nickleby' play, it's her favourite book; she harped on about it during dinner the other evening." His eyes twinkled and Nora smiled slightly. "So. Would you like to come?"

Agnes stared at Humphrey and he arched an eyebrow inquiringly.

"With you and your mother?" Nora asked.

Humphrey laughed.

"Not a chance. Just you and me."

"But what about Mrs Pickering?"

"Oh, mum can go next week with Georgina." He decided.

Nora bit the bottom of her lip, studying Humphrey thoughtfully. Humphrey watched her and slowly his other eyebrow lifted in anticipation.

"It's a bit short notice."

"I'm impulsive."

"When for?"

"Sunday night."

"Just the theatre?"

"Dinner too."

"We've already been out to dinner twice."

"Three's a charm."

Nora's lips twitched.

"Just as friends, right?"

"Just as friends." He nodded, although his blue eyes twinkled a bit more.

Nora glanced at Agnes who was watching with amusement.

"Okay. I'd really like to see the play. And seeing as we're just friends I'd love to go with you. Thank you." Nora finally accepted.

Humphrey straightened up and grinned. He nodded, pleased.

"Great. Well, I've also booked drinks in the bar beforehand. We need to be there by seven so dinner at the restaurant is booked for five."

"Got it all planned have you?"

"Absolutely."

Nora shook her head, amused and pleased.

"I've got an errand to run for Georgina now but then I thought I'd come back here to the shop when I'm done. Georgina said Agnes is leaving at four."

"No way." Nora said firmly. "I might get fed up with you."

"I'm your twenty four hour protection, remember?" Humphrey teased but she could see he was disappointed.

Nora walked around the counter and stood in front of him.

"I'm serious, Humphrey. You have better things to do than hang around The Secondhand Bookworm."

"Believe me I haven't." He smiled. "I'd much rather spend the afternoon with you."

Nora took hold of his arm and attempted to pull him towards the door.

"I have things to do. Ever heard of the phrase 'absence makes the heart grow fonder'?" She said, unable to make him budge an inch.

After a moment Humphrey relented and walked with her.

"I suppose I like the sound of that. I'll see you on Sunday then. Text me? In fact, I'll text you and ask how you are every half an hour."

"I'll text you the address to my parents' house but that's all. Goodbye, Humphrey."

"You're really kicking me out?" Humphrey arched an eyebrow again.

"Yes. Off you go."

He smiled slightly.

"Alright. Bye, Nora."

"Bye, Humphrey."

"I take it he's your boyfriend, really?" Agnes said when Nora was back behind the counter.

"Not exactly."

"Why not? I can see he really likes you."

"We've been distant acquaintances for a few years and have only just become good friends and I can't help thinking of him sometimes like I do my brothers." Nora explained.

"Excuse me." A lady walked up to the counter, interrupting them. "Do you have a 'Mother Goose' book?"

Nora looked blank a moment.

"We do!" Agnes made both the customer and Nora flinch. "I saw one in the children's room when I was getting the annuals for 'The Terminator'. I couldn't help but have a thorough browse through the books while I was in there."

"For the what, dear?" The lady stared at her, bemused.

"We do usually have one." Nora knew, impressed with Agnes and ignoring the question about 'The Terminator' reference.

"Is it a BBC one?" The lady asked.

Agnes looked doubtful.

"No, I don't think so but I can get it if you like and bring it down for you to see?"

"That would be kind." The lady appreciated.

Agnes hurried off.

"I remember 'Mother Goose'. I had one with shiny pages." The woman told Nora. "I had an uncle in those days and he worked for the BBC and he always bought me a shiny book. I ask in every second hand bookshop that I come across. It has to be a BBC publication, with shiny pages."

The phone rang.

"Excuse me a moment." Nora apologised and grabbed the receiver. "The Secondhand Bookworm."

"Yes, hello." A deep male voice greeted slowly. There was the sound of smacking lips. "Yes, mmm, do you have any Folio Society books?"

"We certainly do. Is it a particular one you're looking for?" Nora asked.

"The Seven Pillars of Wisdom' by T.E. Lawrence. It's the yellow thick one with the nice cover." He said and smacked his lips several times.

"I know the one but I don't think we have that at the moment."

"Shame." The voice sounded flat and disappointed.

Nora moved around the counter to scan the shelves. The Folio Society books had their own separate section due to them being lovely hardbound printings of a variety of classic titles of all different subjects. People usually collected them because of the beautiful editions the printing house released. Once, The Secondhand Bookworm had one of King Henry VIII's prayer books which had only had just under a thousand editions printed. Nora sold it one day for eight hundred pounds and received a juicy bonus from Georgina.

"It might be worth checking our Seatown branch." Nora suggested, seeing that there wasn't a copy of The Seven Pillars of Wisdom on the shelves.

"They have it there?" He asked sharply.

"I don't know for certain but we do get it in so it's possible."

"Can you check for me?" He asked.

Nora paused.

"If you phoned them now they can look on the shelves for you while you wait." She suggested.

The man sighed deeply.

"Do you have their number?" He asked.

Nora gave it to him and he rang off quickly.

Agnes appeared holding a couple of books.

"There were three different editions." She said. "But none of them are a BBC publication."

"No, I'd recognise it when I saw it." The woman explained, looking briefly at the books. "It has to be BBC and it has to have shiny pages. Never mind. Thanks for looking though, dear."

"My pleasure." Agnes said, placing the books onto the desk.

The woman left and Agnes and Nora were left alone again.

"It was worth a try." Agnes shrugged, opening the first page of the top 'Mother Goose',

"I think she was determined to find her BBC copy." Nora smirked. "Seeing as you mentioned The Terminator would you like to phone him and tell him we have a selection of annuals? Then put them under the counter in a couple of clear bags from that box over there." Nora pointed. "These little slips here go with the reserved books. Fill in his name and number and write that you phoned him and either spoke to him or left a message, with the date you did so."

"Bonanza!" Agnes nodded and picked up the phone, pushing in the number the Terminator had given.

A man strolled in with bright blue dyed hair and a pink bow-tie. Agnes gawped at him and Nora sat up.

"Hello, Nora." He smiled, pulling out some spectacles on an old chain.

"Hello." Nora greeted.

He nodded at Agnes who smiled back curiously and watched him walk around to the First Edition shelves behind the counter. Agnes squeezed out of the way while listening to The Terminator's phone ringing.

"Hello? Hello. Is that The…is that Harry?" Agnes asked.

Nora bit her lip when Agnes almost called him The Terminator.

"I'm calling from the bookshop. We have some…pardon? No, no I'm not 'the chick with the dark hair'." Agnes glanced at Nora, arching her eyebrows.

Nora shook her head, indicating she wasn't here.

"No, no, I'm sorry she's unavailable at the moment. It's only to let you know we have several Beano and Dandy annuals here you might be interested in. Pardon? Oh, I don't know when she's next in the shop." Agnes grimaced.

Nora grimaced too.

"Yes, we'll keep them by, just come in anytime and have a look through them. Okay. Thanks. Bye." She hung up and looked at Nora. "He was asking about you."

"Lovely." Nora sighed, shaking her head.

Agnes bagged up the annuals, filled in a form and placed them under the counter.

"I think I'll just grab a sandwich." She decided. "Is that okay?"

"Yes, of course." Nora nodded.

Agnes picked up her bag, squeezed past the man with the dyed blue hair, who was still browsing through the first editions, and made a speedy exit as Nora ducked down and disappeared under the counter to rummage through the reserved books with a mission.

When Agnes was gone, Nora straightened up holding a medium sized book in a clear bag.

"Ah, yes." The man with the blue hair noticed it. "I've had three gins so I'll pay for the book now."

Nora laughed, placing the carefully wrapped item on the counter.

"Whenever you're ready."

"You're hoping I'll find another gem behind here, aren't you?" He glanced back, peering over the top of his glasses at her. "Well, I shan't continue looking or you'll be the cause of my bank manager's stroke. How much do I owe you today?"

"Two hundred pounds." Nora said without needing to check the price of the first edition copy of 'Winnie the Pooh'.

"Oh, why do I collect first editions?" He sighed with his eyes twinkling. "But it is rather beautiful."

"It'll be lovely in your collection." Nora assured.

"Quiet temptress!" He warned playfully and drew out his wallet.

Nora wrapped the book in brown paper and placed it in a carrier bag. Blue-Hair took it, handing her his cash.

"Let me know when you want to rob me again." He said cheerfully.

"You're on our database." Nora nodded, counting out the twenties before popping them in the till.

She smiled, watching him leave after asking her to thank Georgina for him. Pleased, Nora wrote the sale in the cash book, sat down and wiggled the mouse. The monitor showed the Skype Chat and Nora typed a quick message to Georgina.

'Mr Blue-Hair has been in for his Winnie.'

She waited a moment and saw the pen start writing at the top. A moment later a message appeared.

'Excellent. What u on now?'

Nora added up the sales, pausing to take fifty pence for two postcards and direct a couple to the tourist information office.

'£572'

Nora Skyped the figure and then jumped.

A woman with dark, narrowed eyes, black hair slicked back into a pony tail and a fed-up expression slammed the door hard behind her and approached the desk. Nora recognised her as a customer who sometimes came in and was very confrontational.

"Where are your books about Indian goddesses?" The woman asked, looking Nora up and down disdainfully.

"Indian goddesses? On the top floor." Nora replied tentatively.

The woman's eyes flashed.

"In Indian history?" She demanded.

"No, in...mythology." Nora explained hesitantly.

The woman stared at her.

"What? Mythology?!" She sneered. "Are you saying they're all an illusion then?"

"It's just where we keep them." Nora explained.

The woman scoffed.

"I shan't waste my time then!"

Nora bit her tongue, watching the woman shove her hands in the pockets of her jeans and move over to the large wall of bookcases to the right, her dark eyes scanning the art biographies. Nora turned and read Georgina's reply on Skype Chat.

'Well done! Rubbish here – just gone over £100.'

"Where are your books about Cubism?" The confrontational woman glared, looking over her shoulder at Nora from before the art section.

"If we have any they'd be under the section where the label says 'art movements'." Nora explained.

"I can't see any. Oh this shop is rubbish!" The woman span around, her pony tail flying out behind her, marched across the room and wrenched open the door.

"Don't come back." Nora said, turning and looking at the computer, shaking her head.

The door slammed but then reopened. The woman was standing on the step staring in.

"What did you say?!" She demanded slowly.

Nora hadn't expected her to hear and met her piercing glare. For a moment they stared at one another.

"I said don't come back." Nora repeated calmly, her heart pounding hard. "Every time you come in you storm out moaning about the shop. If you don't like it then don't come back."

The woman drew a long, slow, deep breath.

"FINE!! I WON'T!!" She shrieked and slammed the door so hard that the windows rattled and a book fell off one of the display shelves.

Nora stood up.

"Psycho." She said, not knowing whether to laugh or cry.

She saw the woman flying off down the road in a rage and decided to laugh. Picking up the book from the floor, Nora put it back, noticing Agnes stand aside to let the mad woman fly past. Nora returned to the computer and wrote on Skype chat:

'I've just banned a psychopath from the shop.'

Agnes came in carrying a sandwich.

"Hello." She smiled. "All the old ladies are sitting on all the benches in town. Can I eat in the kitchen?"

"Sure." Nora nodded.

'Well done!' Georgina replied and Nora smiled.

Agnes disappeared into the kitchen leaving Nora to tidy up the art section and arrange the books on Cubism.

Sometime later, Agnes and Nora were sitting on low stools by the window marking up some paperbacks that someone had carried in and Nora had bought when the door opened to emit a very large woman. Agnes lowered the book and pencil she was holding to stare at her until Nora nudged her arm. Agnes cleared her throat, continuing to pencil the price as the woman stepped down, cursing.

"Oh, the step! It's so flaming deep. What a stupid depth for a freaking step!" She huffed and puffed and Nora almost dropped her paperback.

"Shut up Pansy." A man's rough voice said from behind her.

"Don't tell me to shut up! Oh, flipping heck."

Nora and Agnes stared as the woman named Pansy entered. She wore baggy red tracksuit bottoms and a big tent-like grey t-shirt. She had a large, warty double chin and a hairy upper lip. Several of her teeth were missing and her body odour preceded her.

"Hello." Nora greeted, walking around to behind the counter.

Agnes joined her quickly and backed against the leather books.

"Where's your children's books?" The woman approached the counter and clasped the top, breathing hard and belching.

Nora edged back.

"Pansy!" The man shook his head, closing the door behind him.

"Children's books are all upstairs." Nora replied, knowing what would follow.

"UPSTAIRS!" She roared and Nora almost covered her ears. "What kind of a frigging stupid place...how do I get up there? Do you have a lift? Like hell you do. Okay but if I die then Roddy can sue you."

"Through there." Nora indicated, pretending to scratch the side of her nose but holding her breath.

Cursing with each step, the woman waddled her way through to the back and began loudly up the stairs, taking ages and breathing loudly.

"Let me pass you twit!" Nora and Agnes heard her say.

Agnes covered her mouth. Nora bit back a horrified laugh.

"Oh, oh help me!" They heard Pansy crying.

Roddy was laughing and Nora rushed to see. Roddy was pushing her up the last few steps, hands on her large

240

bottom, as a man pressed himself against the wall of travel books to let them go by.

"Shut up, Pansy." Roddy was calling as he heaved her around to the landing.

The other customer ran down the stairs.

"I'll have this please." He handed Nora a book so Nora took it to the counter where Agnes was smirking to herself.

"I'm sorry that lady was rude to you." Nora apologised.

The man laughed.

"It's not every day you get called a twit." He shrugged good-humouredly.

"Eight pounds fifty for that one, sir." Nora smiled.

He handed her a ten pound note.

"Don't worry about a bag." He took the change and the book and left cheerfully.

Agnes glanced at the clock.

"It's quarter to four!" She was amazed at how quickly the day had passed.

Nora looked at the pile of paperbacks.

"Heather and I can get these away tomorrow if we finish pricing them." She decided.

"Does Heather just work weekends?"

"Heather's my younger sister and she works with me sometimes. She's currently studying at college."

"Cool. Hopefully I'll get to work with her."

"Maybe one day." Nora nodded.

"I'll get back on with these." Agnes said and sat on the already marked up pile of paperbacks before the antiquarian books, drawing some more towards her.

"'Wuthering Heights'. I loathed this until I reached the last two or three pages and then it all just resolved itself and I loved it. Hard work though." She decided, examining the pages of the penguin classic.

241

"Who is your favourite author?" Nora asked, joining her and picking up a Dostoyevsky.

"John Grisham." Agnes replied without hesitation. "I like thrillers and crime fiction, authors like Lynda La Plant and Martine Cole. I also like gruesome stuff about monsters and Stephen King type novels, great for scaring yourself before you go to sleep."

"That's hideous." Nora grimaced. "I don't really read much."

Agnes laughed.

"Don't let people hear you say that when you work in a book shop." She warned.

At four o'clock Agnes gathered armfuls of priced paperbacks to take upstairs as Nora served a customer holding two Chihuahuas.

"This is Frodo and this is Bilbo." The woman introduced.

Nora was stroking them when she saw Agnes backing into the front again.

"Move it you twit!" Came a frustrated voice.

Agnes moved hastily aside to let Pansy and Roddy through. Once they were in the front Agnes exited quickly with the paperbacks leaving the Chihuahuas barking and Pansy huffing and puffing with some children's books.

"Thank you." The lady with the little dogs said, picking up her postcards and leaving quickly.

"Those little yapping twits." Pansy muttered and dropped her books onto the desk. "I found these but I had to bend down to look through the bloody 'Just Williams'."

Nora cleared her throat.

"You can't really speak like that; we get children in here." Nora decided to point out bravely.

Pansy gawped at her.

"Yeah, I did warn you about your flowery language, Pansy." Roddy agreed.

"Yeah well I nearly fell down those stairs of yours." Pansy retorted, stroking her moustache.

"Sorry about that." Nora apologised, opening the first book on Pansy's pile.

"No you aren't you twit." Pansy replied and grinned, showing her gappy teeth.

Nora didn't respond but quickly ran the prices of the 'Just Williams' through the till and bagged them up.

"I don't want a bag!" Pansy objected.

"It saves me carrying them!" Roddy snatched the bag and handed Nora two five pound notes.

"Thank you." Nora quickly gave him the change and they headed off.

Nora watched them leave chaotically and giggled when she heard someone called a 'twit' in the street.

When Agnes came downstairs, Nora was sitting on the stool looking worn out.

"Has the twit gone?" Agnes whispered and they laughed. "I'm working in Seatown tomorrow so I'll speak to you on Skype Chat."

"Okay. It was really great to work with you." Nora smiled as Agnes slung her bag over her shoulder and gathered all her library books.

"You too." Agnes nodded so that her red hair bounced in all directions. "Good luck with Humphrey." She departed waving.

"Bye, Agnes!" Nora bade, waving back and Agnes set off grinning.

Once Agnes had gone the shop fell silent. Nora was able to make herself a cup of tea, choose an art book about collaging and enjoy the best part of running a secondhand bookshop which was when there were no customers to interrupt her reading while she was surrounded by thousands of books.

The Secondhand Bookworm was still empty when Nora brought in the boxes and postcard spinner from outside at five o'clock. She dragged in the last box and turned the sign to 'CLOSED', locking the door behind her. While she cashed up the till two people stood pointing at the books in the window. She could hear them reading out the titles, discussing the authors.

After a final message of goodbye to Seatown on the Skype, Nora turned off the computer, ran upstairs and switched off the lights. She then turned off the downstairs lights, set the alarm, dragged the sandbags in front of the door, brushed the sand from her hands and locked up while slinging her bag over her shoulder.

"Do you have any books about collecting mouth organs?" A man's voice asked next to Nora's ear.

Nora jumped and dropped her keys.

"Oh. Sorry." She bent to retrieve them, looking up at the man.

He was almost buried in a huge overcoat with a bowler hat that Nora stared at.

"Did you drop your keys?" He asked the obvious.

"No." Nora muttered before straightening up before him and pondering his first question. "Actually, I don't think I've ever seen any books about *collecting* mouth organs."

He sucked his teeth.

"Well there are some about, love, but aye, they are few and far between." He shuffled to the door and pressed his nose against the window so that the rim of his bowler hat hit the glass and lifted off of the back of his head. "Is the shop closed?"

Nora pointed to the sign that clearly read 'CLOSED'.

"Hmm, I see. So, is it closed?" He repeated, peering inside.

"Yes." Nora said, almost frustrated.

"Shame. Oh well. I wanted a book about mouth organs."

"Sorry about that." Nora said politely. "Good evening."

She turned and hurried quickly away, leaving him peering inside The Secondhand Bookworm with his bowler hat sticking up comically and muttering to himself.

Further up the street Nora nearly collided with White-Lightning Joe who stepped out of the chemist.

"Oh, hi Nora." He greeted glumly as she let out a small squeal and stopped short.

"Hello!" Nora clutched her chest, straightening her bag.

"How are you?" He pondered her solemnly but before she could answer he made one of his funny little noises. "Eeeeeep, Nora. Can you lend me two quid?"

Nora cleared her throat, already prepared.

"I'm not allowed to lend money to customers." She replied quickly.

White-Lightning Joe's eyes widened.

"Huh?"

"Yes, I get told off for lending money to customers. You're one of our customers so I'd best not or Georgina will have my head on the block. Sorry."

"Oh, but we're friends aren't we?" He asked with a wide smile. "So can you just lend me a couple of quid as a friend?"

"I'd better not." She refused, starting to walk away. "I absolutely value my head." She laughed hollowly, waving goodbye. "Sorry, Joe. I'd better go."

"Okay." He sighed, shoulders drooping.

Nora continued climbing the hill, glancing back to see Joe plod along the road, spot Sam outside the butcher shop and decide to attempt to borrow some money from him.

With a sigh of her own, Nora continued to her car.

"One more day to go." She told herself wearily, unlocked the vehicle, jumped inside and pulled away, leaving Sam digging some change out of his pocket and White-Lightning Joe grinning happily from ear to ear.

12 ELVIS AND THE MAP-BOY

Green and white striped marquees, multi coloured bunting, tables of breads and cheeses, barrows of vegetables, a hog roast, Cole Brew tasting barrels, and tents of endless farming products and crafts lined the streets of Castletown, filled up the cobbles and even reached up the hill to the top walls of the castle ruins.

It was market day in the square, a monthly event that brought many shoppers, browsers and tourists to the historical town, and made parking for regulars and shop workers a delightfully difficult mission.

It was Heather who spotted the little tight parking space down a small road near the old blacksmiths so Nora slammed on her brakes and reversed quickly into it before a greedy visitor snapped it up. Once parked, they grabbed their bags, locked up the car and walked down the streets, pausing to sample some local jam and buying two sausage rolls before reaching The Secondhand Bookworm.

They had eaten them both by the time Nora unlocked and opened the bookshop door, stepping inside the dark shop while Heather moved the sandbags in front of the wall outside.

"Pooh, it's a bit smelly this morning." Nora realised with a sniff.

"Only slightly." Heather agreed.

"The carpet's drying out though. The smell will completely go once it's dry." Nora decided optimistically.

On the mat was a faded old plain white postcard. Heather almost stepped on it but Nora bent down to pick it up, noticing that it had been typed on a manual typewriter. Nora paused to read it before she burst out laughing.

Heather had run to turn off the alarm. After punching in the code she looked back at her sister.

"What's that?"

"It's from Mr Hill." Nora waved the postcard, closing the door behind her.

"Is he on holiday?" Heather was incredulous.

"No. Oh, it is too funny." Nora giggled, dropped her bag on to the desk and cleared her throat. "I quote: *To Georgina Pickering or staff. Please would you cancel my reservation, for book, ANTHONY & CLEOPATRA, as I will, not now, be requiring it.? thanks. regards, Vernon Hill'*."

Heather laughed.

"He is rather silly."

"He'll probably change his mind again." Nora sighed, putting the postcard on the cash book and walking around the counter.

"Shall I do the lights?" Heather volunteered.

"Yes please." Nora nodded.

She dropped her bag to the floor along the walkway that led under the first floor staircase while Heather ran off into the depths of the shop and took the stairs two at a time.

Nora sniffed the air, seeing that the dehumidifier bucket contained only a small amount of water. She took the cash tin out of the safe to fill up the till as the door opened and the first customer of the morning peered in.

"Are you open?" A tall thin man carrying a tub of olives asked.

"Just about." Nora smiled, hastily throwing the money into the till and closing the drawer.

As he stepped inside, Nora could hear Heather running down the stairs.

"Any books about the gunpowder plot?" The man asked keenly.

Nora nodded.

"Probably. If so they would be in the history section but we don't have our books listed." She pressed the button on the computer to turn it on.

His brow furrowed.

"Oh dear." He shook his head. "You don't have them on microfiche?"

Nora stared.

"Erm…no, I'm afraid we don't." Nora apologised, aware of Heather who had returned to the front room and was now standing next to her. "We don't list them because they don't last long enough on our shelves." She added with a polite smile.

The man's lips became a straight line.

"Lucky you. Business is good then." He scanned the room for a way into the back and spotted the walkway. "Where do I look?"

"Shall I show you, sir?" Heather offered.

The man shook his head without looking at her.

"I'll find my way thank you." He disappeared into the depths and Heather looked at Nora.

"I just discovered a puddle of water upstairs." She revealed with a grimace.

"What!?!" Nora stared at her.

"It looks as though some water has come through the roof in the top room."

Nora's eyebrows shot up.

"Really? Oh dear. I'd better have a look."

"I'll start putting things out shall I?" Heather offered.

Nora nodded.

"I won't be a minute."

Nora headed out of the front room, past the first customer who was standing reading the list on the wall that showed where all the subjects of books were located, and started up the stairs.

The sounds from the market could be heard on the top floor; talking, laughing, the calling out of prices and a bell ringing as the large, plump town mayor in her bright red outfit walked around the stalls announcing products and delicious offers in her extremely loud voice. Nora discovered the pool of water. She stood and peered up at the ceiling where a round patch of brown damp-looking plaster glowed nastily above her.

"I believe I've seen you before." Nora mused.

She checked the books in the vicinity to see if any had become wet and when she was sure the water had just dripped down from the ceiling she walked all the way back down to the bottom floor.

"Is it bad?" Heather asked, stepping into the shop after clipping one of the black boxes to the wall.

Nora shook her head.

"No. I think it's probably from the gully that runs between the roofs up there. It must be blocked with leaves. We had that storm last night and because of the past heavy rain all week the water must have backed up and sat on the roof overnight, seeping through the ceiling."

"Are you going to phone Georgina?" Heather asked, grabbing the box of free maps.

"Yes, I'll see if she wants me to phone Elvis. He's mended part of the roof once before."

"Elvis?" Heather repeated blankly.

"He runs up ladders with his magnificent quiff." Nora replied, picking up the phone.

Laughing, Heather carried the maps outside.

Georgina agreed with Nora that it must be the gully causing the leak.

"I'm a little bit surprised because we have it cleared out regularly. Let's hope it's just a build-up of leaves that's caused the water to back up and seep through the ceiling and nothing more serious. Give Elvis a ring and he can have a look." She suggested.

"Will do." Nora nodded, digging out the phone book.

"By the way, Humphrey tells me he's taking you to the theatre on Sunday night "

"Yes, I hope it's okay that I stole your place."

Georgina laughed.

"Absolutely. You should get out and enjoy yourself more often."

"Humphrey said you and Mrs Pickering will be going next weekend."

"Yes, I'm looking forward to it."

"I won't spoil it for you."

"You can't spoil it for me! I've read Nicholas Nickleby." Georgina exclaimed.

Nora giggled.

"Oh yes. So you have."

"Have a nice time on Sunday then. Let me know about Elvis."

"I will."

Moments later a woman's voice was answering Elvis's telephone.

"He's running about on someone's roof already this morning." She explained. "I'll get him to give you a call and come and have a look."

"Great. Thanks." Nora appreciated.

When she had returned the receiver to its cradle she joined Heather outside with the last of the boxes.

"It's been a week battling the forces of water." Nora realised, dropping her box onto the pavement and looking up at the roof.

"It has hasn't it? Let's hope it remains dry until Elvis has checked out the gully." Heather agreed.

"It's an easy access to the roof on the fitted ladder up the side of the building at the back of the Indian restaurant. I've been up there before and you can see the whole town and into people's windows."

"Oooh, that sounds exciting and intrusive." Heather grinned.

"But I suspect Elvis will want to use his own ladders." Nora knew.

The clip-clop of slowly plodding horse's hooves sounded along the street.

"Hey, look." Heather indicated.

Nora turned and stared up the road.

A fully clad knight in armour rode on a magnificent white steed that was decorated in medieval drapery with a squire walking beside him. They were heading along the High Street, probably toward the castle ruins.

"You don't see that every day." Nora smiled.

"Do you have a ribbon?" Heather asked. "For his jousting spear as he goes past."

"No!" Nora laughed.

They watched them pass by and the knight tipped his helmet at them.

"There must be an event on in the castle ruins today." Heather decided. "It will be so exciting when the Duke of Cole rebuilds his estate and moves in."

"Yes, it will be, I'm sure." Nora agreed dreamily.

They returned into the shop where Nora sent Heather off to empty the little bit of water from the bucket under the dehumidifier pipe.

A man in a leather jacket arrived, smiled at Nora and looked around the room.

"Do you have a poetry section?" He asked.

"Upstairs." Nora pointed.

He headed off as two women slowly entered the shop behind him, laden with wicker baskets of vegetables.

"Careful Audrey, the step's deep."

"Yes, very deep. Watch yourself, Genevieve."

"Careful as you go." Genevieve warned. "Oh it's a very deep step. Very deep."

"Shall I take your carrots, Audrey?"

"No I'm alright." Audrey stepped down and made a lot of fussing noises as she approached the counter. Nora was reminded of a snuffling hamster. She stopped before Nora to peer at her out of very pale blue eyes.

"Hello, dear. Do you have any 'Mills and Boon'?"

Nora watched the lady hoist up her knickers, staring at Nora expectantly.

"I'm sorry but we don't." Nora replied.

Audrey sighed.

"Every secondhand bookshop I go into never has any 'Mills and Boons'." She complained.

"Do you have any Danielle Steele?" Genevieve asked.

"Well..." Nora hesitated, wondering if it was worth it. "All of our fiction is in the paperback room upstairs..."

"Oh we don't do stairs." The women said in unison.

"Thought so." Nora muttered to herself.

Audrey picked up her basket of vegetables.

"Don't forget your carrots." Genevieve remarked and gave Nora a stern look. "You should have all your paperbacks downstairs."

"Yes, we should." Nora agreed grimly.

Genevieve gave a short nod and followed Audrey out, lingering on the step while complaining about the depth of it until they were on the street and letting a group of people enter The Secondhand Bookworm in their place.

Heather came back. She put down the freshly emptied bucket and popped the pipe over the top.

"Shall I go and make us a cup of tea? I think we'll need it to start off the day."

"Please do." Nora agreed as she saw more customers approaching, carrying baskets of vegetables and pies or armfuls of corn dollies.

Heather headed off to the kitchen leaving Nora to check the Skype Chat and the shop emails on the computer as the new customers filled up the room.

An ancient looking old man in a tweed suit with a walking stick entered The Secondhand Bookworm accompanied by his middle-aged daughter. She in turn was accompanied by her own daughter, a girl of about seventeen or eighteen with an upturned nose, long red hair and freckles. They had come into The Secondhand Bookworm before, so Nora smiled tentatively. The old man was a retired Major and his family were loud and important.

"Now daddy!" His daughter said loudly. "We're going to look at these books."

"Ah, yes." He nodded. "Ah, yes, good books. Many books. Too many books for one person. Ah, Bishop's Waltham. Grand place. Yes, been there! Been there for tea haven't we Juliet." He said, noticing a book in the topography section.

"Yes, daddy!" Juliet sighed loudly with a long-suffering glance at Nora. "Don't let him leave the shop."

Nora smiled politely and watched her walk over to the art books.

"Daddy. Unity and I are going to the Shakespeare section upstairs, okay? Don't wander off daddy. Wait for us here and look at all the books." Juliet said loudly.

"Oh mummy, don't treat him like a child. We're going upstairs Grandpa." Unity addressed him just as condescendingly.

"A pig in a poke." The Major replied, studying his next book. His long wrinkled fingers grasped it off of the shelf. "Yes, a pig in a poke. Looks good. Good for words. A pig in a poke."

Unity gave a sickly smile to Nora and she and her mother left the front, heading into the back.

"Blue gum clippers and whale ships." The Major next exclaimed. "Large sails. A nice book. Interesting. Very interesting."

Nora watched him thoughtfully, tempted to take a photo of him to send in a text to Cara with his quotes and phrases.

The man in the leather jacket returned.

"Glen Frankland, his life. The years of struggle." The Major exclaimed behind him. "A colourful book. Yes, amusing. Very amusing. Good for reading in the waiting room of a train station."

The man in the leather jacket ignored the Major and popped his own book onto the counter before Nora.

"I'm going to a hole in the wall and I'll pay for that when I come back." He announced.

"Okay." Nora nodded, putting it beside the cash book.

"Blue gum clippers and whale ships." The Major repeated behind him. "Interesting. Very interesting."

Nora felt the urge to laugh. She watched the man in the leather jacket head off.

"Where's the nearest hole in the wall?" He then asked, hand on the door handle.

"Only a few doors away in the wall outside the bank." Nora gestured.

"I'll be back in a moment."

He left and the Major flinched at the sound of the door closing loudly.

"Shouldn't shut doors hard. Damages hinges." He said and took up another book. "Look Juliet. Armies on the Danube 1809. Marvellous. A fantastic book. A good read. I might have that. Yes, I might have that Juliet to read. A grand read by the fireside after tea. I'll buy that Juliet." He opened it, pondering the pages solemnly.

"Daddy, we're going upstairs!" Juliet's voice sailed back impatiently.

"We're through here, Grandpa. Why can't he come up?" Unity's voice accompanied what sounded like the stamp of a foot.

Nora watched the Major turn.

"What Juliet? What? Juliet I have a book I'm going to buy. Where's my money Juliet? Oh. I say, a grand book. Look here. Another grand book." He placed the Danube book aside and took up a different book. "The aircraft carrier story 1908-1945. Hmmm, interesting. Good to study. Maybe the children would like it. Lots of pictures. Hmmm."

The man in the leather jacket came back clutching a ten pound note. He held it out to Nora.

"Thank you." She opened the front of the book. "Four pounds please."

He handed it over and Nora noticed a black stone in the palm of his hand.

"Thank you. Six pounds change. Would you like a bag?" She asked, staring at the stone.

"A paper bag." He replied.

Nora leaned over, picked one up and put the book inside. He took it, pulled the book out and laughed to himself.

"There's a poem in here that reminds me of the Prime Minister. I watch him on TV and think to myself, what does he remind me of, and it's a Betjeman poem. Do you agree? Look, read it. Read it slowly."

"Oh erm…okay." Nora took the book and skimmed the verses which mentioned boils and Hell among other things.

"The Prime Minister says happy things on TV and yet they all have a sad twist about them. You know, kind of like, we went to the sea and we had a lovely time. But we all got burnt by the sun." He popped the stone into his ear laughing and took the book back from Nora.

"I suppose he does." She said, more disturbed about what the purpose of the stone going into his ear hole was.

"Yes I thought so. The church mouse is a nice poem. Do you read poetry?"

"Yes, some." Nora replied.

"Yes, it's nice to read before you go to sleep. Makes you laugh." He said and chortled loudly, turning away. "Goodbye."

Nora watched him leave and then the Major spoke, making her jump.

"Michelangelo." He said. "A good book on the artist. Yes, he was a sculptor and artist. Beautiful art. Interesting read. Nice for framing."

"Do you have any comic books?" A man called in from the doorway.

He had several children around him and one of them barged between his legs.

"Do you have any children's books?" The boy demanded.

"Tobias! I asked the lady if they had any comic books! Don't interrupt." His father exclaimed.

"We have a whole room of children's books upstairs. I don't think we have any comic books though."

"Can we go upstairs dad? Can we dad?" The boy shouted.

"Look! Look at all the books!" A girl joined in.

"Alright, alright, go upstairs and I'll tell your mum and brother where we are." The father sighed. "LESLIE!" He yelled down the street. "WE'RE GOING UPSTAIRS!"

"Dad can I come?" The smallest child asked.

"Yes of course you can you fairy cake." He picked her up and carried her in. "Upstairs, eh?"

"Just follow the others through there; the stairs are in the back room." Nora said, watching the children run off shouting excitedly.

"Okay." He carried his daughter and trailed the others so that soon their voices disappeared into the distance amidst creaks and stamps and several crashes.

Heather appeared with two mugs of tea.

"I cleaned the whole kitchen." She said with a grin.

"Oh, well done! I've been having lots of fun out here." Nora grimaced in a low voice.

"I could hear." Heather nodded and sat down, popping the mugs onto the mouse mat.

The Major made his way towards the back room where they could hear him reading out the different titles of bus and train books. Heather sipped her tea, watching the people outside with their bags of market produce.

"Audrey just dropped her carrots." She noticed and she and Nora laughed.

A Skype message appeared on the computer screen. Nora leaned forward to read it.

'Good morning, ladies. We have the smelliest customers in today. Agnes.'

Nora laughed.

'Ours are all loud.' She typed back.

Heather gave her an amused look. They drank their tea and served a few customers, pleased to sell an expensive book about porcelain from the window.

Once they had finished their drinks Heather ventured upstairs to put away the last of the lingering books about the shop and the remaining paperbacks that Nora and Agnes had priced the day before.

Soon the Major, his daughter and granddaughter returned.

"How much will you sell me those for?" Unity asked Nora, dropping her small collection of books about costumes onto the counter and prodding them will a well-manicured finger.

"Oh...well, whatever is pencilled inside them." Nora replied, slightly afraid of the girl.

The freckles over her upturned nose seemed to flash

"What? For this many? I don't get a discount?"

"Unity." Her mother sighed with a small smile.

"What mother? I'm spending money and I can at least have a discount. How much shall I get?" She asked Nora determinedly.

"A pig in a poke." The Major read and chuckled. "Interesting. Interesting words."

Unity looked at her grandfather.

"Is he getting that?" She asked ironically.

Nora began to add up Unity's books.

"No. Daddy you don't want that. We're getting this book on ships for you daddy."

"Yes Juliet. Where is my wallet?" The Major asked, putting back 'A Pig in a Poke'.

"You already gave me the money, daddy." Juliet sighed and rolled her eyes at Nora.

Nora felt sorry for the Major who stood waiting with a suddenly vacant expression.

"The books come to thirty two pounds fifty." Nora concluded.

"I shall give you thirty pounds shall I? For buying so many." Unity settled, taking out a hideous gold purse.

"Sadly it isn't my decision to make." Nora decided to refuse.

"Why's that then?" Unity shot back sharply. "Where's the person who makes the decisions then?" Her hazel eyes glittered and Nora was sure she heard her foot stamp again.

"Just pay the money, Unity." Juliet laughed falsely.

"I shall put one back." Unity decided triumphantly and dragged the small pile toward her.

"You want them all Unity so just pay for them." Juliet snapped and the snide smile vanished from Unity's face.

For a moment, the young woman seemed to wrestle with wanting to throw a tantrum and Nora half hoped to see her cast her arms in the air and roll about the floor shrieking, but with a small grunt she thrust thirty five pounds at Nora.

"Thank you." Nora picked up the notes from about the counter top.

"Juliet! This book is marvellous, Juliet. A Pig in a Poke." The Major suddenly shouted.

"Oh my…!" Unity clutched her chest. "Please stop him from doing that!"

"I know daddy. But we've decided on this book about ships." Juliet returned loudly. As Nora bagged up Unity's books, Juliet thrust a ten pound note at Nora.

"Have a bag too, mummy." Unity decided. "Can we have a bag for this one too please?"

"Of course." Nora punched the price into the till and bagged up the book just as a white van pulled up outside the shop.

Several large ladders were on the roof rack and rock and roll music played loudly through the opened windows as the van reversed to a stop on the double yellow lines a little further to the side.

"Ugh. *Elvis* is here." Unity grimaced, spotting the source of the rock and roll music.

Nora tried not to smirk as she passed Juliet the bag. It was indeed Elvis who had arrived to look at the roof.

"Come on, darling. Come now, daddy!" Juliet announced grandly and they left the counter, moving aside as a tall, thin man in a blue boiler suit practically skipped into the shop with his dark, oiled hair styled in a magnificent quiff.

"Howdy, Nora! You have a leak." He greeted cheerfully.

"That was quick!" Nora was impressed.

"I just finished a job early this morning and had the ladders on the van so when the wife phoned I thought I may as well pop in and have a look on my way through."

Nora pointed above.

"The puddle is in the front room of the top floor. You can see where the water has come in through the ceiling." Nora explained. "Would you like me to take you up and show you?"

"No need, Nora. I'll go and have a gander." He set off briskly, singing a loud rock and roll song much to Nora's amusement.

Nora's smile soon vanished however when her next customer stepped in.

A boy, approximately ten years of age, wearing the largest glasses Nora had ever seen, ran into the shop at top speed and straight to the Ordnance survey maps through the walkway. A book fell off the counter in his wake turbulence and one of the Shire Book spinners spun slightly around.

"Oh. Map-Boy." Nora grimaced grimly. She leaned to the side and watched him stop before her tidy section of Ordnance survey maps where he promptly pulled out a random pink and white map.

"Yes, this one today, Fairfax." He told his invisible friend, opening it out and examining the layout. "Or shall we? No, maybe another. What do you say, Fairfax? It's your blinking trip after all!"

It was a routine that kept him occupied for half an hour and left the whole section in complete chaos when he was finished.

Map-Boy's real name was Rodney and his mother dropped him off at The Secondhand Bookworm while she went shopping about the farmer's market or town almost every Saturday. Although Nora had once complained to her that her son messed up the entire Ordnance Survey map section she had just smiled sweetly and apologised, saying that it was Rodney and Fairfax's little obsession and they were allowed to buy one map a week for their imaginary trips. Numerous times Nora had tried to encourage Rodney to look at the children's books upstairs with Fairfax instead, but he always relayed Fairfax's rather rude refusals and seemed to get more much enjoyment pulling all the maps off the shelves before he and Fairfax chose one to buy. Nora supposed it was better than his being obsessed with mindless computer games.

Nora peered further around the book shelves.

"Is there a specific one you're interested in today, Rodney?" She asked him.

"No. But Fairfax will find a map sure enough!" Rodney replied, pulling out a large pile and rummaging through them determinedly. He gave Nora a wide, enthusiastic grin.

"Please put them back where you found them?" She asked hopefully.

He grinned.

"Fairfax says that's not my job." He shrugged. "It's yours."

"Cheeky!" Nora rebuked.

"It's not my job is it, Fairfax?" He snorted with laughter and continued opening the maps.

Nora growled, sat down before the computer and told Seatown on the Skype about his arrival in the hope of some sympathy.

A text message arrived on Nora's phone while she waited to hear from Seatown. She dug it out of her back pocket and saw it was from Humphrey. Because no one was around, Nora quickly opened it.

'Hi, Nora. I know we've made a date tomorrow night but I happened to see the Seaside Cinema in Piertown is showing a back to back run of The Lord of the Rings movie trilogy tonight, something to do with the Piertown Tolkien Society celebrating its fiftieth anniversary (are you a member?) It starts at seven. How do you fancy coming along with me? I know they're among your favourite films and the cinema will be filled with your kind of peeps. My treat xx' Humphrey had written.

Nora's eyes widened. She chewed her bottom lip, thoughtfully. It was too tempting to pass up!

'Hi, Humphrey. No, I'm not an (official) member of the Piertown Tolkien Society but that's definitely something I should join! You twisted my arm! I'd love to see the movies with you. Can you actually sit through three films in a row though? Xx' She sent back, dubiously (Nora was a bit of a movie addict and would have no problem sitting for almost seven hours engrossed in the world of JRR Tolkien – she had done it several times with Heather).

A moment later:

'With you next to me, absolutely! I can pick you up from The Secondhand Bookworm when you finish and we can grab something to eat first? Xx'

'How about I meet you at the pier for six? We can go for a walk and then grab some food in the cinema's adjoining café xx' Nora proposed.

'It's a date. I'll be wearing a black baseball cap xx' Nora snorted.

'It's not a blind date, Humphrey! I know what you look like. By the way, do we have to dress up as hobbits? X' Her lips twitched as she pressed send.

A moment later.

'Not likely! Although you'd make the perfect she-elf xx'

Nora chuckled.

'See you later xx' She sent.

'Can't wait xx'

Nora smiled and put her phone away.

By the time Agnes had replied from Seatown, several shelves of ordnance survey maps had been emptied and Map-Boy sat down crossed-legged in the way, absorbed in an open copy of number 121 with a hundred maps surrounding him and discussing a tandem trip with Fairfax.

"Are you sure, Fairfax? Well I won't do all the blinking peddling along that road I tell you!" He folded the map up but then pulled several more off of the lower shelves close to him, stretching out his legs and leaning back against the side of the staircase. "Or maybe this one, Fairfax? What? Too many dog poops on the road? We can't have that."

Nora was about to point out the mess he was making when Elvis came running down the stairs singing loudly.

Map-Boy ignored him, laughing at something Fairfax said.

"As already concluded, it's the gully." Elvis announced, stepping over Map-Boy's legs to stand at the counter. "Hopefully it's just debris and crap blown up there by the wind but I can't tell of course until I have a look so I'll go up now and check it out."

"Okay." Nora nodded as he turned to leave the shop. "The ladder at the back of the buildings is easy access." She called after him.

"I have my own ladders, thanks." He called back cheerfully.

An immense clattering of said ladders sounded barely a moment later. Nora watched with interest as a huge ladder came off of Elvis's van roof. Without any hesitation, Elvis extended it, leaned it against the wall so that it was across the whole pavement and promptly ran up the whole length like Spiderman. Nora had managed to reach the door and look up just in time to see his legs disappear over the top. She shuddered at his total indifference to the height.

"I do hope he has a ladder licence." A man's voice joked as he stopped and looked up.

Nora glanced at him but was distracted by the sudden build-up of people on the pavement each side of the ladder.

"Oh, how awful." An old lady shook her head, stepping into the road.

The sound of a car horn made Nora jump but the woman determinedly walked into the road around the ladder.

Everyone else followed her from both angles. Suddenly there was a queue of traffic as people shuffled in the road, determined to avoid walking under the ladder.

Heather appeared and stepped over Map-Boy.

"People would rather get run over than walk under the ladder!" Nora said, watching everyone, amazed.

Heather joined her by the door to watch too.

"I think it should change to being a source of bad luck to walk *around* a ladder. That lady almost got squashed by a bus." She cringed.

The ladder began to creak as Elvis's legs appeared over the top. In half a moment he had creaked down to the bottom and waited for a stream of tutting old ladies to pass around him before he returned into the shop with Nora and Heather.

"Well, it's going to need a bit of a repair job but I've taken some photos and I can write out a quote for Georgina and get it to her by Monday." Elvis explained cheerfully. "I think the roof will last well enough until then. I've removed most of the mud and leaves that were up there in the whole gully, blocking the flow of rain water into the drainpipes."

"That's excellent." Nora appreciated.

"It's not too much work to patch it up but it might do some damage if I don't remove it all and give it some TLC soon. So, I'll get onto that as quick as possible. Meanwhile, I'd best remove the ladder before someone gets run over and go onto my next job." He stuck his thumb up and left, singing loudly as he took down his ladder, loaded it up and sped away with his rock and roll music fading into the distance.

Map-Boy jumped up and ran out leaving a pile of chaos behind him.

"Aren't you going to buy a map today?" Nora called after him.

"No, Fairfax wants to take a train!" He called back and set off hunting for his mother.

Nora and Heather looked at one another before Nora returned to the seats behind the counter and sunk into the chair.

"I think that's my job before lunchtime then." Heather grinned with a nod at the Ordnance survey section. She promptly set out to reorganise the maps as the town crier arrived in her large red town crier costume and loudly rang her bell to announce that there would be jousting up at the castle ruins.

.

13 THE SECRET WEAPON

Nora and Heather were sitting down after a particularly busy two hours over the middle of the day. They had both had their lunches and were quickly approaching meeting their Saturday target of one thousand pounds in takings after two trade buyers had been in.

A jolly Mr Bennett and his wife had spent two hundred and seventy pounds on gardening books and a grumpy Mr Periwinkle had bought several bags of leather books, some early children's books and a first edition. Nora had watched happily as he had picked out all the ones she had polished the day before.

The shop was relatively tidy. After battling with endless requests for discounts all morning, both Nora and Heather felt quite exhausted.

A man stepped through the doorway and Nora blinked in surprise as a scattering of beautiful coloured lights danced around the room. Heather nudged her arm, motioning to a cane that the man was holding. On the top of it was a big crystal which had caught the sunlight streaming in through the front windows.

The man wore a long ankle-length leather coat and deep red leather cowboy boots. He stood before the Folio Society section.

"Do you think he's a friend of Spencer Brown's?" Heather whispered, biting into a biscuit. "He looks like a magician."

Nora chuckled.

"Spencer Brown isn't a magician." She corrected. "He's a medium. Into the occult."

Heather giggled.

"Oh, well maybe that man is a medium, too."

Nora and Heather were distracted from the man with the cane by another customer arriving.

A woman with blond hair sticking out in a magnificent back-combed style seemed to float toward the counter and Nora edged back a little when she stopped.

"Hello." Nora greeted.

"Where are your books about Zionism?" The woman almost whispered.

"Erm..." Nora glanced at Heather who shrugged, examining the lady curiously.

The lady's eyes widened and she continued to stare at Nora.

"What's Zionism?" Nora asked.

The lady's eyes widened further and her bottom lip quivered.

"Zionism." She whispered with a panicked expression. "Relating to Judaism."

"Oh. Oh yes, of course. I have heard of it before." Nora recalled. "If you wanted religion it would be..."

"Yes!" She whispered tragically. "Religion."

"Upstairs." Nora pointed and watched her seemingly drift away from the counter as if blown along by a small fan and head towards the walkway leading into the back.

Heather and Nora looked at one another but the man with the cane approached them. Nora blinked in the colours that sparkled from the crystal-topped stick as he stopped in a shaft of sunlight before her.

"Can I trouble you for some water?" He asked. "I need to take some pills."

"Yes, of course, sir." Nora saw two white tablets in his hand.

"Lovely Folio Society books by the way. I'll take the set of Churchill and the Anthony Trollope's please. But first a glass of water." He wiped his brow and blinked at Nora.

Heather stood up and Nora nodded for her to fetch him one. Meanwhile, a regular customer stepped down into the shop, curling his lip behind the man with the cane.

"I don't know why I came out on a Saturday and on a market day too. I hate people." Mr Clegg announced to the room.

The man with the cane turned slowly and looked at Mr Clegg.

Mr Clegg was a large, hefty man, not too overweight but built hefty, with small eyes, white hair, thin lips and a big, long nose. He stepped down and huffed and puffed further inside the front room, unhooking the strap of a big satchel from his shoulder.

"May I?" He asked as he dumped the bag behind the counter. "Bloody people everywhere. Still, I might as well have a look to see what new offerings you have. Not that I can buy anymore really as I spend coming onto three hundred a month in both your branches. But I was here buying some bread and thought I'd have a look. But I hate people."

Nora bit back a smile.

"Well hopefully you won't find anything you want today, Mr Clegg." She said.

He huffed on a laugh and started to browse the antiquarian books.

The man with the cane ran a hand over his clammy face, waiting for some water.

"Could you please box up those Folio Society books for me?" He asked Nora.

"Certainly."

"I'll pay for them now but collect them in a few hours." He added.

"That's fine, sir."

Heather arrived with the water and passed the glass to the man with the cane. She joined Nora by the Folio Society books and helped take the chosen books from the shelves.

"You see who's here?" Nora whispered.

"Who?" Heather whispered back.

"The man behind the counter looking at the antiquarians." Nora elaborated.

"Oh. *Him*." Heather rolled her eyes with a smirk.

"He has a secret weapon." Nora whispered and screwed up her nose.

"What?" Heather almost laughed.

"You won't be laughing if he uses it." Nora warned.

Heather continued to giggle as she took the Anthony Trollope's to the counter. They ran the prices through the till and the man with the cane passed back the empty glass.

"Thanks." He nodded, taking out his cheque book. "Don't worry. It's not catching."

Nora smiled sympathetically, hoping he was right. He looked frail, clammy and pale. He paid for the books and left Heather and Nora to box them up, stepping out of the door with one last smattering of coloured light.

Mr Clegg was rummaging through the leather books behind the counter so Heather moved the box of Folio Society books out of the way.

A family entered, headed by a man in a long black coat, a huge beard and a cane of his own. His wife had waist-length red hair and their son had a matching cane.

"What is it with canes today?" Nora whispered warily.

"Theirs have skull-heads on the top." Heather nodded.

Nora's eyebrows shot up.

The young boy looked sulky and moody and stamped towards the motoring shelves.

"Look at these, Merlin." The woman called to him.

"Ain't interested." He brushed her off.

He left his mother and father by the art area, spying the leather books. Nora nudged Heather's arm, gesturing at Mr Clegg who saw the boy approach. When Mr Clegg noticed him coming, he shook his head and edged away. The boy named Merlin took a leather book from the shelf and scoffed at the price.

"Yeah...right." Merlin mocked and went to take another one off when the enormous sound of breaking wind came from Mr Clegg.

Merlin almost dropped his cane and he and the skull on top of it gawped at Mr Clegg.

Mr Clegg scowled at him.

Nora covered her face while Heather did her best not to laugh. Merlin ran back to his mother, leaving Mr Clegg alone, just as he liked it.

"That's his secret weapon." Nora whispered and Heather almost doubled up with silent laughter. "It's not funny, Heather! It's obscene."

Heather was laughing so much that she had to retreat to the kitchen. When she came back shortly afterwards she was surprised to see Nora alone at the desk.

"Did Mr Clegg with his secret weapon scare everyone off?" Heather asked, still laughing. She popped two freshly made cups of tea next to the mouse mat.

"Hmm!" Nora frowned but her lips twitched.

"What a terrible tactic for getting rid of people." Heather decided.

"No shame." Nora agreed.

Heather chuckled.

"None at all. But it looks like it worked."

"Mr Clegg has never liked people and can't bear looking at books with people near him." Nora explained. She shuddered. "It might be useful for him but one time he did that next to my ear and I'm scarred for life."

Heather squealed.

"Bleurgh! The ups and downs of working in The Secondhand Bookworm." She giggled.

"And there are a lot more where that came from." Nora sighed. "Well, let's forget about Mr Clegg. We have some books to look for from Seatown."

She scrolled up the Skype messages and found the requests.

"Ooh, I'll go and have a look." Heather volunteered after a slurp of her tea.

Nora scribbled them down and passed the slip of paper to Heather who put down her mug and headed off.

The market was being dismantled out in the town square and the constant sound of metal poles bashing the cobbles began to make Nora's eye twitch as the marquees were taken down.

She watched the large town crier stomp across the square and almost trip over a green pole that was waiting to be loaded into a truck. Her bell rang out as she dropped it on the cobbles so she decided to shout alongside it.

"Oh yey. Oh yey." She yelled, straightening her red coat and britches. "Hear ye all." She bent down and picked up her bell. "At three o'clock there will be Morris Dancing in the Square. God save the Queen."

"Oh, great." Nora grimaced, glancing at the clock. She saw that there was half an hour to go before a long ordeal of jangly bells to give her a headache.

A young man entered the shop and grinned brightly.

"Hi! How are you?" He greeted over-enthusiastically.

"Fine." Nora replied warily, spotting an enormous bag he was practically dragging with him across the floor.

"Lovely day, isn't it!" He stopped before the till.

Nora remained silent.

He grinned at her, winked and then gestured his head of brown curls down to the bag at his feet.

"Now I'm sure as the cold weather starts to close in on us you'll be wishing you had a warmer quilt?" He said dramatically.

"Pardon?" Nora stared at him.

"Well madam, we're doing a large deal on quilts from a warehouse sale today and would like to offer you a variety of togs from duck and goose fifteen togs down to the lighter polyester eight togs..."

"Do you have quilts in that bag?" Nora stood up to see.

"I certainly do, madam. Sadly I only have ten togs quilts left as the rest of your surrounding work colleagues have cleared me out of the other togs today but I can offer them to you at a price to make them burn with envy." He opened the bag with a flourish. "One ten togs quilt for fifteen quid madam, that's fifteen quid for a ten togs quilt to you today."

Nora shook her head, wanting to laugh.

"No, thank you."

"Thirteen quid for you madam, thirteen quid for a ten togs quilt." He said without his grin moving. He eased one half out of his bag.

"I actually have a quilt that erm...works quite well thank you." Nora declined.

His grin faded.

"Right you are." He stuffed the quilt violently back in his bag and closed the case. "Sure I can't..."

Nora shook her head.

"Have a nice day." He concluded drearily and dragged the bag towards the door, up over the step and out into the street where he stopped the first person he came to and repeated the same discourse all over again.

Heather returned with the list.

"No luck with any of those requests." She sighed, sitting down and taking up her tea.

"You just missed the opportunity to buy a ten togs quilt." Nora told her grimly.

Heather snorted into her tea but didn't get a chance to say anything as another customer entered.

"Oh no. The man with the breath." Heather whispered hard and shrank back behind her tea mug.

Nora watched the accused man step down and close the door behind him hard on the sound of the metal poles still banging on the cobbles.

"Hello. I really shouldn't, I know I shouldn't but I must have a look." He grinned, rubbing his hands together and cracking his knuckles like gunpowder as he walked across the room and headed for the stairs.

Nora smiled but when he had gone Heather waved her hand frantically before her face and sipped her tea.

"What do you mean the man with the breath?" Nora asked once he was creaking loudly up the stairs.

"I was here on my own once and he spent ages looking at the books behind the counter. I thought old granny Parker was in here wearing her fur coats." Heather explained cryptically.

Nora paused.

"Do you mean that his breath has the scent of mothballs?" She deciphered.

Heather nodded with a grimace.

"It engulfed me."

"Maybe he doesn't want the moths eating away his wooden teeth." Nora suggested.

Heather laughed but shuddered.

The telephone started to ring. Nora hoped it wasn't Mr Hill. She picked up the receiver.

"The Secondhand Bookworm." Nora greeted cheerfully.

"Hi, Nora. It's me." Georgina's voice sailed back.

"Ah, hello. How are things?"

"Good. I'm writing a profile on an internet dating site."

Nora blinked. Before she could say anything, Georgina continued.

"Elvis told me all about the guttering. We'll get that sorted out next week. Fluffy! That's not edible! Chubby! Don't sit on Fluffy." Georgina next said, speaking to one of her Leonberger dogs. "Honestly, it's like having children sometimes."

Nora grinned.

"It certainly sounds like it." She agreed. "Er…Georgina, about that internet profile?" She prompted.

"Yes! I wanted to ask your advice. How would you describe my hair? Humphrey's not been much help. I keep telephoning him but he's in another one of his meetings again up in London as I expect you know. He keeps giving me one word answers such as 'black' or 'short', not poetical, alluring or helpful at all!"

Nora bit back a smile.

"What is this internet dating site? Is it safe?"

"Yes, I had Humphrey check it out for me last night. It's one of the good ones, where you pay a lot of money and can meet wealthy businessmen and politicians." Georgina enthused.

Nora screwed up her nose.

"Each to their own."

"We're not getting any younger. If you like we can do you a profile in case things don't work out between you and my brother, which I wouldn't be surprised about because he's annoying. He described my height as midget-like."

Nora smothered a laugh.

"I'd be happy to buy you one. It's only ten pounds a month." Georgina urged.

"No thank you, Georgina! That's very kind of you but I don't think internet dating is for me."

"Suit yourself." Georgina chuckled. "There's a section here about interests. Hmm. What do you think? I don't want to put off a man who doesn't like Barbie-dolls and they are my secret collecting fetish."

"As long as you write positive things and take care with your grammar, oh, and also maybe avoid clichés then you should be fine." Nora advised.

"That sounds good."

"You should write 'must like dogs'." Nora next proposed. "Then you rule out the horrid men who don't like dogs. And don't put in things like your height or your weight or your hair colour; maybe be a bit of a mystery and let them check out your photos."

"I like the sound of that!" Georgina enthused. "Thanks, Nora. I'll phone Cara and pick her brains, too. I've a good feeling about this. Hopefully I'll meet Mr Right and if not then I'll agree to settle with Mr Make-Do as long as he's mildly good-looking! I'd better go and take the dogs for a walk before they eat Fluffy!"

Nora shook her head, bemused.

"Is this what happens when you reach thirty-five?" She teased.

"I guess so." Georgina laughed. "Enjoy the rest of the day in mad town!"

"Speak soon." Nora grinned and they hung up.

"Dare I ask?" Heather smirked.

"Best not." Nora chuckled and picked up her tea.

A man arrived with a box of books which he told them he had acquired from sorting out his ancient gran's house during the week, warning them against catching The Bends or Space Madness from the tatty tomes about diving or astronaut-ing.

Nora suspected he was serious.

After turning him and his books away and selling some cheap paperbacks, giving directions to the chemist shop, the short term car park and telling people the time when the Morris Dancers would be dancing, Mothball Man returned. Heather picked up the empty tea mugs and hurried into the kitchen to wash them up.

"I can never resist when I find what I'm looking for, no matter the cost." The man shared, and immediately memories of old granny Parker and her fur coats overwhelmed Nora.

Nora coughed, leaning back slightly as she looked at the book he placed before her.

"Ah, we don't actually get many books about gypsies and Romani." She nodded behind her hand, seeing the first book on his pile.

"I can believe that. Lots of people are interested in the subject now." Mothball Man agreed.

He had two more books about boxing and one about herbs. Nora quickly ran the prices through the till and popped them into a bag.

"Thank you. Must rush today so I can't browse your antiquarian books but I shall be back, I shall be back." He said, taking up the bag and heading off.

"Bye." Nora coughed.

When he had left she picked up the dusting spray and cleaned the counter with an inhale of the dispersed scent of lemons which made her sneeze.

"Oh good. He's gone." Heather sighed with relief, coming back.

"And thankfully the market has finally gone too!" Nora noticed.

The large form of a man loomed in the doorway. He met Nora's eyes and stared at her questioningly.

Nora smiled in return, shaking her head.

"Na, na, see, see, we don't even have to speak now. Ah, one day, one day. One day you'll have some Muffin the Moo." He mumbled, turning and walking off.

"Muffin the *Moo*?" Heather looked at Nora.

"He means Muffin the Mule. It's the way he pronounces it sometimes." She explained as the telephone rang once more.

This time Heather answered it. When she started speaking cheerfully with a customer, Nora watched a woman bound into the shop. She closed the door behind the sound of approaching jangling bells that heralded the arrival of the Morris Men, and bounded up to the counter, looking about her.

"Hi!" She greeted, peering through giant square rimmed glasses. "Are these books all secondhand?"

"Yes." Nora nodded.

"Ah. Shame. I'm an author and have just had my first novel published." She pulled a paperback out of her bag and extended it towards Nora. "It's set in the First World War and it is based upon my grandfather's life during that time."

"That's interesting." She nodded politely.

"Oh thanks, yes, thank you, thanks! Here, I'll sign a copy for you." She pulled out a bright blue pen with pink feathers on the top. "Now, what's your name?"

"Erm...Nora." Nora replied, watching her, slightly bemused.

"Hi Nora. Enjoy the story. Love Helen Martina. XX." She said as she wrote and passed it to Nora.

"That's nice." Nora smiled.

"I was hoping to have all the local bookshops stock it, sale or return, but as you're all secondhand...?"

"Sorry, I'm afraid we wouldn't be able to do that." Nora assured, flicking through the pages of the novel.

"It's a great story." Helen Martina pointed out. "I had to fill it with coarse language before they would publish it, my grandfather probably spun in his grave, not that he had one because he was actually blown to smithereens on the beach at Normandy, that's how it ends, but look on page one; I gave him Tourette's Syndrome so the first word is..." She glanced about and stopped herself with a chuckle.

Nora closed the book.

"Oh dear. They wouldn't publish it unless you did that?"

"No, said it was too boring. Ha ha, it is funny though. I hope you enjoy it!" She closed her handbag and slipped the strap over her arm. "Bye. Thanks, thank you, thanks." She waved all the way to the door and closed it behind her.

Nora threw the book over her shoulder into the bin.

Heather's eyes widened and she hung up from speaking with her caller.

"What was that all about?" She asked, half amused, looking at the book in the bin.

"A new author signed their new book for me."

"And you threw it away?!" Heather laughed.

"That was rather mean wasn't it, but it didn't look like my kind of thing. It was full of eff words." She explained as Heather fished it out.

"I'll give it a read. I like to support new authors." Heather volunteered. "I'll give her a review on *Good Reads* when I'm done."

"Just cover your ears against all the swearing." Nora suggested.

Heather giggled.

She and Nora then stood before the bay window, peering through the shelving to watch the Morris Men set up outside in the square. A small, eager crowd gathered.

"What a treat! An afternoon of dancing men." Heather grinned as they watched sticks and swords and handkerchiefs fly about the square.

"A real delight." Nora laughed, shaking her head.

Towards the end of the day a few customers milled about The Secondhand Bookworm, passing the time until their buses arrived or their trains were due in at the station. Nora was getting ready to send Heather around with the shop umbrella to open it up and oust them all out, but first she was counting up the small change in the till and bagging it up into money bags.

The man with the cane had returned to collect his box of books. He had been grateful to Heather for carrying the box to his car where she had returned contemplating getting a crystal-topped cane of her own. They had spent half an hour looking up Swarovski Crystal Dress Canes on the internet until it was time to start packing up.

"Excuse me." An old lady stuck her head in the opened doorway. "Can I have a free map of Castletown please?"

"Oh. Have they all gone?" Heather was bent over picking up giant leaves that had blown in through the doorway throughout the day before setting about bringing in the wares from outside.

"There are only maps of Seatown in the box." The lady pointed out.

"It's the same one." Heather explained helpfully.

"I assure you it is not!"

"The Castletown map folds out."

"Oh! Does it?" The old lady shuffled off and pulled one out of the box. "It folds out Barney." She said loudly.

"It folds out?! IT FOLDS OUT?" An old man's voice repeated. "Well, they could have made that clearer!"

There was the sound of unfolding paper and a big discussion about where to get a glass of Prosecco on the map. Eventually they set off across the road, arguing.

"Maybe we should fold the free maps all the other way around." Heather suggested.

"Be my guest!" Nora offered wryly.

Gradually, the last of the customers wandered down and left The Secondhand Bookworm while Nora and Heather brought the postcard spinner, free maps box and cheap paperback boxes inside. Heather left Nora cashing up the till to check nobody was lingering upstairs, tidying books that had been pulled out and left on the sides of units and to turn off the upstairs lights.

Nora deterred several people who wanted to come in and pass the time while they waited for their coach. They shook their fists at Nora when she pointed to the CLOSED sign and stomped off angrily. Shaking her head, Nora headed into the back to lock up the kitchen and discovered an old man browsing the nautical section.

"Any books about pirates?" He asked.

"They would be there if we had some." Nora stood next to him and scanned the shelf. "It doesn't look like we have any in stock at the moment."

"Any books about lumberjacks?" Was the next question.

"I don't think I've seen anything specifically about lumberjacks lately!" Nora admitted.

"Hmm." He rubbed his chin.

"Any science books?"

"We have a section upstairs..."

"Oh grand." He started away.

"But the lights are off because we close at half past five on a Saturday." Nora added, following him out of the back room.

"What's the time now?" The man asked flatly.

"Just gone half past five." Nora replied.

"Have I got time to go and browse?" He asked, foot on the first stair.

"Sadly not." Nora refused, leading the way into the front.

He sighed, checking his watch.

"My train isn't for another twenty five minutes." He tried to persuade her.

"I'm sorry but we do close at half past five." Nora glanced at Heather who was zipping up her coat. "And we must get going. I have a date with some hobbits."

The man gave her a look as if she was potty.

"Okay. I'll be off." He finally submitted and Heather opened the door to let him out.

Once the shop was finally empty of customers, Nora turned off the computer and closed the cash book.

"Well, that was a good day." Nora said as she shrugged into her jacket.

"Yes, Georgina will be pleased with the takings." Heather agreed.

They set the alarm, turned off the front lights, hurried out and closed the door behind them, dragging the sandbags before it and brushing the sand from their hands.

"Oh, are you just closing?"

A man stood behind Nora and Heather. Nora turned her key in the lock and glanced over her shoulder at him.

"I'm afraid so." Heather nodded.

"Do you have any books about clown noses?"

Nora dropped her keys.

"Specifically about clown noses?" Nora repeated flatly.

"Yeah." He stared at her expectantly.

"Is there such a book?"

"Must be." He nodded. "There's a variety of noses that we use."

"Are you a clown?" Heather asked and Nora nudged her arm before bending down to pick up her keys.

"I perform on some occasions, yes. But it's a delicate art form and the positioning of the nose is quite critical." He explained gravely.

"I'm afraid we don't. Sorry." Nora said, beginning to drag Heather away.

"Okay." The man peered through the shop door glumly and Nora and Heather hurried up the road.

"Is that a first?" Heather grinned.

"A request for a book about clown noses?" Nora asked, chuckling. "Yes, I think that's a first. But I doubt it will be the last."

"Maybe he could go for a job at Seymour's theatre when he opens at Christmas."

"I doubt Seymour will need clowns in his plays."

"You never know. So what's next for Castletown and The Secondhand Bookworm?" Heather asked keenly.

Nora linked her arm with her sister's, glancing back to where the bookshop stood nestled neatly among the Tudor buildings on the edge of the old cobbled square.

"I think we shall have some typical bookworm fun over Poppy Week in November." She decided with a wry smile.

"I can't wait, Nora." Heather grinned. "I just can't wait."

They reached Nora's car, climbed in and Nora reversed out of the steep, hilly road, joining the steady stream of traffic moving slowly out of the town.

Sombre organ music sailed out of the little Catholic Church of Castletown; crows, rooks and ravens flew noisily overhead to nest in the trees of the castle ruins; the Morris Men danced happily towards the Black Hart for a round of Cole Brew and a man stopped before the window of The Secondhand Bookworm.

His eyes honed in a book displayed in the window about Tree Surgery and he made a mental note to call in to speak to Nora at The Secondhand Bookworm first thing Monday morning and see if she'd knock anything off it for cash.

Piertown was overrun with elves, hobbits, wizards and a few trolls, heading in droves to the art deco cinema located on the seafront for *The Lord of the Rings* movie marathon. Nora met Humphrey at the pier and walked with him through the wide cobbled main street of the town, spotting a display of JRR Tolkien books in the window of Waterstones.

"It's always nice when a bookshop gets into the theme of things." Nora admired, pondering the different editions of the classic fantasy books on show.

Humphrey was distracted by a troll stomping past, dragging a club.

Nora's gaze was drawn to several other books, including a hardback tome titled: '*The history of the Dukes of Cole and their Historical Properties throughout England*'. Her heart stuttered unexpectedly when she saw a photograph of the current Duke of Cole on the cover. Nora pondered it for a long moment and smiled.

"You know, I'm starting to worry these trolls will eat all the food in the cinema café before we get there." Humphrey frowned, watching a party of orcs hurry past next, looking ravenous.

Nora straightened up and smiled.

"Then we had best get going." She said and linked her arm with his.

Humphrey grinned.

They set off towards the cinema, Nora casting one last thoughtful look back at the Duke's book in the window, before setting her mind on a truly obsessive *Lord of the Rings* movie night.

Almost four hundred and fifty miles away, in a large, stately castle near the Scottish borders, light filtered through a tall, mullioned window in a vast private library, casting colours from stained glass shields and figures onto balustrades and stone walls below.

James, the Duke of Cole, took a sip of tea, placed the cup onto a saucer and picked up a sheet of paper from his desk top. His blue eyes focused on the information and he rubbed his chin, thoughtfully.

Around him, thousands of rare, leather-bound, collectable, inherited or specially accumulated books occupied rows and rows of shelves in ornate wooden cases. Numerous tomes were open or piled in small tottering columns on his desk, among blueprints and brochures, leaflets and booklets all about a single topic – one of his family's historical properties.

James continued to rub his chin, reading and musing, thinking and frowning, until his gaze reached the bottom of the page. His blue eyes rested upon the photograph of a young woman with the title '*manager*' written beneath. He stared for a long moment, and slowly smiled, his mind made up.

Reaching for his desk phone, the Duke of Cole placed his information about The Secondhand Bookworm onto a folder and pressed a button that would contact his valet.

"Jeeves." James said, leaning back in his chair. "Contact Peterson, my surveyor. We're heading down to

Castletown first thing in the morning. What was that?" James paused and then chuckled, shaking his head. "Jeeves, my man. You know me so well. Yes, it was indeed the bookshop that made up my mind."

THE END

ALSO IN THE SERIES

'The Secondhand Bookworm stories continue in book two:

'Nora and the Secondhand Bookworm'

Also in the ongoing series:

'Christmas at The Secondhand Bookworm'
'Summer at The Secondhand Bookworm'
'Halloween at The Secondhand Bookworm'
'Black Friday at The Secondhand Bookworm'
'Book Club at The Secondhand Bookworm'
'Valentine's Day at The Secondhand Bookworm'
'Lockdown at The Secondhand Bookworm'
'Strange Things at The Secondhand Bookworm'
'Winterland at The Secondhand Bookworm'

Available in paperback and Kindle

Watch for more novels in the Bookworm series

Also by the author

'House of Villains'
Available now from Amazon

ABOUT THE AUTHOR

Emily Jane Bevans lives on the south coast of England. For ten years she worked in, and helped to manage, a family chain of antiquarian bookshops in West Sussex. She is the co-founder and co-director of a UK based Catholic film production apostolate 'Mary's Dowry Productions'. She writes, edits, produces, directs, narrates and sometimes acts for the company's numerous historical and religious films on the lives of the Saints and English Martyrs. She also likes to write novels based on her bookselling experiences for fun.

MARY'S DOWRY PRODUCTIONS

Mary's Dowry Productions is a Catholic Film
Production Apostolate founded in 2007 to bring the lives
of the Saints and English Martyrs, English Catholic
heritage and history to film and DVD. Mary's Dowry
Productions' unique film production style has been
internationally praised for not only presenting facts,
biographical information and historical details but a
prayerful and spiritual film experience. Many of the
films of Mary's Dowry Productions have been broadcast
on EWTN, BBC and SKY.
For a full listing of films and more information visit:

www.marysdowryproductions.org

Made in the USA
Middletown, DE
17 August 2023